The Rose
and the
Sword

OR

The Story of a Lotus Flower and a Dragon

By Gina Marinello-Sweeney

Gina Marinello - Sweeney
Christmas 2018

Front cover art by:
Crossvalley Smith; Kreuztal, Germany (1953–2015)

Back cover photo by:
Anja Osenberg; Aachen, Germany

Sword on back cover by:
pixabay.com/en/users/209144-209144/

"Celebra la vida" (2008), Written by:
Axel Fernando, Nicolás Urquiza, and Norma Teresa Villa
Olivares; Performed by: Axel Fernando

"I Am Blest" (2004), Written and Performed by:
Chris Muglia

Chapter headers and rose scene break designs by:
Obsidian Dawn, www.obsidiandawn.com

Sword scene break designs made by:
Freepik from www.flaticon.com

Used with Permission. Thank you!

The Rose and the Sword

Published in the United States by Rivershore Books
9011 Pierce St. NE, Blaine, MN 55434
www.rivershorebooks.com

ISBN-10: 0692662502
ISBN-13: 978-0692662502

Printed in the United States of America

Dedication

I dedicate this novel to my mom, who is always there for me, and to our Heavenly Mother, the Blessed Virgin Mary, who, by saying "yes," delivered Christ our Savior into this world and continues to intercede on our behalf with the Immaculate Heart of a loving mother.

"If you are what you should be, you will set the whole world ablaze."

-St. Catherine of Siena

 *Prologue*

I stood, the wind rippling through my hair, tearing across my shoulders, burning my cheeks.

I stood at the peak of a gray silk mountain-guardian, at an altitude that provided little moderation in climate or speed of wind.

I stood, not knowing how I had gotten there and feeling moisture, a sudden dampness, on my left cheek that I also blamed on the wind and its mountain.

I felt a hand lightly touch my shoulder and turned.

She stood, tall and graceful, elegant, yet not proud. She stood, her eyes sapphires of the morning sky and light, gauze-like robes of a like hue billowing softly about her, moving only slightly in a wind apart from that of the mountain.

The Lady in Blue.

Her eyes, large and sympathetic, spoke to me, and a single tear that I could no longer ignore fell across my cheek. She stepped forward and lightly wiped it away.

"Will you pray with me?" I asked quietly, my eyes tired

and lifeless.

The Lady in Blue nodded and gently took my hand to guide me toward a nearby crook in the crevice of rock. And here we sat in silence and in word, gazing far, far above, seeking her Son, and praying from the depths of our hearts.

As the sky above us darkened in the quickening nightfall, the Lady in Blue squeezed my hand and slipped away with a quiet smile as suddenly as she had appeared.

I woke up with the light of dawn, rosary beads clasped in my hand.

Tell me the story of the lotus flower and the dragon.
Did she escape its wide grasp?
Her soft dance continue?
A melody vibrant,
A story untold?
And did she see
The rose and the sword?
Did she see the rose and the sword
As she bent to look in the underbrush?

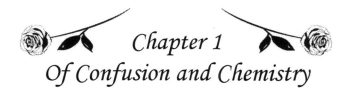

Chapter 1
Of Confusion and Chemistry

"Excuse me; do you work here?"

I looked up from the stack of books that I was organizing to quickly form an employee-of-the-month smile. "Yes; may I help you?"

The young man in front of me fumbled with the paper in his hands, looking around at his surroundings as if in unfamiliar territory. "I was just looking for my books for this semester."

A freshman or a transfer. He looked pretty young, so probably a freshman.

I nodded in understanding. "Is that your class schedule?" I asked, indicating the paper in his hands.

"Yep." He nodded, handing the scrap of paper to me. As I quickly examined it, I felt the pressure of a stare directed toward me. Sure enough, when I looked up, Freshman was grinning openly at me, brushing back his hair with a more casual expression to replace his initial nervousness.

Oh, help.

"Um, right this way." I suppressed a groan and pointed two aisles to the right. He followed me, dragging his feet in what I suspect he thought was a "cool" gait. When we finally arrived at the Science section, he nearly crashed into me.

"Sorry, babe," he said, almost popping bubble gum in my face that he must have inserted during his slow meandering.

"That's Reb—" I paused. *No need for him to know my name.* "Call me Employee 34."

There. That should be weird enough to scare him off.

"Employee 34, huh?" He winked, quickly bobbing his head up and down as if sharing an inside joke. "That's hot."

"Um, Chem 101 with Gersher, right?" I thrust the book into his surprised arms without waiting for an answer and headed to the next aisle. "Follow me, please."

We moved from aisle to aisle as if running a race . . . Freshman staring and popping his gum— occasionally leaning against a row of books to wink at me and ask, "So, what year are you?" or "Does Employees Only *really* mean Employees Only?"—me, all the while, throwing books at him.

Throwing would be an exaggeration, I decided, as we finally headed to our last stop, Psychology. *Placing firmly would be more accurate.*

Psychology. First it had been Chemistry, then Sociology, followed by World History, then German, complete with Beginning Law and Creative Writing, not to mention Logic (He could use that course.) and Environmental Toxicology. He *is*, by all indications, a freshman, I reminded myself, as I handed him his last book. *It's a time to figure things out.* Yet I couldn't get the thought out of my head that he was purposely selecting all these random classes just because he found it to be amusing. And *nine* classes at that.

He was insane.

And that was the least of his problems.

"That's the last one, right?" I asked, relieved, wiping moisture from my brow that had resulted from the two-minute dash we had just completed.

"You got it, Babe 34." Freshman popped his gum and stared intently about five inches below my neck. *And that was it.*

Freshman fell, sprawling, to the floor, his nine books of nine different subjects flying everywhere. "Ouch!"

"Sorry." I smiled sweetly as I helped him pick up his books. "My doctor has always commented on my excellent reflexes. I guess they were inspired to act."

Freshman stared at me in complete and utter confusion.

"To the Front Desk?" I carried half of his stack as he followed, no longer attempting to walk the "cool guy" walk.

The college bookstore was a splash of life, culture, and society. As a psychology student, I often found myself intrigued by the behavior, ways of thinking and feeling, and general schemata of others, and this was the perfect spot to engage my senses.

Other times, I was just annoyed.

As we approached the register, another student materialized, standing pleasantly with the familiarity yet youth of a sophomore.

Oh, great. I hope he hasn't been there long.

I dashed behind the counter with a smile, leaving Freshman to take a spot behind Sophomore (?). "Find everything okay?"

"Sure did. Thanks for asking."

I nodded in return, scanning his books and then placing them in a bag as I waited for his receipt.

"Hey, are you a Christian?"

I looked up, caught slightly aback. "Yes, I am. Catholic, to be precise."

"Catholic, huh?" He leaned forward eagerly. "You worship saints, don't you?"

Once again, I suppressed a groan.

Every year for the past *ten* years it seemed that I was constantly bombarded with this misconception.

At least it allows me to correct all those crazy ideas people have about my faith, I told myself, regaining my composure.

"No, not at all. We worship only God."

"That's not true. Pastor McCarthy told me that you worship saints."

Pastor McCarthy, who surely knows more about Catholics than a Catholic herself.

"He has clearly been misinformed," I said patiently. "We ask saints to pray *for* us, that is true. But we do not pray *to* them in a worshipping sense like we would God."

Sophomore scrunched up his nose as if he still did not believe me (and he probably didn't). "But you worship statues?"

Oh, brother.

"Not at all."

"The Pope?"

"No."

"Mary?"

"No."

"Rosary beads?"

"No."

"Easter lilies?"

Oh, goodness.

"No. Just. God. Like. I. Said. Before."

He shook his head. "I'll have to consult with my pastor. Until then, you're not a Christian."

Sophomore grabbed his book bag, dropping a pamphlet for True Word Church on the counter.

Freshman stared at me, this time with a clear sense of disapproval, as I rang up his order. When I finally handed him his bag, he shook his head, now a grouchy old man wagging his finger at noisy children in the neighborhood. "I can't believe you're Catholic."

"Really?" I managed to keep my voice even.

"Yes." He shook his head again. "I can't date someone who isn't Christian. So long."

And, with that, Freshman disappeared as quickly as Sophomore had, tossing a piece of paper on the floor as he left.

When it came between curiosity and irritation, curiosity usually won out with me. I knelt in front of the counter and picked up the piece of paper.

Visit Faith Community Church. Special classes for recovering Catholics are available.

I leaned against the counter and finally let out a sigh.

Well, hey, at least anti-Catholicism had some benefits in this case, I retorted to myself sarcastically. *Gets rid of annoying guys who try to pick you up.*

"You look like you just heard someone insult Italians."

I turned around and, automatically, a smile began to replace the already deeply-planted frown as my favorite co-worker and assistant store manager, Jeffrey, strode over to the register.

Jeffrey was nothing short of an anomaly . . . an anomaly, and a contradiction. His hair came in billows down to the middle of his back like that of a hippie, yet he discussed matters of business with all the air of a professional in the accounting section of the bookstore. He spoke of philosophy as he readjusted his cowboy hat, and got together with questionable characters for a smoke while always leaving a loaf of bread for his aged grandma on the way over. He was liberal and unpredictable and had probably slept with dozens of girls, yet he had always been respectful to me. He spoke of a father who was in and out in jail, yet was saddened by the choices he had made in life. He was the kind of person I never thought I would consider a friend, even within the confines of a business relationship, and, yet, his hearty laugh, good humor, and genuine desire to grow closer to God and farther from his faults had made me grow fond of him, I realized with a smile. Even if both he and I knew that we lived in different worlds, and those worlds could only mix so far. Even so, he had risen above his circumstances, his difficult background.

He had a good heart.

"Even worse." I rolled my eyes, both in response to his remark and in an effort to shake myself from my ponderings.

"Worse than insulting Italians?" Jeffrey raised an eyebrow. "I thought it didn't get worse than that."

I laughed. "Well, there aren't many things that do. But this one takes the cake."

Jeffrey surveyed me with an anticipatory glance before nodding quietly.

Jeffrey, being Jeffrey, realized that I didn't want to talk about it. In that way—but only that way—he almost reminded me a bit of . . .

"So," Jeffrey strummed his hands rhythmically on the countertop, "it's the big day, huh?"

In the rush of the daily bookstore duties, intermixed

with unforeseen irregularities in that agenda, I had briefly forgotten what had enveloped my mind for the last few weeks.

The next big step in graduate psychology. My first day of a semester-long, full-time psychology internship.

1,000 hours that could determine all future hours in my life.

No pressure.

I managed a smile. "Well, there will be enough psychos in the city to keep me busy, no?"

Jeffrey laughed heartily. "You could say that. You nervous?"

I shrugged hesitantly. "It should be an experience."

Jeffrey said gently, "You're not in Cedar Heights anymore, Rebecca."

He was right. Cedar Heights, the place that I had called home for twenty-two years, had been temporarily left behind me for a psychology internship. In the place of the sleepy little suburban town I had grown to love and cherish was the big city of Los Angeles, wild, unafraid — perhaps too unafraid — and unknown. No longer did the night end at 9 p.m. and the local news stations boast of a world with relatively no crime, of the status of one of the safest locations in the United States of America. Los Angeles was forever wide awake, pulsing with the vigor of a diverse culture, yet, at the same time, pulsing with the danger of a Safari chase. This was no place for a girl in her early twenties, relatively alone and on her own.

And, yet, here I was.

I nodded. "I know."

I thought back to the young man who had been flirting with me earlier. He, with all his cliché (if clichés existed) remarks and drooling winks, was probably one of the more innocent, upstanding citizens in the city. I recalled an earlier scenario three months prior . . .

I was standing, leaning against a tree outside, during my dinner break. Three men of identical attire and the aura of a less innocent world approached me. **Gang members** *was my instant thought as I quickly formed a calm demeanor, staring curiously at my apple.* **Confidence, apart from arrogance, was instrumental in my safty.** *I casually met their gaze, seemingly without a care in the world. In the back of my mind, I noted the proximity of the bookstore and my heart beating wildly in my chest.*

The tallest, who stood slightly in front of them and appeared to be their leader, addressed me.

"How old are you?"

"Two hundred four," I responded coolly.

Leader paused, taken aback. He opened his mouth as if to utter a word and then closed it.

I slowly backed away from the tree with an irresistible smile. "He hath indeed better bettered expectation than you must expect of me to tell you how. Shall quips and sentences and these paper bullets of the brain awe a man from the career of his humour? Dost thou not suspect my place? Dost thou not suspect my years?"

When all else fails, talk Shakespearean, and it will confuse them enough to keep them at bay.

Leader and his followers stood, gaping in bewilderment, as I entered the bookstore, exhaling deeply.

Jeffrey, upon hearing the story, called campus security. Afterwards, he surveyed me with a somber expression, lecturing me with his eyes. If it hadn't been such a serious moment, I would have been amused by such a change in Jeffrey's eternally laidback demeanor.

"You should have left from the start."

I nodded, assenting. "I know. It was stupid of me."

"Although," Jeffrey relaxed, smiling, "you handled

*yourself well. You didn't anger them or let them scare
you,"* he paused, observing my hands, which were
shaking, *"or, at least, didn't show them that you were scared."*
I smiled. *"Thanks."*
"But next time . . ."
"I know."

Now, three months later, Jeffrey once again
surveyed me with a knowing expression. "Any guys
bother you today?"
"No one dangerous, but," I exhaled in annoyance,
"a less-than-chivalrous nuisance."
Jeffrey smiled. "Well, in that sort of case, I'm not
worried."
I cocked my head slightly in curiosity.
"You can handle yourself well with the regular idiot.
It becomes obvious to them soon enough that you're not
game."
"What do you mean?" I looked at him, this time the
one held at bay by confusion.
"The way you carry yourself tells people a lot."
"It does?"
"Yeah, I mean," he strummed his hands on the
counter again before finally looking up with a smile,
"they don't have to see a ring to know that you're . . .
pure. And that nothing they do or say can change that.
It's . . . you. It's Rebecca."
"Actually, I came across a ring that rather took my
fancy and was thinking of getting it."
He smiled, shaking his head slowly. "Don't ever
change."
I grinned. "I'll try not to."
Jeffrey bowed, a mischievous grin inching across
his face. "And, Miss Rebecca, we must find your Prince
Charming."

I hardly had time to respond when he pulled my hand forward and began to passionately sing the first line of "That's Amore".

I giggled as he spun me around to the joint lunar-pizza imagery of love.

Jeffrey often viewed the bookstore as his personal dancing—and singing—studio. And sometimes he didn't bother to wait until the customers left.

"And when . . ." he paused, "the sun hits your eyes like a bowl of lasagna?"

I snorted. "Somehow I don't think that was the next line."

He grinned, bowing again.

"But it was still funny."

"Thank you, Madame." He glanced at the clock, his eyes returning with an even brighter beam. "Hey, wanna grab a bite at the café before you leave?"

I followed his gaze back to the clock. *How time flies.* It was only a minute until closing time, and no customers had ventured hither since Freshman and Sophomore.

"Sure."

We "walked" the bookstore, making sure everything was in order and reorganizing anything that was not. Jeffrey took out the trash as I vacuumed and wiped down the windows and door. With a sigh of relief, we finally headed to the back to gather our belongings and clock out. A few minutes later, the locked door closed quietly behind us.

We walked easily, a companionable silence filling the breeze that lightly touched our shoulders.

Companionable silence.

Peter.

Two and a half years ago, a student from Canada had come to Cedar Heights, California during the season of Lent . . . and, by no dramatic exaggeration, changed my life in a mere month and a half. In the midst of trials that we had both endured and joys that we had shared, he had become my friend . . . No, more than a friend. A . . .

I glanced at Jeffrey, the off-beat, somewhat questionable older brother from another mother.

A brother, then? *No, I found myself shaking my head, brother just doesn't seem right.*

Then, what was he? An honorary cousin, a next-door neighbor?

I shook my head.

He was Peter, and that was all that came to surface.

I paused, trying to remember where I had heard that before.

"What's up?" Jeffrey had evidently observed me shaking my head, and he eyed me inquisitively.

"Nothing. Just thinking."

"Of Peter?"

I laughed. "Do I talk about him *that* much?"

Jeffrey smiled. "Kinda."

"He's a good friend."

And I missed him. Sure, we emailed once or twice a week and talked on the phone about once or twice a month, but it just wasn't the same.

Jeffrey nodded, understanding. "I know." He indicated the café door that had, as if by magic, suddenly appeared before us. *I had really been sidetracked.*

"Sure, go ahead."

He opened the door, and we walked in.

Adoro te devote, latens Deitas. Peter, come home.

I took a deep breath, surveying the tall screeching building before me while the theme song of an obscure horror movie played. *This was it.*

"No, it isn't." I yawned, opening my eyes reluctantly. "Not 'till tomorrow."

I surveyed my actual surroundings and gulped. "No, that would be . . . today."

I was sitting at a small table at the café, attempting to review my psychology notes before the internship started at 4. *I don't actually need to review notes, I reminded myself, after all, it isn't like I am being tested.* But Jeffrey had already left, I still had half an hour to kill, and I thought it might be a good idea to brush up . . . just in case.

I looked at the time display on my cell phone. *Actually, that would be ten minutes.* Ten minutes to *get* there.

While I lost track of time often enough, I never fell asleep like that unless I was sick. *Why now, Rebecca,* I lectured myself. At least, I had planned my schedule so that I would be a few minutes early. I relinquished my seat, quickly gathering my belongings together.

"Hey, Rebecca!" I looked up to observe a class-mate from one of my graduate classes walk over, her boyfriend by her side.

"Hey, Teresa!" I gave her a hug and nodded pleasantly at her TARDIS companion. "Long time no see! What are you up to these days?"

"Not much. I'm off to my first internship in a week." Her eyes met mine with a contagious grin. "I'm pretty much thrilled."

"Oh, nice!" I slipped on my jacket. "Who's it with?"

"Same as you. Dr. Yin, on Second Street. Only," Teresa offered a teasing smile, "I don't have the official Everson Seal of Approval."

I blushed. I had been recommended for the scholarship by Dr. Everson, the head of the psychology department. The Everson Psychological

Center had been founded by his grandfather and was considered one of the best in the nation. Dr. Yin was the current psychologist presiding over the center and would serve as my mentor as I grew from a preservice psychology student to one ready to enter the field. Teresa was also considered one of Dr. Everson's best students, but she had lost the scholarship honor to me.

"I—" I turned red again. "Um . . ."

"Rebecca! Seriously, I was just teasing you." Teresa tapped me playfully on the arm. "I'm glad that a friend got the scholarship. If anyone deserved it, you did."

A friend. That was nice, I thought to myself. I guess I had always thought of Teresa as a friend, but we didn't talk that much. This would be a nice opportunity to get to know her better.

I shook my head with a smile. *I'm such a friendship nerd.* I loved getting to know people, each with their own unique qualities, and watching the friendship blossom.

Blossom into random insanity, more than likely.

I grinned.

"Well, I'll see you soon then." I returned my mind to the present. "What time does your shift start?"

"3 p.m."

"Starting next week, right?"

"Yeah. I'm . . . starting later than you because I have to go on a trip this week."

She looked down, smiling almost apologetically. My overly curious mind wanted to ask her about it, but my polite demeanor demanded otherwise.

"Gotcha. Well, hey, I'm set to start in the mornings after today, so I might run into you when I'm on my way out. It'll be fun!"

"Definitely! Well, we're going to grab something to eat." Teresa indicated her boyfriend, who had remained silent the entire time. "Nice to see you!" She gave me another hug.

"Nice to see you, too! Later."

I waved at the retreating couple and made my way toward the door of the café. Just as I was about to exit, my backpack, planted firmly on my back, caught itself in the double doors. I was stuck.

I cleared my throat, attempting to regain any dignity that I had left as I managed to squeeze myself out.

Hope no one saw that.

Chapter 2
Of Hot Chocolate and
Unexpected Visitors

As I walked to a tall structure with the words "Everson Psychological Center" highlighted in gold — but without any ominous black towers that I could discern — I decided to double check my cell phone for any last-minute messages.

None.

Oh, well. I wanted to read my last conversation with Peter anyway.

I clicked on the Facebook app and selected his name . . .

Peter Asturian: *So, have you met your mentor yet?*

Rebecca Veritas: *Nah, not until Tuesday . . . I got an email from her, though.*

Peter Asturian: Yeah?

Rebecca Veritas: Yeah. *She wanted me to write an introductory letter to the staff and one for the clients. I had heard that at least one of her clients was Hispanic, so I wrote back asking if she would like me to translate the letter. I didn't know if he was fluent in English, but thought I'd mention it just in case.*

Peter Asturian: And . . . ?

Rebecca Veritas: *And she said, "Yes, both letters need to be translated." Which . . . I mean, is fine. It was just kinda a weird way of putting it. Being bilingual isn't exactly a requirement for this internship.*

Peter Asturian: *I wouldn't worry about it. Sometimes tone can be misinterpreted online.*

Rebecca Veritas: *Then . . . how come we never have that problem? ;)*

Peter Asturian: *That's different. :D*

Rebecca Veritas: *Haha I know. And you're probably right. I mean, it doesn't HAVE to mean anything. Besides, she may have been in a rush or something.*

Peter Asturian: *Exactly.*

Rebecca Veritas: *So, how's Alberta? As lovely as ever?*

I closed my flip phone—an older model that I refused to replace due to my secret suspicion that it was really a Starfleet communicator—and walked the last few feet to the door.

I peeked into the window, hoping for a first glimpse of my new world.

Really, Rebecca? I told myself. *What are you, five?*

"Nope," I said aloud. "Just seems more romantic glimpsing first before fully seeing."

I cleared my throat, reminding myself to not allow my inner ponderings to come forth verbally in the presence of my new mentor, and opened the door.

As soon as I entered the room, my eyes were greeted with a simple office that reminded me much of my dentist's office. A small desk was in the right corner, labeled, "Ms. Cornell, Secretary to Dr. Yin." The tall, light-haired woman seated there nodded in my direction. I walked to her desk, glancing back for a moment to observe a large mirror near the entrance from which I had just come.

That's probably the only thing in here that doesn't look like typical office fare, I noted to myself before leaving my thoughts with a smile at the secretary's desk.

"Rebecca, right?"

"That's me," I confirmed.

The secretary handed me a badge with my name on it. "Dr. Yin will be right with you. You may have a seat over there." She indicated the many cushions and chairs scattered about with a wide sweep. "Anything I can get you to drink? Coffee? Hot chocolate?"

"Ooh, hot chocolate would be lovely! Thank you."

The secretary nodded pleasantly and left her seat, evidently in search of my hot chocolate.

I sat down on the nearest loveseat and tried to ignore the nervous feeling in my stomach.

When the secretary returned, I had nearly forgotten about my hot chocolate.

"Here you go." She handed it to me with a smile.

"Thank you, Ms. Cornell!" I responded formally.

"You can just call me Christy."

I nodded in acknowledgement.

Christy returned to her desk. I lifted the mug and took my first sip.

"Oh, Rebecca?"

"Yes?" I looked up.

"We have a small entrance fee, which you may pay now if you'd like," Christy said, her voice rising agreeably.

"Oh, right! Twenty dollars?"

"That is correct."

I put the mug down on the small adjacent table, picking up my purse next to it. Taking out my wallet, I scanned the dollar bill designations. "Ah, a $20," I said aloud, finally locating the correct one. Just as I removed the bill, a ten-dollar bill fell from behind it, leaping boldly into my hot chocolate mug.

I stared in disbelief as the money slowly descended the chocolate depths before I finally snapped to attention and retrieved the sunken article.

I held up the ten-dollar bill and blinked. "Well, that's . . . different."

After relocating the newly bathed money to a paper towel on that same table, I arose, offering the more dry and substantial bill to the secretary.

"Thanks!"

"Sure, no problem." I returned to my seat, my attention sporadically captured by the anomalous ten-dollar bill and followed regularly by an incredulous shake of the head.

As I was pondering over the possibility of a hot chocolate-themed dollar store, I heard the quiet metallic twist of a retreating door and looked up.

In the doorway stood a thin, petite woman with wiry

spectacles and an angular nose. Her short black hair was brushed back neatly. I was reminded of the girls at my college who never seemed to have a single hair out of place, causing my bafflement. She was wearing a high-necked, black silk blouse and matching skirt. Her lips formed a small smile as she took in the waiting room.

"Ms. Veritas, I presume?"

I got up quickly, nearly spilling the rest of my hot chocolate in the process. "Yes, that's me." I walked over to the door and shook her hand. It was rather cold. *That happens*, I thought to myself. *Rather warm day, though.*

Her eyes flickered over me briefly again before reaching Christy. "Paperwork in order, Christy?"

Christy looked up from the counter. "Yes, all ready. I also collected the entrance fee."

"Wonderful. Thank you. The lab fee?"

"Oh," Christy turned slightly red, "I forgot about that. I will . . ."

"No need," Dr. Yin answered briskly but pleasantly. "I will collect it myself."

She turned back to me. "We have a small lab fee. Would you like to pay now?"

"Sure! How much is it?"

"Ten dollars."

I winced.

"Sure, just . . . one moment."

I walked back to the small sofa as if it were a death sentence. *This was going to be so embarrassing.*

I looked at my purse. One last check.

Nope. No more ten-dollar bills. No ten one-dollar bills. Or a five-dollar bill plus five ones. Or . . .

I picked up the hot-chocolate-bathed ten-dollar bill from its place on the table. It looked back at me with a mischievous hot-chocolate-infused face.

Now I've truly lost it.

I wiped it again as best as I could, hoping that no one was watching, and walked over to give it to my new boss.

Dr. Yin looked at the bill without betraying any expression.

I coughed. "It unfortunately had a run-in with some hot chocolate." I attempted a laugh, hoping that she had a random sense of humor.

She smiled effortlessly. "That is quite all right. Just put it in the box over there, and then follow me down the hall. I will give you a tour of your new workplace."

Good. I didn't make my new mentor and possibly future employer touch it.

I dropped it in the box and followed her down the hall.

"This is where you will be most of the day." Dr. Yin opened a second door three doors down on the left and beckoned for me to follow.

It was a rather large and spacious room, not the typical psychologist's office one might see on TV during psychotherapy sessions. The walls were bright and colorful, filled with scenes of exotic locales, happy smiling faces, and floral artwork.

"Wow." I turned around. "This is great."

"Glad you like it." Dr. Yin's lips formed a thin smile. "We like to keep our patients happy."

"For sure." I looked around again and saw what appeared to be a small water fountain on the far right corner of the room. Two sea creatures of a type that I did not recognize chased each other around the water spout. One was dark; the other white.

"Oh, wow," I said again. "That's pretty neat!"

"Thank you. We like our patients to have something to focus on as they are working. Water has a calming effect on a person."

"Definitely!"

"Will you have a seat?" Dr. Yin indicated the chair directly opposite hers at her desk.

"Yes, thank you." I sat down and waited. Dr. Yin sat in silence for a few moments, looking over a sheet of paper.

"So, you worked with Dr. Everson on a behavioral theory research project."

Ah, probably my resume.

"Yes, it was wonderful! He is a great person to work with. It was also an honor," I added quickly, caught between the desire to appear as a colleague and not sound like I was putting myself on the same level of one of the "greats."

What was more professional anyway?

Dr. Yin nodded. Even her nod was done as neatly as her hair arrangement. "I'm glad to hear that."

She slid another piece of paper across to me. "This will be your schedule. We will start with observation and then move more into active participation on your part. First you will observe patients with emotional trauma, then move on to more intense behavioral issues."

"Understood. May I ask how old the clients are?"

Clients. My grandfather had told me to use that term. He disliked the term "patient," throwing it aside as less human.

"There is a wide range. Most of the patients are middle-aged. However, one of our emotionally traumatized is in his early eighties."

"Oh, goodness . . ." My forehead instantly creased in concern.

". . . and a pair of seven-year-old twin girls who have emotional difficulties coupled with learning disabilities."

"Oh, wow . . . I didn't realize that any of the clients

would be kids."

"Is that a problem? Do you dislike working with children?" Dr. Yin questioned me over her spectacles.

"Oh, no . . . I *love* kids. In fact, if I hadn't gone into psychology, I probably would have gone into elementary school teaching . . . like my friend . . ."

I let it trail off. *Too much personal information.* Professionalism did not necessarily allow for casual conversation.

"I see." Once again, it was difficult to tell what she was thinking.

Did she like kids?

"Tell me a bit about your background. What made you go into psychology? And, don't worry." Dr. Yin smiled lightly. "This isn't an interview."

I laughed. "Sure! Well, I think that . . . it all really started with my grandpa. He is a retired psychologist and was always well-respected in the field. Ever since I was a little girl, I wanted to know what exactly all this was about. I knew that he did something important. He taught me over time, and I realized that I was fascinated by how the human mind works. Why people behave the way that they do. The entire network of emotions. All this complicated, yet simple, interaction. And then I realized that . . . I wanted to help people. People whose network was starting to break down and get confused. Or those who just needed a little extra help. My grandpa always said that everyone needs someone to talk to . . . maybe that is a lot of what this is about. Sometimes . . . with more complications. With more crying and screaming. But still . . . ultimately, someone who just needs someone to talk to. Like we all do."

I cleared my throat. "I apologize. I rambled a bit there."

"Do not worry. You are very articulate."

"Thank you!"

Dr. Yin really seemed nice. My concern over the email appeared to be unwarranted.

She stood up, once again the china doll without a blemish.

"Let's take a look around."

In airy breaths I fly anew
Uncontained by earth or mortal coil
I remain free, as if in distant land
Circling on and on without false step
Breathless, I glide, a maiden swept
In the wonder of ice-capsuled chandeliers
Laughing without reserve or fear
Touched by the vibrant glow
Of a treasure chest
Sought and found.

I ran around the room giddily, forgetting to dance, but dancing all the same. *This was it. This was what dreams felt like.*

I was on my way to becoming what I had always wanted to be. I was so close. Everything was like Taylor Swift's song. It was *starlight*.

The doorbell rang.

Slightly vexed that my daydream dance had been interrupted, I left my bedroom and walked down the adjacent hall. When I opened the door, I was greeted by a familiar — but rather unexpected — face.

"Dude," Adriana grinned widely, "what's up?"

"So, you just decided to come to Los Angeles on the spur of the moment so that we could eat frozen yogurt?" I sat at the other end of the coffee table, shaking my head with a barely suppressed grin. "Are you serious?"

"Um, yeah." Adriana moved a chess piece with relish. "That basically sums it up."

"Okay, dude, you are like . . . officially the best friend *ever*."

"Yeah, I know." Adriana offered a grin before casting a cursory glance around the apartment. "Not bad. And—" her eye caught sight of pink floral accents throughout the room, including, but not limited to, a lamp in the shape of a coral primrose, "very *you*."

"I like to keep it real."

Adriana and I both burst into laughter simultaneously. Oh, it was so good to have someone I *really* knew back here in the unknown.

I squeezed her shoulder. "Good to have you around again, dude."

"Likewise, dude. Now how about that fro yo?"

"¡Ahora mismo, pero ya!"

We grabbed our purses and ran out the door.

Long live the echoing pathways of Mary Poppins laughter.

As we walked outside, I heard the faint sound of rustling from the direction of some nearby underbrush.

The ravens were unusually active of late.

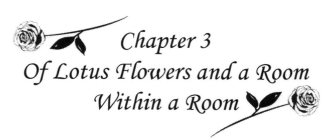

Chapter 3
Of Lotus Flowers and a Room Within a Room

I took a deep breath before opening the door to Everson Psychological Center. *This was it.*

Dr. Yin had suggested that I arrive half an hour early so that we could go over logistics. The first client would arrive at 10:30.

"Hi, Christy!"

The secretary looked up. "Oh, hi, Rebecca! Right on time. Just sign in here." Christy indicated a pen and clipboard on the counter.

"Thank you!" I wrote down my name and the time and then sat down in the waiting area in anticipation of Dr. Yin's arrival. My palms were wet and sweaty in my nervousness. I wiped them hurriedly on my freshly pressed black pants as Dr. Yin opened the hallway door.

"Come on in, Rebecca." Dr. Yin nodded pleasantly

with the same calm, collected tone I remembered from my last visit. I quickly got up, relinquishing my seat with a silent plea to our Father that all would go well.

We walked to the same office as before. Dr. Yin sat down.

"So, Rebecca, I asked you to come here earlier for a little psychoanalysis. Sit down."

I sat down, puzzled.

"Do you see the mirror on the right side of the room?"

"Yes, I do." At that moment, I also recalled the one at the entrance of the facility, an unusual placement. My unease quickly turned to excitement as I realized Dr. Yin intended to teach me something. Clearly the mirrors were part of some new psychological approach. I took in the mirror eagerly.

"Stand up so that you can gaze upon the mirror more fully. This should be a learning experience."

I obeyed, walking to stand in front of the glassy surface.

"What do you see?"

"Um . . ."

Did she mean literally or metaphorically or—

I decided to avoid asking and say both. "I see a girl. Me. A student of psychology. A . . . lotus flower."

Lotus flower. Bad mistake. Calling oneself a flower sounded self-complimentary. But before I could correct my error, Dr. Yin's voice came from behind me.

"Lotus flower?"

"Yes, um, it's just something that a friend of mine calls me." I thought back to my bookstore friend, Jeffrey, and what he had said upon giving me the nickname. "He said that it was the Hindu symbol for purity. That it had a lightness of spirit and joy that suited me."

"He is Hindu?"

"Actually, no, he just likes the symbol."

"And why did you select an image given to you by someone else? Do you not have a name for yourself?"

I shifted uncomfortably, my face burning. *Obviously another psychological technique. She was good!* "I understand your concerns, and I share them. Surely we should not define ourselves by how others define us or wish us to be. But, at the same time, I do not think we should reject a meaning that suits us. That is to say, I should wish to be more like the lotus flower. The lotus flower is what I want to be and what I hope to flourish more deeply into as I grow as an individual and child of God."

Child of God. It had slipped out quickly in my fervency, but my public school education instantly chastised me for it. The fact that that politically correct thought entered my mind instantly dismissed my concerns. *It's not like I'm trying to convert anyone. She wanted me to be honest, clearly. And I can't be honest without mentioning my faith.*

"It is a name that I make for myself," I said softly.

There was a slight pause, a silence. I waited, forcing myself to not turn around. That would seem too pushy. I wasn't quite sure why, but it would seem that way.

"I see. That is all, Ms. Veritas."

I continued standing, uncertain.

"You may have a seat."

I returned to the desk.

"Well done."

Once again, Dr. Yin's tone was hard to decipher. I wasn't sure if she was really satisfied with my answer or not. But, at the same time, I felt that I could not have given her anything else.

At least, not without more advanced notice.

I glanced again at my new mentor. "A quick

question?"

"Sure, go ahead."

"Will we be working with clients in this room today?"

"No, the larger room across the hall."

"Oh, right." My face reddened again. We had gone over this on the tour. The awkward silence had begged for conversation, and I had submitted to its request too easily.

For the next twenty minutes, Dr. Yin had me fill out a set of confidentiality forms for each of the six clients that we would be seeing. I read the background information carefully, eager to know more about how I might best serve these individuals, even if only as an assistant. Each of the documents held a story. I moved the description of the first client to the top to read it again. The man was suffering from PTSD from his time in the Korean War. The war that took place only a few short years after the one in which my grandfather fought.

I heaved a sigh. *He had been one of the lucky ones, my grandpa. We all were.*

I reminded myself of everything I had learned about PTSD, and, in no time, I heard a knock at the door. Dr. Yin was still poring over some paperwork of her own, so, after a slight hesitation, I went to answer it.

An old man, gray eyes set back far in his face and a tattered blue shirt sitting in contrast to his newly pressed dress pants, looked at me in confusion.

"Who are you?"

"I'm Rebecca," I responded cheerfully, looking deeply into his eyes. "I'm the new intern."

The man did not answer, staring quietly into space.

I bit my lip, a tear nearly cascading downward. *So this was PTSD.*

"Albert, you have arrived." Dr. Yin finally looked up, offering her client a glance over her wide spectacles. "Are you ready to enter the room?"

Enter the room? Hadn't he already— Oh, yeah, that room. My stupidity was felt more fully as I made the same mistake twice.

In actuality, that had not been what she had meant.

"Rebecca, follow us out, please."

We all walked out of the room, Albert with a slow, deliberate pace as I was caught between catching up to Dr. Yin's vibrant stride and staying with our client.

I finally walked ahead, the student teacher standing beside her cooperating teacher at the head of the class.

My eyes were soon greeted by a familiar sight, a larger, but equally bright, version of Dr. Yin's office. I stopped to help Albert make his way in, his eyes still lost, on the battlefield or at home, I did not know.

"Dr. Yin, where shall we—"

"Beyond this room." I looked ahead to discern what she meant.

At the far end of the room was a door with a brass handle. Typical, almost too ordinary.

"In here." Dr. Yin gestured for me to guide the man into the room. I opened the door tentatively. Much to my surprise, it was completely dark inside.

I moved a hand in search of the switch.

"Don't worry about that." Dr. Yin cleared her throat. "Albert needs some time alone and will take care of it himself."

Interesting.

"Um, okay! Should we both—" I gestured toward the door to see if we should enter.

"No, completely alone. It's a new psychological strategy for those dealing with PTSD."

"Ah, I see."

Albert looked between us and the door in confusion. "Go in," I coaxed automatically. "Everything will be fine."

He walked in.

"So, why didn't you want me to help him in? Or follow him in myself? I hope you don't mind my candidness. I just want to understand better."

We had left the auditorium and were once again in Dr. Yin's office. I turned toward my new mentor with what I suspected was an inquisitive gesture.

"It's a new psychological strategy," Dr. Yin said once again. "We will discuss it more at a later date."

I nodded, deciding to not follow it up with any more questions.

Clearly it was for another day.

Chapter 4
Of Snake Charmers and Trampolines

"There's an albino cobra on the loose."

I looked up from my ice-blended drink at the local Coffee Bean to observe the frenzied gestures of one of the baristas.

A young woman, picking up a cup to hand to a customer, dropped it in her nervousness. Coffee spilled liberally over the surface of the counter. She barely noticed the resulting rebuke of "Crystal!", quickly surveying her surroundings, as if determining the best exit should the need arise. "An *albino* cobra? An albino *cobra*?!"

I would go with the emphasis on cobra, personally.

No, I had never heard of albino cobras before.

But I *had* heard of cobras, and that was the problem. That was enough for me to take one look at the female barista and follow suit, turning my direction toward each and every exit as if I expected the cobra to suddenly materialize out of thin air.

Number 1 on Rebecca's List of Fears: Snakes.

A middle-aged man at a nearby table observed us with a barely contained chuckle. I would normally ignore such an occurrence, but something about that in conjunction with my greatest fear coming to life made me swallow my usual inhibitions.

"Excuse me, sir, but I am deathly afraid of the creature in question and don't appreciate your masochistic gesture of superiority."

The man blinked, appearing to be genuinely surprised at my outburst. He recomposed himself with a slight smile. "Quite a mouthful."

"Thank you."

What in the world was I doing?

Whatever it was that I was doing inspired the man to stand up and tip his cap. "My name is Arvind," he said gallantly, with what I soon realized with a slight Indian accent intermixed with a British accent. "I meant no offense, surely, but I am from India, where snakes abound."

I took a deep breath. "It's all right. I'm the one who should apologize. Snakes just freak me—"

"*Where* is the snake?" The young barista, Crystal, was still in a frenzy, nearly pulling The Snake Announcer to the floor. "Is it . . . is it *here*?!"

"No." The male barista edged away carefully, straightening his clothes. "It's not . . . you know, that close by. Just . . . um, down the street!" He ran toward the back of the café, whether away from Crystal or the cobra, it remained unknown.

Crystal followed him with the Barbie equivalent of a warrior cry.

My eyes followed the retreating figures, not sure whether to laugh or run with them due to the proximity of The Creature. I turned back to Arvind.

"How quickly can cobras break through glass, leap in the air at warp speed, and kill people?"

Arvind searched my face to see if I was joking.

I was not.

"Not that quickly . . . I didn't catch your name."

"Rebecca. That's my name. I'd like to keep my name . . . alive."

"Calm down, Rebecca. It is venomous and one of the most dangerous snakes in the world, but that is no reason to—"

He stopped, probably because I had turned an even lighter shade of pale than was customary.

"It's outside, Rebecca."

I nodded. "If you say so."

Arvind cleared his throat. "If it helps to know, I happen to be a snake charmer."

An albino cobra on the loose. A snake charmer who happened to be in a local café while the cobra's departure from captivity was announced. How nice.

I'd take it.

I took a deep breath. "Mind watching my back while I head to my car?" I fingered the pepper spray can in my bag just in case the man wasn't as benevolent as he seemed.

But My Worst Fear was also on the loose, and I didn't want to take any chances with that, either.

"Of course."

He casually strolled to the front of the café, opening the door for me with one hand still holding his drink. "After you."

"Thank you."

I walked outside, the fresh air invigorating me.

No, Rebecca, don't let down your defenses. I stood taller and walked with all the purpose of a soldier going into battle.

Is this real life?

Arvind remained behind me, darting to and fro like a spy from one of the *Mission Impossible* movies. Was he making fun of me?

I squared my shoulders and moved forward.

We arrived at my car.

And that was when I saw The Albino Cobra. It slithered like a shimmery ribbon of doom near the passenger side of the car next to mine.

Apparently I wasn't the first person to see the cobra, either, because cameras clicked and voices were raised with the collective chaos of media coverage and (hopefully) people who knew what to do.

The Albino Cobra did not like the noise. He raised his head, as if to strike, with that scary hiss that you might have heard imitated but never really expected to hear outside of a television box.

I made the Sign of the Cross.

I was too young to die.

Arvind broke through the crowd. "Excuse me, may I be of assistance? I am a snake charmer."

A group of people huddled in discussion, "Animal Control" printed on their jackets, turned. "You have any experience with albinos?"

This wasn't the time to ask for credentials.

"Not exactly, no, but I think the same rules apply."

One of the men in the circle nodded. "We could use the help."

I turned away. I had seen enough snake movement for one day.

After a few moments of near silence, I heard a voice call out from somewhere in the crowd. "Watch out!"

I turned swiftly back to the scene. The Albino Cobra was moving quickly, slithering a few cars over before climbing across the last vehicle in the lot.

I took a deep breath and, almost as an involuntary gesture, moved my hand to my purse.

In one quick movement, I aimed my pepper spray at the serpent in question.

"Rebecca, what are you doing?" Arvind grabbed my hand. "Are you trying to antagonize it?"

"I wasn't going to shoot! I was just . . . preparing myself! In case it attacked!"

Arvind shook his head. "Women."

I shot him a glare.

Five minutes later, The Albino Cobra was curled luxuriously on top of a trampoline at the adjacent park. Every few moments, it circled around, causing the typical bouncy movement of the device.

If the scene hadn't been so terrifying, I would have laughed.

Animal Control carefully retrieved the creature and put it into a safety box. Arvind assisted, helping remove something from its neck. Once it was at a safe—but still discernible—distance, I leaned forward to see better.

On the 'collar' of the snake read: *William James' Charming Creatures Backyard Exhibit.*

I looked at Arvind.

The snake charmer shrugged. "Don't trust people with two first names."

I leapt up abruptly in the middle of the night, breathing heavily.

Really? An albino cobra?

I shook my head with a smile. I was not only bolder in my dreams, but more insane.

I turned over to my back, the position I always took when I was contemplating something when I was supposed to be asleep.

Did I *want* to be bold?

The next day at work, I could barely look at the tall, dark-skinned employee organizing textbooks to my left. When he glanced my way, I turned away, biting my lip to conceal the grin that wished to break forth.

These crazy work-related dreams needed to stop.

I finally couldn't take it anymore.

"Arvind." I cleared my throat, walking over to him. "You don't happen to be a snake charmer, do you?"

He looked at me blankly. "Um, no."

"Right." My face reddened. "Just thought I'd check." I moved away as quickly as possible without making it obvious.

From behind me, I heard a faint chuckle.

Chapter 5
Of Mirrors and More Mirrors

"You're not pretty."

I blinked, looking up from the ham and cheese sandwich I was eating.

A slim brunette wearing hip-hugger jeans and a distasteful expression stood in front of me.

"Um . . ." I fought for words but couldn't find any. *Did she seriously just—*

She rolled her eyes and, in an instant, had left the scene. I watched her retreating figure. She walked down the hall slowly, brushing back a lock of hair with the air of a supermodel princess.

Did that just— I shook my head, attempting to clear it. *Did some random girl just randomly walk up to me and say that I wasn't pretty for no apparent reason?*

And this wasn't even a dream.

I used to like randomness.

I returned to my sandwich with a dazed expression.

My lunch break ended, so I returned to the psychological center for the second half of my internship session. Dr. Yin had a late day, so I had spent the morning organizing her files and looking over the notes that I had made on Albert. As part of the requirement for my graduate studies at the university, I was to write a case study paper focusing on one of the clients with whom I worked. I had yet to meet the others, but I already felt drawn to Albert's story.

"Hey, Christy!" I waved at the secretary as I entered the double doors.

"Hey, Rebecca!" Christy smiled back amiably. "You can go on back. Dr. Yin is ready for you."

"Thanks!" I headed through a second set of doors in what was starting to feel like a routine.

Dr. Yin was in her office, seated in the usual spot behind her desk. She looked up in acknowledgement. "Hello, Rebecca. Have a seat."

"Thank you." I sat down at the indicated chair across from her, staring absentmindedly at the rather large, gray handbag laying near her desk.

Enough room for a small elephant. Perhaps—

I was jolted back to reality as Dr. Yin cleared her throat.

"Since we had an unusual schedule today, our first group will be from the beginning of the mental challenges segment. Do you remember anything about them?"

"Two seven-year-old girls. Twins. Abigail and Adelaide, right?"

"Correct. Good."

I thought briefly to myself of how my first two days of work had actually not been full days, as far as the arranged schedule was concerned. I didn't know in advance but was informed soon after my arrival at the facility or later on in the day.

No matter. Probably a good thing to break into it more slowly.

"They should be here any minute." Dr. Yin returned to the papers in front of her without another word.

My eyes were once again drawn to the mirror at the far end of the room. The mirror in which I had identified myself as a lotus flower. As I continued to look into its reflective surface, its image shifted and changed in my mind's eye.

I no longer saw myself. I saw a tall brunette with hip-hugger jeans.

There was a knock at the door.

"Would you—" Dr. Yin gestured at the door.

I moved from my seat and opened it.

In front of me were two girls, not too different from how I had imagined them the night before. I had imagined all of my clients, I admitted to myself, after meeting Albert. I wasn't really sure why, but something about him had made me want to know them before I *knew* them.

The young girls looked at me with curious eyes, their wavy brown hair and matching yellow and pink outfits standing in perfect unison. "Who are you?" one of them asked in a shy voice, words taking me back to an earlier visit to the center. The other girl (was it Abigail or Adelaide?) bounced excitedly up and down in agreement.

I bent before the children. "I'm Rebecca." I smiled, looking into their eyes.

They were so adorable and sweet that I just wanted to hug

them.

Abigail (Adelaide) and Adelaide (Abigail) took my smile as a hint to do just that. They threw their arms around me, giggling.

"I like you," one of the twins said brightly, as she finally pulled back. "I'm Abigail, and this is my sister Adelaide!" She giggled again as she pointed to her sister. "But you can call us Abi and Adi!"

"Nice to meet you, Abi and Adi."

There was a slam on the desk behind me. I turned around.

Dr. Yin shot her a warning glance over her spectacles.

"I like you, too," I said in a quieter voice. With a small hand in each of my own, I approached the desk.

"What did I say about nicknames, Abigail?"

"I . . ." The girl seemed to think for a very long time. I looked at her and remembered the record, that Abigail had a minor mental challenge.

"Adelaide?"

Adelaide stared ahead, beyond Dr. Yin.

"Abigail, what is our rule about nicknames."

"I . . . don't remember."

"Adelaide, what is our rule about nicknames? Adelaide?" Dr. Yin's tone took on a more severe tone.

Adi's hand began to tremble in mine. I looked at her, surprised by her reaction, and knelt before her. "Adi— Adelaide, do you understand what Dr. Yin is saying?" I asked gently.

Adelaide shook her head.

Dr. Yin cleared her throat. "That's enough for now. Girls, sit."

I helped the two sisters to the smaller chairs placed to the left and right of mine.

"Adelaide and Abigail, there is no need to use nicknames or to tell someone that you like them. Walk into the room without a word," she said shortly.

The two girls nodded in unison, their shoulders hunched over.

Guess Dr. Yin is just one of those stricter teachers, I thought to myself, as I observed their interaction. *Strict can be good, but . . .*

"Rebecca, can you pull the blinds please?"

"Sure!" I walked over to the windows and pulled the blinds.

"Lights, as well."

I paused. Why would the lights need to go out?

Apparently I wasn't as up-to-date on the latest psychotherapy techniques as I thought I was. I turned off the lights.

And that was when I heard screaming.

The high-pitched moan of a frightened child.

I turned the lights back on.

Abigail had her arms around Adelaide, who was sobbing hysterically. "Adi gets scared when it's dark."

"Sweetie, it's okay." I rushed over. "It's just the light—"

"Rebecca." Dr. Yin offered me an expressionless gaze. "The lights must be off for this procedure. The girls will adjust."

I hesitated before finally nodding, walking back to the light switch to turn it off.

We all sat in silence, the plaintive moans of Adelaide filling the room, but now more subdued, as if out of fright.

I finally heard a voice, disembodied. "Think about your worst memory. But no crying. No talking."

Reverse psychology to get over a fear? I shrugged. *I don't know . . .*

When I finally was told to turn back on the lights, both girls were visibly shaken, tears rolling down their faces.

I moved toward them to dry off a tear, but Dr. Yin cleared her throat behind me.

"They must adjust," she said.

They're only children, I thought to myself.

But I only nodded and sat down again, looking once again into the mirror on the far right side of the room.

As I walked down the street to my car from Everson Psychological Center, I heard a slight rustling in the bushes to my left.

I turned around, scanning my surroundings with an uneasy feeling at the pit of my stomach.

Probably just the wind, I thought to myself. *Or perhaps a lizard.*

I rolled my eyes. *Seriously, Rebecca? You sound like you're the heroine of one of those murder mystery novels. Chill out. It's just the effect of the time of day. You were doing paperwork at the center late. You're just acting skittish.*

I finally reached my car. With my hand on the door, I looked up at the night sky.

Black. Pure blackness.

Where were the stars?

The next few days of the internship went more smoothly. I felt more at ease with my surroundings, my mentor, and the methods that were used. I noticed some strategies and techniques with which I was more familiar as a psychology student. I met two more clients and began to adjust myself to the daily routine of the practice.

I also was getting to know Dr. Yin a bit better. During

lunch hour, we would occasionally stay in the room and chat. She was a wonderful conversationalist and was familiar with many of my favorite philosophers and psychological theorists. We also shared some personal anecdotes that had us both laughing long into the day.

Was she a kindred spirit?

Peter Asturian: *That's about it on my end. How's that internship going?*

Rebecca Veritas: *It's going well! Much better!*

Peter Asturian: *Much better?*

Rebecca Veritas: *Yeah, I mean . . . I wasn't sure for a bit if maybe it wasn't a good match. Dr. Yin's methods seemed more . . . caustic than the approach I would take. But I think my overactive imagination blew it out of proportion. We're getting along great, and our approaches seem more similar than . . . well, than I previously thought. And I'm sure I could learn a lot from her to add to my practice once I'm officially in the field.*

Peter Asturian: **nods* That's good.*

Rebecca Veritas: *Yeah. It is. :) I'm glad. So, on another topic, it's about time for our monthly phone call, isn't it? When do you want to talk? :D*

He took a few minutes to respond. I waited, yelling at myself inwardly for my impatience. I just really . . .

Peter Asturian: *Oh, about that . . . I'm really sorry, Rebecca, but I'm pretty swamped this month with papers and my own internship at the local elementary school I* *mentioned. I'd like to do it when there's a good block of time so we can really talk, given the long distance calling and all. I don't know if I'll have the time this month.*

Oh.

I swallowed my disappointment and wrote back:

Rebecca Veritas: *Oh, of course . . . no worries! There's always next month!*

Peter Asturian: *Yeah. I'm actually . . . not sure if I'll be able to next month, either.*

He didn't know that I looked forward to those phone calls like Christmas and summer vacation.
Nor would he know.
I wrote back:

I understand. :)

The ballerina left her flight
And became a simple girl
Onward she walked
        alone
On her road
And alone she would find her place
In the cobbled streets
Of that fair-weather realm.
She looked up and whispered, "I can."
But there was a tear
In her eye.

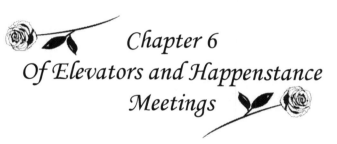

Chapter 6
Of Elevators and Happenstance Meetings

I pressed the button outside of the elevator, waiting for the door to slide open. As a child, I had always been fascinated by this moving, transportive "box" that glided up and down like some sort of teleporter. Now, as an adult well-versed with elevators, it still reminded me of something out of a sci-fi movie.

The door opened with a precise ring, and I stepped forth.

When I entered, however, I found myself jumping in surprise. "Christy," I exclaimed. "Small world!"

The secretary from Dr. Yin's facility looked back with a polite smile. "Nice to see you, Rebecca! Where are you headed?"

"Oh, I'm going to meet some friends for coffee. Well, actually," I smiled, "I can't stand coffee. It just sounded sophisticated putting it like that. I'm meeting friends at Coffee Bean for anything *other* than coffee."

Christy laughed, now more easily, the formality of the situation seeming to wear off. "That's so funny. I thought I was the only person who couldn't stand the taste of it."

"Oh my gosh, I know, right?!"

We spent the rest of the short, yet seemingly-longer-than-usual, elevator ride discussing other mutual areas of food and drink snobbery.

Interesting, I thought to myself. *I see this person every day, and yet I've gotten to know her better in the few moments of an elevator ride than any time before.*

*It's **nice**.*

The elevator stilled, coming to a stop. I took a step out, followed by Christy, who was carrying a large, black bag over one shoulder.

"See you later, Rebecca! I'm off to my weekly gym workout. So far," she laughed, "I've managed to keep to my schedule of coming every Tuesday."

"Good for you! See ya!"

We parted ways, waving goodbye, my heart left with the giddy joy and quiet satisfaction that comes when you feel that you have made a new friend.

I surveyed my surroundings, looking past various clothing stores and a bookstore of which I made mental note for future perusal, before finally spotting the object of interest.

"Coffee Bean" was printed in neat, dark-brown lettering, providing an appealing contrast to the lighter hues of its overall composition. I made out the figures of Teresa and another psychology classmate and walked more quickly.

"Hey, girl!" Teresa gave me a big hug. "So glad you could make it!"

Madeline, a girl with short, brown hair, smiled at me pleasantly from the other end of the table. "Hey, Rebecca!"

"Hey, Maddie!"

Maddie was a "school friend." I didn't know her very well, as we had never spent much time together outside of the classroom, but we had collaborated on various graduate projects, often with Teresa as a third team member. She always seemed nice, so I was glad that Teresa had invited her to join us. It would give me the opportunity to get to know each of them better. With the start of my internship, I knew that these opportunities would be few and far between, so I embraced it even more fully.

"So, anything new?" My eyes shifted quickly between the two girls, a dual purpose inquiry. "Work going well?"

"Oh, yeah," Maddie said. "I've been enjoying my internship. Already started writing up my first case study."

"Oh, already? That's amazing."

"What?" Teresa offered me a teasing glance. "The honors psychology student hasn't already finished her case study?"

"Ha, ha, very funny." I shook my head with a smile. "I'm not *that* crazy."

"Wanna get our drinks now?" Maddie pointed in the direction of the short line, which was arranged in a delicately cascading pattern originating from the register.

"Sure!" Teresa and I followed her to the end of the line.

I looked at the menu and decided upon a vanilla ice-blended drink. As I waited for the order to be filled, I began to feel a slight tension in my abdomen.

"Ow," I said aloud before I could stop myself. I didn't really like to broadcast physical discomfort.

"You okay, Rebecca?" Teresa eyed me in concern, Maddie quickly following suit.

"Oh, yeah, I'm fine."

I didn't elaborate further, and they didn't ask.

I was glad.

By the time the drinks were ready, the pain was gone. I wondered what it was. Maybe I'd pulled a muscle or tensed up.

I retrieved my drink and headed back to the table with my friends. The rest of the evening was relatively unremarkable, at least to the outside. We didn't discuss anything life-altering or paramount to international security. We discussed normal things, from school to members of the opposite sex, to career dreams beyond our school days, to life in general.

But, to me, it was *nice*.

I looked at the other two girls, laughing and joining me in their effervescent—but quiet—chatter, and images collided.

Strange how feelings of nostalgia can occur only a short time removed from the related events.

I saw a trio, and I smiled.

Approximately two hours later, we stood up, embraced, and went our separate ways. I put on my long, black, button-down coat and looked around. I could either make my way back to the elevator now or stay for a bit longer.

I chose to stay.

As I walked around the mall, window shopping, I discovered something that I had never found in my youth. When I was a teenager, I was supposed to have been enthralled at the prospect of visiting the mall. For me, that had been far from the case. I didn't mind the occasional trip—it served a practical purpose, there was the occasional fun store, and, as I thought to myself with a smile, I suppose my childlike nature had found something interesting in the way that the department store shifted into the mall, like a portal between two worlds. But, other than that, I found nothing too remarkable and, in fact, was a bit disenchanted due to its connection to giggly, boy-chasing, 'typical' teenage girl activities. I vowed to never be the girl who was "going to the mall" with her friends on the weekend.

Yet, as I walked, wrapping my coat around me thoughtfully, there was a new element to it. As blatantly immature as it would have sounded, I felt *older*. There was something about that walk that made me *feel* older.

Maybe it was just the coat and high-heeled boots.

But I think it was also something in the atmosphere, in the air . . . or maybe in me.

I had encountered an old place with a new perspective, and perhaps that made all the difference.

Now all I needed was an independent single woman anthem to spontaneously play.

The bookstore caught my eye again, beckoning me closer, and I finally assented, temporarily halting my window-shopping, quiet-pondering adventure as I stepped toward it.

As I opened the door, chimes dancing lightly in the air with the movement, my eyes took in a small, quaint room, filled with the sight and smell of books in varying stages of wear, dangling invitingly as they circled around and around in an arrangement of whirlpool delight. Some appeared as if they had been barely used—perhaps read, with care, once—but others looked years, perhaps decades, old. My eye was drawn to a large, dark green volume of swirling elaborate design that sat, seemingly in wait, near the register. It had the appearance of something ancient.

I cleared my throat, causing another occupant near the register, who was bent over some boxes facing the employees section, to turn around.

"Do you have a question?" The Ancient Book's friend materialized into a tall, slim woman with medium-length, gray-brown hair.

"I was just wondering—is this a bookstore for used books or rare?"

"Both. Some of the books," the woman pointed to an arrangement of shelves a few feet away, "could be found on Amazon at a higher price. But others are rare finds that I picked up in my travels."

"Oh, that's amazing—where did you find them?"

The tall woman leaned forward thoughtfully. "Oh, all over the place, really. Indonesia. England. Canada." At that last one, my mind instantly turned to Peter. "I do a lot of traveling and collect rare editions and rare books as I do."

"Wow. Very impressive. Do you have any special recommendations?"

Over the next hour, I browsed books, listened to tales of Tara's (That was the bookstore owner's name) travels, and decided that, when I grew old, I would not only be a lighthouse keeper, but a lighthouse keeper whose lighthouse was filled with books, from top to bottom.

Why have a *regular* lighthouse when you could have a Library-Lighthouse?

I grinned.

With much reluctance, I made my way toward the exit, noticing the time on the clock.

This was a great day, I thought, leaving the bookstore with a content heart. *Once again, the little things.*

I began to walk in the direction of the elevator, about half the mall away.

When I reached the mid-way point, my abdomen began to pulse with pain once again, about ten times worse than before. I pushed my hand against the wall forcefully.

What is going on?

I finally moved onward, although the pain had not dissipated. I hoped that the movement would help.

And that was when I saw a tall figure before me.

He was lean yet muscular, which seemed to make little sense. His eyes were light blue, without much depth to them, yet the sort that most girls would have found to be attractive. His heavy coat was gray, a lighter hue of the boots he wore. He stood before me with an impenetrable gaze.

I did not know who he was or what he was about to do, so I began to move quickly.

"Hey, girl." He stopped in front of me, his hands outstretched as if in a gesture of peace. "I didn't mean to scare you. But . . . are you Rebecca Veritas?"

He didn't need to know my name. I glanced toward the bookstore again, remembering how safe I had felt only a few minutes earlier.

"Oh, don't worry. Tara and I are old friends."

That reassured me. I had only just met Tara, but, unless my perception skills had taken a serious derail, I didn't detect any malicious intent from her.

He must be okay then.

"Yes, I'm Rebecca." I smiled hesitantly. "Well, I'll be on my way."

The man's eyes penetrated mine. "Nice to meet you, Rebecca."

"Same! See you later."

I walked quickly toward the elevator, remembering the time.

I only need to rush because of the time.

Time. What is time?

As I reached the elevator, I turned back briefly. Several yards away was the man with the dark gray coat, seemingly not an inch from where he had previously stood. He watched me fixedly with his cool blue eyes and smiled, a friendly smile of pearly white teeth.

I pressed the elevator button and walked through the door.

Oh, hey, Peter, this isn't really important. But it's Rebecca and —

Hey! I'm really short on time, sorry,

But what's up?

Oh, no worries! It's nothing, really.

Chapter 7
Of Eyes and the Sea

His dark gray eyes sank into his face, the tendrils of white and gray washed across his thinning hairline, wrinkles of time asperously making their mark. As I watched Albert, the first of the clients I had met, awaiting the next steps of Dr. Yin, whose own eyes remained encapsulated by the notebook before her, I found myself reminded of Cedric, the elderly usher at my home parish of St. Vitus.

They both must be about the same age, I mused, as I watched him. *They have the same dark gray eyes, when it comes to features. The same markings of the passage of innumerable days.* And yet how fundamentally different they were. Cedric was nearly ageless due to his timelessness, due to the sea captain in him, while Albert had seemingly been cast aside by time itself in its quick measure of thought, tossed in its dissonant quells.

No, he had not been cast aside. It was simply his eyes, lost in the time that had eluded him, in the time that would have it so. He had not been tossed aside by time, but lost in it. And, at that moment, as I watched Albert, his face fixedly impenetrable, I firmly decided that I would do my best to help him understand something of Cedric and fix his eyes with peaceful serenity upon the ceaseless ebb and flow of a forever-running tide.

"Albert," Dr. Yin addressed her client from the pile of papers before her, pulling me from my thoughts, "what did you accomplish this week?"

She did not look up, so I did, my eyes fixed upon his face, waiting for eyes to turn.

But they did not.

Albert sat, immobile, a Narnian statue that knew not how to transform back into his original state.

"Let us start with something simple. Did you go in the room before your session today?" Dr. Yin persisted, casting a measured gaze upward.

His eyes remained transfixed, as the corners of his mouth moved in a mere flicker. "Yes."

"Staying in the room helped you re-focus."

There was a silence broken only by the sharp, but steady, flow of the old man's breath.

"Albert," I said gently, once again reaching for his eyes, "Dr. Yin wants to know if it helped to do the therapy in that small room."

He did not answer.

Dr. Yin's eyes returned to mine. "Sometimes it is difficult to retrieve a clear answer from a client," she explained, taking on the voice of a teacher, in a sidenote that momentarily forgot the presence of a third individual. "Do not expect answers to always or immediately come."

She was right.

I nodded. "I understand."

"But there may be a more roundabout way of addressing it." Dr. Yin cleared her throat, once again addressing Albert. "Albert, you will go to the room again tomorrow."

He stared ahead, eyes unmoving. "Yes, I will go to the room."

"Good. Now, let's move on to our next goals . . ." Dr. Yin once again glanced down at the sheet before her. "Albert, you came back from the Korean War sixty years ago with a moderate level of PTSD that was successfully treated in five years . . ."

I snapped my pen open, taking notes. Dr. Yin was likely saying this as much for my benefit as Albert's, even though I had already viewed his file.

". . . when the Vietnam War brought the death of your nephew, the boy you looked after for over a decade following the fall in combat of your only brother, this panic intensified. Unchecked for many years, it only worsened over time, until the Veterans Health Administration became aware of your case three years ago and took action. Now you are in a safe place where you can get better."

The pleasant plethora of colorful paintings and bubbling water of the fountain of opposites murmured in agreement.

"Worse," his voice fumbled through the fog.

"What's worse, Albert?" I earnestly inquired, still seeking his far-cast eyes.

Dr. Yin cleared her throat, shooting me a look of mild reprimand.

"Oh, sorry," I mouthed, closing my mouth quickly, my face reddening.

It was time for me to learn from her, not to speak out of turn. For someone who had gone through much of her life avoiding the anxiety of speaking up voluntarily in class—let alone speaking out of turn—choosing instead to quietly complete work apart from the rest, I did not know why I was suddenly compelled to speak now. Certainly the nervousness of my high school years had abated significantly, but I was still that shy, unobtrusive girl. I only broke that inner pact within myself when the force of the circumstances was so strong as to evoke an inner pull from within that was stronger, compelling me to speak.

Unlike what I was facing now.

"He is reiterating that he became worse over time," Dr. Yin continued, brushing aside pages in her notebook, "but even repetition is a good sign, as it establishes his recognition of facts."

Of course. I nodded again, soaking in her words.

"Unfortunately, he is even less communicative than usual today, so another period in the therapy room may be required. It is a more intensive probing of the mind that you will observe in a future session." Dr. Yin glanced in my direction.

My mentor certainly has a good memory, I thought to myself with satisfaction, recalling the curiosity I had expressed to her in a previous session in regards to the small therapy room that Albert had then entered.

"But, for now," a line of amusement crossed her brow, "I have mounds of paperwork, especially with the addition of a new client shortly before you began your internship. It is relatively self-explanatory, but also rather tedious, so I would be thoroughly gratified if you assisted in this most grievous of circumstances."

I laughed. "Of course. Would be happy to help."

Dr. Yin escorted Albert to the door, his thin, frail body prodding slowly behind her.

As he walked past me, I suddenly reached out a

hand and lightly touched the sleeve of his worn blue shirt, the same old garment that he had worn during the previous session, if memory served me.

It was a nearly involuntary movement, spontaneously surfacing in my mind the instant that I put it into action.

And, yet, as it occurred and he continued toward the door held open by Dr. Yin, seemingly without any notice of what had transpired, I watched quietly, my eyes barely perceiving a flinch of movement across his cheekbone, drawing the surface of his cheeks slightly downward, as if relaxing briefly into its natural shape.

But perhaps it was my imagination.

Chapter 8

Of Half-Made Plans and Hurried Agendas

I knocked on the white-washed wooden door.

"Come in," came a faint, familiar voice from within.

I obeyed, opening the door.

Dr. Everson sat behind an impressive, dark mahogany desk. He was never one for understatement, but his office at the Los Angeles extension of my old university always seemed to have a more luxurious bent than the one that I had visited so many times before as an undergrad. Every time I stopped by, it seemed to develop a new addition.

For a moment, I was caught in an awareness of how far in the past my graduation—five months ago—now seemed.

"Rebecca," he said in that booming voice of his, "have a seat." He indicated the chair across from him.

I took a seat, reminded momentarily of my first meeting with Dr. Yin. But this was very different. It was a meeting with an old acquaintance.

"Nice desk," I observed.

He laughed, a laugh as booming and contagious as his speaking voice. "Thank you. I thought it was about time for a replacement of that old metal contraption. This year we had a bit more money in the budget to spend for our department, and I took advantage of it."

He said "advantage" like he was some sort of corporate spy.

I smiled.

"So," he said, drumming his fingers thoughtfully on his desk, "how do you like working with Dr. Yin?"

I paused. "Very well. She is very knowledgeable. I wasn't . . . as familiar with some of her techniques at first, but I'm learning."

I had looked up the fear replacement tactic she had used with the twin girls. It was called exposure therapy, used in the treatment of phobias. According to the theory, repeated exposure to fears in a non-threatening environment could lead to the overcoming of those fears.

"Excellent. I have never met Dr. Yin myself, but her credentials are sound." Dr. Yin's voice softened. "I am glad that she brings honor to my grandfather's name."

In that moment, I was abundantly glad that I had not said anything negative about my mentor.

Good thing I had scheduled this meeting a week later than initially planned.

"So, here is your schedule for the rest of the semester." Dr. Everson handed me a marked calendar, in addition to a rather large packet. "And the guidelines for your internship and related course study. I know you have the preliminary summary, but this is a more in-depth look." He nodded in my direction. "Let me know if you have any questions."

I glanced at the stack of papers before me. "I will."

On my way out, I met Teresa in the hallway.

"Becca!" she called out to me from the other end.

I ardently disliked that nickname but would forgive it in hallway meetings.

"Hey!" I reached her. "You here for your meeting with Dr. E?"

"Yeah, and," she ran a hand distractedly through her hair, "that's the problem. You see, I totally forgot that I was supposed to be staying with my little sister this afternoon. She goes to a private school and has the day off. Anyway," she looked at me hopefully, "you wouldn't have a spare hour or two, would you?" She continued breathlessly, "I'm going to be working with Dr. Everson as an administrative assistant this semester, so it might be a long meeting. We have a lot to set up."

Teresa made a face. "I'd just have her wait here, but she already made a scene in the lobby."

"Sure!" I said, wondering in the back of my mind how much of a scene she had made. "How old is she?"

"Fourteen."

"Fourteen?" I lifted an eyebrow.

"Yeah, I know. She's a real brat. Could use some supervision. You can just take her to the mall or something, whatever you want. Anyway," Teresa waved in the direction of Dr. Everson's office, "I'd better run. You're a real lifesaver, Rebecca. I owe you!"

And, with that lightning-speed farewell, Teresa disappeared into the distance.

"No problem!" I called after her.

I shook my head with a smile and headed for the lobby.

A short girl with auburn hair highlighted with

blonde streaks sat in apparent discontent on the fourth cushion of the spacious lobby.

"Hey." I cleared my throat. "Are you Amelia?"

I hoped that was her name. Teresa's chipmunk explanation left me to my memory, which seemed to record that name as the identification marker of Teresa's one and only sister.

"Yeah." The auburn-haired teenager looked up, her countenance a mixture of curiosity and instantaneous disapproval. "What do you want?"

"I'm a friend of your sister. Teresa asked me to keep you company," I said, hand outstretched with a smile.

Amelia made a sound halfway between a gasp and a sigh in evident indignation. "That would be *so* like her! Whatever. You can hang. I'm bored anyway."

I sat down in response to her reluctant invitation. There was a moment's pause.

Amelia glanced in my direction. "You a Christian?"

"Yeah, I am," I said, the moment calling to mind a certain perplexing day in the college bookstore.

"Oh, I guess you're okay then." She paused. "Sorry for my mood, by the way. Did Teresa tell you why I was annoyed?"

I paused, considering my options. *Do I **really** want to know the answer?*

My bullet-proof honesty once again won out.

"No, why?"

"Because it's not *fair!*" she exploded, beginning to launch into a twenty-minute dissertation on how her friends got to wear the hottest clothes and go out more than she did, "ughhh," and how the other kids at school—the ones who weren't her friends—were "so lame, like, really."

I listened patiently, in what I hoped was an empathetic way.

Note to self: Try to connect better with teenagers than you did when you were a teenager yourself.

"And it's *so* unfair," she finished. She looked at me. "Don't you think?!"

"I think," I said evasively, "that it can be difficult to stand out, but that . . . your parents just want what's best for you."

"Ugh, you sound just like Teresa! No wonder you two are friends." She groaned. "Well, at least you're both Christian."

I took this turn in the conversation as an opportunity to switch gears . . . or, in this case, locations. "Want to go to the mall?"

She stared at me. "I take that back. You are way cooler than my sister!"

Actually, I thought to myself, as we left the lobby and headed to my car, *it was your sister's idea.*

"I take that back *again*."

Amelia and I stood in front of Tara's bookstore. We had hardly reached the approximate vicinity of the store before the disgruntled teenage sister of my new BFF staged a protest.

I ignored her objections and entered. She reluctantly followed.

I began to browse a shelf of rare books that had recently been shelved.

"A bookstore?" She stood with her hands on her hips, mouth widening in the continuation of her rant. "You have *got* to be kidding. I don't want to go to some dumb bookstore!"

I looked at her. "I don't care." I pointed to the chair ahead. "Sit."

She blinked, half in protest and half in disbelief, as if no one had ever dared to say such a thing to her.

And then she sat down, fixing her eyes upon the wall ahead, her mouth forming a formidable pout.

A smile tiptoed across my face. *For a brat, she was starting to grow on me.*

I bit my lip, shaking my head as the smile grew into a grin.

"Rebecca?"

Tara came out from the back of the store, her eyes bright. "Thought I would see you again soon!"

I had visited the bookstore a few more times on my way home from the internship. It seemed that talking to Tara never got old. There was so much history in her story.

In that way, she reminded me of a lighthouse keeper.

I smiled. "Hey Tara! You still have that rare edition of *Pride and Prejudice*?"

"Oh, I'm sorry, honey, it's been sold already! But I do have another Jane Austen book — *Sense and Sensibility*. Not as old, but it's still quite beautiful." Tara surveyed the bookstore shelves, her eyes pausing on Amelia, who was scowling in my direction. "Friend of yours?"

"Um," I paused, "my friend's sister."

Tara nodded in understanding, a smile curling at the corner of her lips. "Ah, yes, babysitting."

"I heard that!" Amelia stood up quickly, her eyes narrowing. "How can you babysit a fourteen-year-old?"

My question exactly.

"Poor choice of words, my dear," Tara responded amiably. "Need help finding anything?"

"No, I don't even want to *be* here." Amelia sat down in a huff. "I wanna go to the cool stores."

"Amelia," I looked at her severely, "That's no way to talk to the store owner."

Tara waved it away. "Don't worry about it, Rebecca. I'll find that book for you."

While the bookstore owner looked through a few stacks on a cart that had yet to be put on the shelves, I pulled up a chair and sat next to Amelia. I was about to open my mouth when I saw, through the store window, a familiar man with cool blue eyes. He was standing near the entrance to the beauty salon across from Tara's bookstore, and, with those eyes, stared back at me.

He made no move to enter the salon or the bookstore, maintaining a steady focus in my direction.

I shivered involuntarily, and, once again, a sharp pain accosted my abdomen.

"You looking at that guy over there?" Amelia leaned over for a better view. "Is he cute?"

"Amelia!" I grabbed her arm, speaking more sharply than I intended, as I cast a quick glance in the direction of the exit. "Let's go."

"But we just got here!"

"I thought you didn't want to be here."

"Well, we haven't checked out the rest of the mall yet. And," she waved a flurry of paper in my face, "Vintage fashion magazines."

Despite the feeling of—hyperbole aside—impending doom, I couldn't help but smile. "Well, I'm glad you found something 'cool'."

"What's with the guy?" Amelia returned to the original subject, not missing a beat.

She was too smart.

Okay, well, I could make it a teachable moment.

"I'm not sure," I said carefully, "But I don't like the way he's looking at me. So, I think we should exit through the back. Just in case."

To my surprise, Amelia nodded, relinquishing her seat quietly. She followed me as I made my way toward the back door.

I fingered the pepper spray in my purse. It was still daytime, but . . . just in case.

"Rebecca?" Tara looked up from the cart as we inched toward the door. "Leaving already? Should I put this book aside for you?" She held up the copy of *Sense and Sensibility*.

"Yes, please! Sorry we have to rush out."

"Oh, no problem. I understand." She waved us out.

Amelia followed me to my car and buckled herself into the passenger seat.

With one hand on the door, I looked back, the stabbing pain in my chest pulsing with renewed vigor.

The red robin on the fencepost lost his focus and dived downward.

The grasshopper jumped into the car.

Chapter 9
Of New and Old

I propped my chin against my hand, smiling, as I read the email displayed on the screen.

It was from Teresa. She reported that Amelia could not stop talking about me for the remainder of the day when she returned home. It was a running commentary of observations and questions that literally took her to bedtime. It was not a monologue free from criticism, Teresa noted humorously, so I was now in the same or at least a similar boat as her. But she said that, underneath the complaints, she could tell that Amelia liked me.

And that, she wrote, *is the accomplishment of the century.*

Yet the email was not without its mark of sadness. Due to personal complications, Teresa had had to put off her internship with Dr. Yin for another semester. She had only had the opportunity to meet her before the news struck her that her family was in difficult financial straits caused by the bankruptcy of her father's corporation. The family was now without a stable source of income, and, after much prayer and reflection, Teresa had come to the conclusion that those she loved most would be best served if she assisted by taking on another job.

So, I'm sorry I won't see you after your sessions this semester, but I'm sure we will get to hang out at other points. I'm excited about what this new year will bring!

I sensed the disappointment of my friend behind the typed words and over-cheerfulness that could not mask her attempts to be more positive than she felt.

Poor thing. The internship had meant the world to her, and even a temporary delay would break her heart. I clicked on the "Reply" button, mulling over in my mind what I would say.

But I was saved from that immediate decision, as the repetitive ringing of the apartment phone broke through my inner thoughts.

"Hello?" I dashed to the phone, throwing the receiver to my ear.

"Hi, baby."

"Oh, Mom!" I grinned, holding the receiver more comfortably against my ear. "I'm so thrilled you called! I missed talking to you the other day when I fell asleep in front of the computer."

"Rebecca," the voice on the other end was severe, "if you are not taking care of yourself in this overrated city of Los Angeles, your Italian mama is going to come and—"

"Mama, I'm fine, really," I protested, as my smile

grew. "But thanks for caring."

"I'm not sure if 'fine' is as high a standard as I would like, but I'll give you another month."

I laughed. "Okay, Mom."

"So," her severe voice transformed, warming into the curiosity that comes with love, "how is your internship going? Do you like your mentor?"

I paused. "Yeah, it's going great. It's just a bit hard, you know, with the clients."

"How so?"

"Well, I haven't really started working with them actively, though I incidentally just got an email from Dr. Yin suggesting that I begin some minor cooperative work with her to assist clients in the next session. I guess she noticed how eager I was to begin." I laughed. "But, anyway, I digress . . . What I mean is that the clients I have seen so far have a rough time. Especially Albert. He has PTSD and . . . Mom, he barely even looks at anyone. It's like he's stuck, stuck in his recollections and unable to be freed from it. I don't really know much about PTSD and whether that's common or not, but . . . all I know is that he is really bad off. And I may not know him, but it still . . ." I paused. "It still breaks my heart."

"That's because you care, Rebecca. I'm proud that you are that kind of person."

I nodded, even though she couldn't see it. "Thanks, Mom. I really appreciate that."

"Don't worry, sweetie. I know I'm not exactly an expert at not worrying" —at this, I laughed heartily— "but it's true that worrying doesn't solve any problems. Just do your best as I know you will, and leave the rest to God."

"I'll try."

"Good girl. I'll be praying for him. And for you."

"Thanks, Mom."

"Of course, sweetie. So, who are your other clients?"

"Oh!" My voice rose in excitement. "They are so adorable! Just absolutely . . . adorable. I love them."

"And . . . who is adorable exactly?"

I laughed again. "Sorry, Mom, I suppose I should have provided an introduction. The members of the human race that I referred to a few moments ago carry the names Abigail and Adelaide . . . though I like to think of them as Abi and Adi. They are a set of very, very sweet twins. They're only seven years old. I love their innocent little facial expressions and loving hearts. And I love how I can say that after only having seen them a grand total of three times."

"They sound perfectly adorable. I'm glad you get to work with kids. You always had that in common with Peter."

"Oh . . . yeah, I did. I do."

"Are you two still keeping in touch?"

"Sometimes. We try to. It's hard this semester, but . . . we try." I closed my mouth, allowing a pause of silence to continue the conversation.

"I understand."

Like dandelions they flew across the expanse
Of desert calm without advance
They filtered through the stilled "become"
Returning to the land they knew.
They knew no more than where they flew.
And so they gathered, one and all,
And scattered it throughout their path.
Only golden-shafted majesty could still their might.
And so they flew onward, without a path.

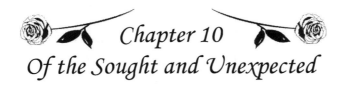

Chapter 10
Of the Sought and Unexpected

"Okay, St. Anthony," I said, looking squarely ahead. "This is a crisis situation."

I stood in the middle of my apartment, the warmth of morning air casting light shadows on the wooden floor.

"Could you have a chat with God for me? Because I could really use your prayers right about now. I'm almost late for my internship," I gestured toward the door, "and I can't find my notebook anywhere. Literally . . . anywhere."

I had searched the room for nearly an hour to no avail, finally throwing up my hands in exasperation.

"So, it would be great if you could intercede, preferably before internship begins . . . if that works."

"You know," I added, "I was reading Revelation 8:3–4 the other day, the part about incense mingling with the prayers of the saints . . . and I instantly thought of *you*. Because we're buddies like that."

I cleared my throat. "And that was not an attempt at flattery. At all. I just. really. need. to. find. my. notebook."

The patron saint of lost articles remained silent.

I sighed and turned to my desk to retrieve my purse. *Guess I'll use a separate piece of paper today and remember the rest as best as I can.*

I bent over, unzipping the middle section of my purse to find my sunglasses.

A slight pressure directed upon my head—accompanied by the sound of a small object falling—impeded my actions, inspiring a glance upward.

I blinked, staring blankly at my internship notebook, which sat cheerfully on my head.

Speedy delivery.

"St. Anthony?" I said haltingly, looking up at the ceiling—and beyond—inquisitively.

After a moment's pause, I returned to my purse. "That's pretty chill. Now, if I could just locate that mantilla," I mumbled, "I could attend my first Latin Mass next Sunday as planned."

The phone rang.

I froze. *No way.*

Probably a phone spammer.

I picked up the receiver. "Hello?"

"Rebecca, it's Mom."

"Hi, Mom."

"Something . . . unusual just happened." The puzzlement in her voice was indisputable. "I had put down some library books on the sofa—saint biographies for our religious discussion meeting—and left the room for a few minutes, ten at the most. When I returned, I found your missing mantilla on top of the pile. Not sure how it got there, unless it fell down from somewhere or

I completely forgot . . . No one else was in the room . . ."

"Mom," I interrupted, "Do you remember which saint book was at the top of the stack?"

"Um," there was a brief pause, "it looks like . . . the Saint Anthony one. Why—"

*Catholic nerd-out begins . . . **now**.*

"Mom, one second?"

"Sure, hun!"

I threw down the receiver, running gleefully in a frenzied manner around the room, a spontaneous reel which climaxed in an energetic leap into the air.

Dude.

I returned to the phone. "Back, Mom. Actually, I'd better run so I'm not late for my internship. Yes, I do. Okay then. Talk to you later. Bye."

I put down the phone, grabbed my purse, recovered notebook, and keys, and headed for the door.

At the last moment, I turned back, a wry smile lifting itself across my face.

"Well played, St. Anthony, well played."

My eyes were covered by thin hands the moment I stepped into the room.

Two identical pairs of giggles trickled into my hearing.

"Okay, Abi and Adi," I said, a smile inching irresistibly across my face. "I know it's you."

Further giggles subsequently followed, as those two pairs of small hands were lifted from my face.

"Scared ya." Abi's eyes beamed at me with rambunctious energy; she was standing next to her sister, whose face was similarly aglow.

I feigned a sigh of defeat. "So you did, girls; so you

did."

The twins giggled again, and, at that moment, I happened to look up.

The entire office was decorated to the brim. Streamers of pink, purple, and white cascaded in shimmering beams of bright light, welcoming a spacious festivity to the office room. Confetti fell to the marble floor, as Abi and Adi circled about in effervescent flight.

In the center of it all was a large, hot pink banner with the words, "Happy Birthday, Rebecca!" written across with an elegant flourish.

At that moment, Dr. Yin, previously a background image that passed my notice, moved from her desk with a wide, composed smile. She wore a yellow lacey blouse, still formal with the cupped collar at her neck, but less business-like than anything I seen her don previously. In her hands was a large, white cake, decorated with delicate swirls of the same colors that bedazzled the room.

"Happy Birthday, Rebecca," she said, with a back chorus of two young voices now receding to the background. "We thought you might like to celebrate with us at work today." She smiled again, her demeanor pleasantly adorned in the same festivity of the room.

"Thank you." I blinked. "But . . . my birthday is January 29th."

"Your *true* birthday. The day you presented your thesis on behavioral theory. Once in the field, you will find that that is a more significant celebration than that of the day you were born."

I smiled, shaking my head in wonder. "This is really sweet of you. Thank you, truly."

"It is my pleasure. Now, shall we dig in?"

Chapter 11
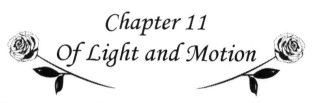
Of Light and Motion

"Albert, would you tell me a little about your family?"

I took off the cap of my pen and waited. For the past several minutes, I had tried to coax Albert into saying something—anything—that would bring him to reality. But I had had little success. He maintained his gaze outward, or perhaps inward, staring into the distance without any clear indication of its destination.

Dr. Yin cleared her throat. "Perhaps it is best that I take over for now."

I glanced over at Albert, who remained standing with the same vacant expression imprinted on his face, before nodding. "Of course. I . . . have a great deal to learn." I managed an embarrassed laugh.

"Just some strategies. It will all come in time. Would you hand me the notebook on top of the files?" She gestured to the large, wooden cabinet ahead. "It appears that Christy forgot to put it on my desk."

"Of course," I repeated, relinquishing my seat to retrieve the object of interest. As I did so, the pulsing sensation of a vibrant melody emanated from my left pocket.

My cell phone had apparently decided that now was the best time to say hello.

Embarrassment at maximum levels.

"I am so sorry!" I rushed to explain, reaching to pull my cell phone out, my face warming as I did. "I always turn it off before entering the office. I have no idea why I forgot . . ."

My words trailed off as a distinct tapping sound inspired me to look up.

Albert stood, one foot in front of the other, moving in hesitant, but distinguishable, steps.

Dancing steps.

"Albert, you like to dance?" I forgot my cell phone, letting the melody of Axel Fernando's "Celebra la vida" continue to play.

He did not answer, but, after a moment, I perceived a slight inclination of the head.

A nod.

Communication.

"Hey, you know," I said enthusiastically, "I have the full song on my playlist, along with some others. Maybe we can dance together." I moved my hand quickly across the screen, swiping a few buttons before finally reaching the desired input. "Here it is . . ."

No sé si soñaba, no sé si dormía, y la voz de un ángel dijo que te diga . . .

The soft voice of Axel Fernando glided through the airy expanse of the small, brightly furnished room.

Albert moved slowly, his body rocking back and

forth, finding the beat.

I don't know if I dreamt nor if I slept.

The quiet melody broke into an energetic salsa beat.

And the voice of an angel told me to tell you . . .

I took his hand, slowly reaching out, uncertain of how he would react.

He did not pull away.

Faster, faster.

We spun around, slowly and then with less hesitation.

¡Celebra la vida!

Albert took my hand and twirled me around. I fell into the movement, circling around and around with renewed energy before returning to face him.

Que nada se guarda.

His face was flushed with the same energy, his eyes brightened. While there were hints of the hazy mist surrounding his countenance, it had largely retreated.

Que todo te brinda.

I smiled.

The corners of his mouth moved uncertainly before they, too, formed a smile.

We shifted through the movements of the dance, free and alive.

Christy entered, pausing to stare with wide eyes at the scene. As for Dr. Yin's reaction, I remained unaware, only that she remained silent.

I grinned, holding out a hand. "Join us, Christy."

Christy blinked, held at bay by disbelief, before an innocent joy filled her eyes. She grinned back, and moved forward, taking one hand of Albert's and one of mine.

Time did not seem to exist as, together, we spun around the room, laughing in the ecstasy of the moment.

Laughing. Albert was *laughing.*

My eyes grew moist, but I was smiling. *Oh, I was smiling.*

The song reached its conclusion, lingering for several moments in the air as each of us wiped moisture from our brow.

I curtsied deeply to my partner. "Thank you for this dance, Mr. Albert."

He did not bow, but he was grinning from ear to ear. Christy looked back and forth, from Albert to me, in unveiled wonder.

"Dance again!" Albert exclaimed, his eyes alight as he reached his hand out.

It was the first time I had ever seen him happy.

"Oh, I would love to! But I don't know if—"

From behind me, Dr. Yin cleared her throat.

"It's best that we get back to work."

"Of course," I said quietly, indicating with a smile for Albert to follow me. I picked up the notebook that I had long forgotten and turned back.

Albert's eyes focused on mine, the trusting expression of a child.

"Dancing girl," he said.

"Dancing man," I said with a smile.

Rebecca Veritas
It was . . . incredible, Peter. This man has lost so much. It usually seems like he has lost himself, too. But today . . . there was something there.

Peter Asturian
nods
That's incredible, Rebecca. :) I'm glad.

Rebecca Veritas
:)
So, what's new?

Peter Asturian
Well
things are pretty busy around here with the winter festivals coming up.
It's a pretty popular attraction around here in Banff.
and all of Alberta, really.
We get a lot of tourists this time of year.

Rebecca Veritas
Oooh that sounds epic! :D

Peter Asturian
Yeah, you'd like it a lot. :)
Especially the Ice Magic Festival.

Rebecca Veritas
The Ice Magic Festival? :D

Peter Asturian
Yeah, ice carvers from all around the world come together to sculpt these really incredible pieces out of ice.
They're like something out of a fairy tale, really, so I think you'd love it.

Rebecca Veritas
Wow, sounds beautiful. I hope I can . . .

Peter Asturian
?

Rebecca Veritas
Oh, I just meant that I hope I can see it one day.

Peter Asturian
Yes, you should.

Rebecca Veritas
:)
So, what's your favorite part of the festival?

Peter Asturian
I like the ice carving, too, but my favorite is probably the parade of lights. I remember watching Santa's sled fly across the night sky ever since I was a little boy. Somehow it doesn't seem to matter that I'm older now. It still holds something for me . . . not because I believe in Santa (other than the real Santa, St. Nick ;)) anymore, but because it's something that the world at large has lost.

There's beauty in it. An innocent joy.

Rebecca Veritas
nods I think you're right.
I hope you have a beautiful time watching the lights this year.
:)

Peter Asturian
Thank you.
I'm afraid I must go, but

Rebecca Veritas
Have you been writing at all? I mean, you must be busy trying to fit the festival in when you're going crazy anyway
Oh sorry, didn't see your reply until now.

Peter Asturian
That's OK.
I'm helping out a little with the festival. It's a small town . .
. and my dad actually is on the festival committee, so that's
a given. But it's more a feeling of busyness rather than much
direct involvement.
And, no, not much time for writing at the moment.

Rebecca Veritas
sighs I know the feeling. I've written a few poems here and
there, but that's about it. I haven't written more than a few
pages of an actual story in months. Maybe I'll have more time
this summer. It feels weird not writing.

Peter Asturian
nods Yes.
Well, I have to run. Take care.

Rebecca Veritas
TTYL.

Peter Asturian
TTYS.

I closed my laptop and crawled into bed. Ice
sculptures danced before my shut eyes, delicate
figurines come to life.
I wish . . . was the last thought before I drifted off to
sleep, a withhold sigh forgotten in its wake.

In the reverie of night
Lost thoughts assemble and form a truce

To create out of jumbled plethora
A something
A tale with half sense and partial truth
But a story is a story all the same
As unsuspecting traveler emerges in nightgown or cap
To partake in its imagining.

In the reverie of night
Lost thoughts inform, but scatter still
When an unsuspecting traveler
Creates not with scattered thoughts
But scattered hearts
Dreams once started.
Are they better left in partiality?
Or is it worse that they have begun at all . . .

The traveler continues on
And the heart remains with the lost thoughts
Of half-realized dreams.

Rebecca Veritas woke up, her eyes burning with lost sleep.

I woke up, my eyes killing me. A quick glance in the mirror revealed drooping eyelids and bags underneath. With a sigh, I closed my eyes again, banishing any extraneous thought.

And, with it, the poem in my mind.

Chapter 12
Of What I Thought and What I Think

I walked into Everson Psychological Center in what, by now, felt like a well-rehearsed routine. I brushed off the weekend sleepiness and set my book bags on a nearby couch, digging through my purse for my cell phone. Taylor Swift's "Fearless" was playing with enthusiasm, letting me know that a caller was trying to get through. As I balanced the cell phone precariously against one ear, I cast a quick glance at the secretary's desk to wave at Christy in greeting.

But, as my eyes took in the familiar sight of desk and chair, they noticed an absence.

No Christy.

Instead there was seated a tall woman with light brown hair busying herself at Christy's desk.

She looked up at me, as if noticing my observation.

I looked back, listening to the call that had become a message.

She looked a lot like Christy. The same stature, the same hairstyle.

But also very different.

I flipped my phone closed, put it away, and walked up to the front desk.

"Hi, I'm Rebecca."

"Donna," she responded amiably, shaking my hand with a contagious smile.

"Nice to meet you. By the way, have you seen Christy around?"

"Christy doesn't work here anymore."

"Oh, I see," I said, caught by genuine surprise.

"I'm the new secretary," she said, by way of explanation.

"Ah, gotcha. Well . . . again, nice to meet you." I laughed awkwardly.

She laughed. "Same to you."

I returned to my seat.

"Oh, Rebecca?"

"Yeah?"

"Dr. Yin is ready for you." She pointed to the headset that she was wearing. "She just called you in."

Guess we've had a technological advancement in one week's time, I thought to myself as I followed Donna down the hall, even though I knew my way.

"Hello, Rebecca," Dr. Yin addressed me over her wiry spectacles as Donna left, closing the door behind her. "Won't you have a seat?"

I sat down, a bit perplexed at the formality in Yin's voice. But I then remembered that, despite our laughs and casual conversations, she was still my superior.

I sat down, finding that I had been sitting down, opening doors, closing doors, and walking around an awful lot lately.

I sat down and waited.

"Well, Rebecca, you have been an incredible asset to the team with your assistance and, no doubt, by your observation. But now," she looked me straight in the eye, "it's time for you to move on to the participation segment of this internship."

I involuntarily sucked in my breath, both in nervousness and excitement. *This was it.* Well, part of it . . .

"Don't worry," Dr. Yin interjected with a laugh. "You'll still be observing. But it'll be half and half. And . . . about a month down the road, you'll be taking over with full responsibility of my clients for a period of four weeks."

That was it.

"So," Dr. Yin passed a folder to me, inviting me to open it, "as you see, there will be one additional time slot on your schedule. You already know the twins, Adelaide and Abigail, as well as Albert—"

This was the first time I noticed that there were so many "A" names on the list.

"—Diana—"

Diana was a kindly, middle-aged woman with a severe aversion to heights. While her struggles were seemingly minor when compared to those of the other clients, every night she faced a chaotic stream of images related to her fear. It was starting to have an impact on her career and marriage.

"—Tybalt—"

Named after the character in Shakespeare's *Romeo and Juliet*, Tybalt took the role seriously because of his multiple personality disorder. In a different way than Albert, he seemed disconnected from reality half the time. Sometimes he waved his hand in the air as if he were engaging in a swordfight.

Only it wasn't funny.

"And, now, I'm going to add Stacie to your list."

I opened my notebook and clicked my pen, the AP student ready to take notes. "What is her difficulty?"

"Self-concept."

I nodded, writing it under the new page I had started, as for every client. "Got it."

"Please be here one hour early, at 9 AM sharp tomorrow," Dr. Yin said. "You may take an early lunch now."

"Will do. Thank you." I reached my hand across the table, shaking her hand, in the final gesture of formality.

Then I took my book bag, preparing to leave . . .

And walked out again.

It is almost Thanksgiving, I thought to myself as I shivered in the cool evening breeze. The world was hushed, as if waiting a bit early for Christmas, icicles dancing across its vision.

Only, I noted with some slight bitterness, *it won't snow around here.*

It had been a relatively uneventful day. After lunch, I had helped Adi and Abi with their confidence in speech. It seemed that, when Abi started to make a breakthrough, her enthusiasm carried weight and shifted to the shoulders of Adi. But Yin was very clear about use of instructional time, so, once satisfied with some progress made, she moved on to the next lesson, asking me to leave the room to file some papers. Albert had been missing all week—on some hospital recess, I think, but Yin couldn't tell me—so all that remained of the afternoon was Tybalt and Diana. Neither seemed any better, I noticed with the frustration of a newbie, but not particularly worse either. At least it was better than the alternative.

So, once I was done with the filing, I was permitted to leave early.

Easy day.

"Hey, hey, special jewelry for sale!"

A few doors down, a jeweler, tall and dressed in flowing garments, was selling her wares, reminding me of the medieval marketplace that I had always romanticized.

I couldn't resist.

Without a second thought, I walked over. *Perhaps I would find some Christmas presents.*

A flute played in the distance, a yearning, plaintive voice lifting in quiet echoes of starry tales once told. And, yet, it was as clear as if it had been told yesterday, as certain as the passing of sunlight each day.

My eyes followed the source, heart also yearning for the same sweet song, as I temporarily forgot the jewelry stand before which I now stood. They soon took in an old man playing by the side of the road. There was something comforting in his presence, as if his song spoke beyond his instrument. I found myself, for the first time in a long time, reminded of a certain old sea captain I once knew. Beside him, a middle-aged woman sat, selling her wares much like the jeweler before me that I had quickly forgotten. And, despite the wonder and beauty of the scene, I knew from their appearance that they were there because they had no other place to call home.

As these thoughts and others collected in my mind, the woman took note of me; her eyes turned toward me pleasantly as her lips formed a cheery smile. The old man, clad in rags but appearing to be a lord of the court, then saw me, too, and lifted his hat to me as if we were not living in the 21st century, but years past. And, with that salute, I found a gesture of not just "Hello," but "Would you like me to play my song again?"

I nodded, and he lifted the instrument to his lips.

I stood there, listening, as I took in my surroundings. As I took a deep breath, filling my spirit with the brisk, cool air that greeted me in its own welcoming party. It filled my entire being as I saw a place, a world, once again. As I finally sighed and moved to purpose, springing to action like the transition between "pause" and "play," to look through the jewelry before me. As I found a shell keychain among them, fingering it lightly before handing it to the seller. *It would be for Peter.*

The song remaining in hearing and heart, I walked, window shopping, and, perhaps, just *being*. A smile formed on my lips—I felt it now—as I became lost, yet found, on a road and its leaves of poetry.

My gaze flickered across the two individuals who marked the start—and soundtrack—of my trek, noticing that the woman, who had since tied her hair up with a scarf, was laying out scarves of varying hues and designs on a small table. They glimmered in the remaining sunlight of the quickly departing day in delicate elegance.

Scarves were my one material weakness.

I eagerly walked back to the beginning in long, brisk strides.

"Hello, dear." She nodded pleasantly in recognition. "Did something catch your fancy?" She gestured to the table lined with scarves. Closer up, they appeared even more irresistible, shimmers turning to sparkles, like jewels around a young courtier's neck.

"All of them," I blurted out without thinking before

blushing furiously. "I mean, they're all lovely."

And I have a few at home. But Christmas is coming . . .

"I'd like to buy one for my mom."

The woman nodded. "A thoughtful gift, dear."

I searched the supply. "Perhaps the red and white one with the sparkles. Mom likes red best, and it would suit the season . . ."

As she folded the scarf carefully, preparing the order, I heard the sound of shuffling feet and looked up.

Albert stood, his appearance a scramble of mismatched clothes and vacant eyes.

And suddenly all became clear to me. Albert had skipped his regularly-scheduled appointments because he could no longer have them.

Oh.

"Albert," I said quietly, my voice breaking.

His eyes met mine, and, for a single instant, there was clarity, a recognition in them.

"Dancing girl," he spoke slowly.

"Yes." I bit my lip, trying to stop the tears that threatened to cascade downward. "It's me. It's Dancing Girl."

He turned away, his tired eyes once again lost in the distance. I thought of how I had, only a few moments before, been lost in something, too.

But it was a very different kind of *lost.*

I looked back at the old flute player and—was it his daughter? She handed the bag to me wordlessly, her sympathetic eyes touching mine briefly in understanding.

She knew. She was a stranger, but she knew.

The old man sat there silently before once again lifting the flute to his lips with his eyes focused on me intently.

The flute carried its song once again, lifting into the

air with sweet surrender.

I took the bag in my hand and prepared to leave . . .

Then, a voice—

"Happy," the words were deliberate, and, as I turned to observe Albert looking back at me, I realized it was a struggle to get them out, to break through the haze and set them free, "to see you. Happy to see you, Dancing Girl."

He reached his hand for mine.

I took it, putting my own—a small form over one large and worn with age—over his.

"Good to see you, too, Albert."

On the way home—on the walk to the car and the silent drive—I clung to the scarf of red and white in my mind, bidding it remain at my side. It overlapped with the image of a dancing man, confused but alive.

The flute played on as I burst into tears at the traffic light.

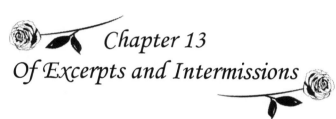

Chapter 13
Of Excerpts and Intermissions

"Does that settle things?"

"Thank you. It does."

"Let me know if you have any further questions that may help facilitate your university report," she said.

"Thanks again."

"My pleasure." Dr. Yin's eyes returned to the spiral notebook in front of her.

I paused. "There's something else. I was passing through town and . . . ran into Albert. He's staying at a homeless shelter."

"Yes, I know," Dr. Yin said dismissively, the pace of her notes not missing a beat. "He ran into a bad deal when going through one of his spells. Needless to say, he lost everything."

"That's terrible!"

Dr Yin nodded, a slight inclination of the head.

"I don't know if I should ask this, but . . ." I hesitated.
"Will he—"

"Continue as our patient?" Dr. Yin finally looked up with an expressionless gaze. "That depends on whether his caseworker can provide the appropriate number of funds for him to continue. If he does not, then no. His files will be removed and transferred to the social workers."

His eyes were beautiful. Confused, but beautiful.

"I see." I nodded, my eyes filling. "I'm . . . really sorry to hear about all this. I hope he will be okay."

Dr. Yin's eyes pierced mine, the shrewd look of a hawk. "As psychologists, it is important that we do not develop a hero complex. You cannot save everyone, Rebecca."

My face warmed. "I know. But, still . . . I would like to help as much as I can."

"It's like a test tube in a laboratory, Rebecca," Dr. Yin said, maintaining her fixed expression, her back poised elegantly. "You study it in fascination. You take notes. You caress it with your mind. But, once you have the information you need, it may be discarded. Knowledge is what we ultimately seek."

Knowledge.

"But, surely," I said quietly, "there is a human element to it, too."

"The human element may prove useful as a means to our goals. However, most often, it is an illusion."

Was humanity an illusion? There was a rhythm to her syntax, but I couldn't decide whether or not it was right.

My mind was jumbled by a riddle.

"I . . . guess we will see what happens," I finally said.

"Yes," she said firmly, "we will. You may go now, Rebecca. See you next Tuesday."

"See you next Tuesday."

I walked to the door.

"You any good at math, Rebecca?"

I blinked, looking up from my cell phone to address Teresa, who had just walked in the room. "Um, I suppose so. I'm more of an English and history person, but I tended to ace math classes when I was in—"

"Good, thought as much." Teresa grinned. "Hey, so . . . Amelia has been struggling with algebra, and I was wondering if you would be interested in tutoring her." She paused, smiling. "She seems to like you, and that's a good thing. She's already been through two tutors. I know you have the bookstore job and the internship work, so I'd totally understand if you can't." She ran a finger idly through her hair. "But it would just be every so often. And you'd definitely be paid."

"Sure," I said. "I should be free on Saturdays."

"I still don't get the point of x's and y's," Amelia announced, as she closed her math book, flopping onto her bed. "If I wanted to learn about letters, I'd buy a phonics book."

I laughed. "Well, I see your point. But, whether you like algebra or not, you're starting to catch on."

"Yeah, I guess so."

I dug into my purse to check the time. When fingering for my cell phone, rosary beads peeked out of the handbag.

"What's that? A necklace?" Amelia peered closer for a better look.

"No, it's my rosary," I pulled out the entire rosary

and held it up so Amelia could see it better.

Amelia's eyes widened. "A rosary? But those are for idolaters! It goes against the Bible!"

God, give me the words.

I paused, thinking how best to express what I was about to say. "Well, actually, Amelia, the rosary is about as biblical as you can get."

"I'm pretty sure that makes no sense." Amelia scrunched her eyebrows together skeptically.

"Well, first off," I said, "the prayers said during the rosary are biblical. Some of them even have direct quotes from the Bible. Like, take Hail Mary, for instance. That's the one that a lot of non-Catholics don't get. But, listen to the first words . . . 'Hail Mary, full of grace, the Lord is with thee.' Sound familiar?"

"Wait," Amelia said slowly, almost in disbelief. "That's what the angel Gabriel said when he told Mary she'd be with child."

"Exactly!" I responded enthusiastically. "In fact, that's one of the 'mysteries' that we focus on during the rosary. The Annunciation. You see, while praying the rosary, we meditate on the life of Christ. In other words, each 'mystery' of the rosary—Joyful, Sorrowful, Glorious, and Luminous—is about a specific period of Jesus' life."

"It is?"

"Yep!"

Amelia paused, as if in thought, before finally throwing her arms up in frustration. "But why are you still focusing on Mary if it's all about Jesus?"

"Jesus is always the focus," I said gently, "but, well . . . hmm, you know how you ask friends on Earth to pray for you?"

Amelia nodded.

"Well, we're doing something similar when we ask

the saints to pray for us. You see, as Catholics, we believe that the Church is like one big family in Heaven and on Earth. So, it makes sense to have these really special, holy people pray for us, too. And," I added, "Mary is especially important because she was chosen by God—among all women—to be the mother of Jesus. It doesn't get more special than that. We honor her as Christ does. As His mother."

We sat together for a few moments in silence.

"Oh," Amelia finally said. "I see."

"So, yeah," I said, attempting to fill the silence. "It's all about Jesus, but Mary walks with us on the path to her Son. We journey together, meditating on the different stages of His life. It's like the Bible coming to life, kinda like—"

"Spiritual time travel?" Amelia looked up with a smile.

I laughed. "Something like that."

Amelia leaned forward, her elbows propped up under her chin as she pointed to my rosary. "Do they come in pink?"

"Um, no," I said, "I think I'll watch from here."

We were standing by an ice skating rink, watching indistinct figures glide by with a grace that I did not hope to imitate. Teresa bit her lip, hiding a smile, while Amelia tapped her foot impatiently.

"Rebecca, you're going. You can't turn back now."

"Yes, well . . . now that I'm here, it doesn't sound like such a good idea." I paused, pointing toward the skaters. "See, they're practically dancing. If I go out there, the only place I'll be dancing is toward the ground."

"Oooh, Miss Perfect can't fall down! C'mon, Rebecca; no one is going to be grading you!"

I cleared my throat, smoothing my clothes. "You're right. No one will know I didn't ace this test."

"It's not a test!"

"Yes, it is!"

"Girls," Teresa interrupted with the air of a primary teacher, "I think—"

"Besides, I thought you were a dancer," Amelia continued, ignoring her sister. "As you said, this is pretty much the same thing."

"I never said I was a dancer. I said I *liked* to dance. On firm ground. On firm, *dry* ground."

Amelia folded her arms. "Coward."

"How dare you! I will have you know that—"

"Girls!" Teresa stated again, this time more loudly.

We shuffled our feet, staring at the ground with all the remorse of a child who was caught flushing her brother's toy medical kit down the toilet.

"Rebecca," Amelia said reproachfully.

"I can take notes! Maybe I'll write a blog post on my observations of your skating!"

Amelia grabbed my arm and pulled me toward the rink. "No."

"There is a reason that ice rinks are not common in Southern California," I protested, trying to break free from the surprisingly firm grip of my fourteen-year-old friend. "We don't know anything about ice skating! This rink is probably flawed in some catastrophic way—"

"Three tickets, please," Amelia said cordially to the ticket manager, as Teresa caught up to us at the booth.

"This is a forced entry," I said. "Do you really want to begin a criminal record at 14?"

"Thank you." Amelia grabbed our tickets and pulled each of us by a hand as we approached the small gate enclosing the rink of doom.

"Rink of doom?" Amelia finally paused to address me, lifting an eyebrow. "Really, Rebecca, isn't that a tad dramatic?"

Note to self: Do not think your thoughts so loudly that they escape your mouth.

"I was talking to myself," I muttered. "Now let's get this over with . . . if we must."

Amelia grinned. "I *knew* you would come around!"

And, so, there we went, Teresa and Amelia throwing on their skates and entering the rink with all the excitement of a chimpanzee who discovered wireless Internet, with me dragging my feet behind.

Romanticism, I thought to myself bitterly. *That is what made me agree to this.*

I should have stuck to bridges and balconies.

I took one step out onto the ice and fell to the ground.

"What did I say?" I moaned, examining my knee, which was turning a delightful shade of purple. *"What . . . did . . . I . . . say."*

"You said," Amelia smiled, reaching down to help me up, "that you wanted to dance in an upside-down world."

The three of us burst out laughing, trickles of laughter echoing across the ice-covered land. A few skaters turned around to observe us with a smile.

"I will not allow this ice to dominate me," I proclaimed, determined. "Onward, my friends!"

With those words, I slipped again.

"Ouch." I winced, holding onto the railing.

Teresa eyed me uncertainly. "Maybe you should try another day . . ."

"No!" Amelia and I exclaimed simultaneously.

Not when I have embarrassed myself twice already.

"She'll never try again." Amelia glared at her sister.

"It's now or never."

I nodded emphatically.

Teresa looked back and forth between the two of us, evidently puzzled as to the sudden change of heart. "Well, I guess third time's the charm . . ."

And, with that, Amelia grabbed my hand once again, sending us flying into the ice.

My feet wobbled as we circled the ring, but I managed to stand upright, determined to not fall prey to its machinations again.

"Teresa, come on!" Amelia called out to her sister, who was still steps closer to the edge.

Teresa met us just as a close encounter with nearby skaters—a middle-aged couple—nearly sent us flying toward to the ground once again. Her eyes were distracted, flitting back and forth sporadically, as they ultimately dodged our current position for one in the distance.

I followed her gaze to the east side of the ring, where a familiar young man stood.

"Oh brother," Amelia groaned.

She pulled me away as Teresa sped off to meet her boyfriend.

"You are not allowed to get a boyfriend," she told me severely as we spun around.

"I'll try to avoid it," I responded with a wry grin, "but I can't make any promises."

Amelia grinned and moved more quickly across the ice, dragging me with her.

The uncertain steps of a new skater faded, and soon we were gliding.

I closed my eyes, feeling the rhythm of our movement. Icy pillars of serenity, spun from airy mist, entered my quiet vision in echoes of worlds unknown. With a new turn, we met delicate flowers of snow, majestic in their purity, leading to the beyond. They beckoned toward a forgotten palace standing tall in the distance, encapsulated in the same frozen fervor of shrouded mist.

I spun around giddily, caught in a dance of the past and present, time unknown. When I opened my eyes, I saw that Amelia's eyes were caught in the same wonder, her cheeks flushed. For a moment, the scrutinizing eyes of a teenager retreated, becoming once again childlike and overflowing with unmasked joy.

I smiled and squeezed her hand.

October 20, 1999.

The cool air was filled with the lightness of baby's breath.

I twirled her around, relaxing myself into unrestrained movement.

Mom sat, her hands folded, in the doctor's office. Her eyes shifted nervously.

He entered.

We dropped hands and spun around, alone yet together.

"Mrs. Veritas, I am so—"

I washed away the scene from my mind.

The mountain palace danced in the distance, sheltered by a moonbeam, as we left to meet it. We joined hands again, giggling for no reason—and every reason—at all.

And so we spun around and around in winter wonderland, gliding across the icy surface in ecstasy, until the day turned winter wonderland to dusk.

Chapter 14
Of Mirrors and Motions

I took a deep breath before entering the lobby. This was my first day with a new client who would actually be my client.

Donna did not speak to me as I approached the receptionist desk, but simply nodded and pointed toward the familiar hall down which I had walked many times.

I guess Dr. Yin was ready for me.

I nodded in response and followed her instruction.

As I stepped toward the remaining feet separating me from the office door, I was thrown headlong into a hurrying figure.

"Oh, I am so sorry! I am *stupid.*"

She said the word "stupid" as if she actually meant it, rather than the exaggerated meaning it usually took in such a scenario.

"Really, it was nothing at all," I said. "It happens to the best of us."

"*And* it happens to me," she concluded, running a hand nervously through her gray-brown hair.

There was a brief pause as I stood, uncertain of what to say. "Well, I um . . . it was nice meeting you! I'm Rebecca. Sorry, I didn't catch your name . . . ?"

"Stacie," she responded, her hand now shaking as she dropped it from her hair down to her side.

Stacie. My new client?

"You wouldn't happen to be Dr. Yin's client, would you?" I asked.

"Yes." Her voice trembled ever so slightly. "Yes, I am her patient."

"Well, then," I smiled brightly, "I am Rebecca, Dr. Yin's intern. I look forward to working with you."

Stacie nodded, smiling uncertainly. "It's real nice to meet you."

I shook her hand. "And you. Shall we . . . ?" I indicated the door to Yin's office with one hand.

"Oh, yes," she said, all aflutter again. "She hates when I'm late."

I held open the door, allowing her entrance, before stepping in myself.

Dr. Yin looked up from her desk. "You're late."

"Sorry, Dr.—" we both burst out simultaneously, but Dr. Yin's eyes were only on Stacie.

"I was looking at the mirror, Dr., and then I ran into—"

"Rebecca," I said quickly.

She said the word "Mirror" as if it were in caps.

"Yes, Rebecca." Stacie cast her eyes downward in timid remorse.

"And what did you find in the Mirror?" Dr. Yin's eyes examined hers with the narrow precision of a hawk.

"I saw . . ."

"Answer, please."

Dr. Yin motioned for me to sit down but held her hand up when Stacie attempted to follow suit.

I remained standing.

Dr. Yin's eyes narrowed, but she said nothing.

Stacie continued to stammer, once again brushing through her hair nervously with one hand. "I—"

"Then you will look into this one." Dr. Yin's eyes followed Stacie to the large mirror at the corner of the room.

The mirror where I once saw a lotus flower turn into nothing, with the flashing image of a haughty girl in blue, hiphugger jeans.

Stacie took two tentative steps forward, and then stopped. She covered her face with her hand.

Why?

In an instant, Dr. Yin was before her, taking her arm with an iron grip and pulling her forcefully toward the mirror. Stacie struggled, kicking and trying to pull her away. Her mouth opened, but no sound came out.

Had she once screamed?

I froze, staring at the scene before shaking it off, bursting forth in the direction of Stacie and Dr. Yin.

"Dr. Yin, you are—I think you're hurting her." I grasped Stacie's other hand helplessly. In that moment, she looked at me, her eyes wide with terror. Dr. Yin turned her head slowly, fixing her eyes upon me coldly.

"You will observe now," she said evenly.

I moved helplessly, reaching for my seat. Perhaps my mind had exaggerated the force with which Dr. Yin had—

"Now, Stacie," Dr. Yin said calmly, "what do you see in the mirror?"

"I see a girl who . . . well, I have freckles and my skin

isn't very smooth—"

"You see an ugly girl."

The words resonated throughout the room, sending a deafening pause. I caught my breath. *Where am I?*

"Say it!" Dr. Yin shook her arm, raising her voice an octave higher. "Say it."

"I see," Stacie gasped, breathing heavily, "an ugly girl."

"Good, Stacie. Very good. Look at your hair now. Your nose. Your hands. Your *snail* brown eyes. Take note of it all. Each part separately is as hideous at the whole. Say it."

Stacie repeated it, a large tear dripping down her cheek.

"And that is what you should have said when you walked in." Dr. Yin's eyes stared back at her blankly. "And that is what you will tell your reflection when you leave today. You are nothing. You are dirt. You look worthless . . . and you *are* worthless."

My chest burned with the pain of Stacie, my eyes too empty for tears. *Who is this woman?*

"And now," Dr. Yin turned toward me with a plastic smile that I realized now had been her smile every day, "you will practice."

"Practice," I said helplessly, swallowing the word as I remained glued to my seat. "I—what will I—"

"You will practice the routine I just modeled with Stacie," she said coolly.

Stacie had become a heap on the floor before the mirror, her body wracked with sobs.

I didn't move. I couldn't. But Dr. Yin's hawk—or vulture—eyes flashed at me again, and then I was up.

I walked toward the crumpled figure, my mind vacant. I offered her a hand.

Stacie looked at me pleadingly, her figure still bent

toward the floor. She appeared as if she would fall down again at the touch of a finger.

"Now then, Miss Veritas," Dr. Yin said, "you will begin."

I opened my mouth, but, like Stacie only a few moments earlier, nothing came out. "I—"

Dr. Yin's voice floated before me in ironic tones. "Perhaps I should model again as you say it. Repeat after me. 'Stacie, look into the mirror.' "

"Stacie . . . look into the mirror." My voice shook.

She lowered her eyes and cast them into the reflective surface before her.

Mirror, mirror, on the wall.

"See yourself." The words broke like ice.

I repeated them, my mouth dry. "See yourself."

Who's the fairest of them all?

"You are ugly. You are worthless."

"You are . . ." I bit my lip, halting my words.

No. The new word, never spoken, resounded through my mind.

"You are . . ."

I trembled, but it would not leave me.

"You are . . . beautiful and worth more than you can possibly imagine."

In that moment, I heard the drum of a sentence, but could not care.

My heartbeat would not steady, but it was strong. It was strong.

I turned toward the girl at the mirror, her reflection now beside my own. The reflection turned away from the mirror.

Stacie looked at me in wonder, her eyebrows furrowed in confusion, but there was more light behind her eyes.

Dr. Yin stood up, her eyes blank yet somehow

focused.

"Rebecca Veritas, I will speak with you. Stacie, leave." She pointed toward the door, and Stacie scurried away like a mouse fleeing its captor.

Like the creature that Yin called her to be.

The door closed with a slam, and then Dr. Yin and I were alone.

Dr. Yin's eyes addressed mine coldly, her composure remaining. Did she ever lose her controlled poise? "Miss Veritas, you did not follow my instructions."

I swallowed, but steadied my voice. "I could not."

"Do you question my methods?" Dr. Yin looked at me over her spectacles, adjusting them in a mere flicker of movement.

This was it. This was the moment in which I could take it all back, claim that it was all a mistake. This was the moment in which I could save my internship—for, I knew, no matter what logical reasoning passed through my mind, that it came down to that.

But I could not save my internship by ruining another person.

"Yes," I said quietly. "Yes, I do."

Dr. Yin's eyes flickered briefly with surprise before returning to their measured stare. "I see."

That "I see" echoed throughout the room and emptied my lungs.

"You will learn," she said, "and you will mimic my methods the next day and those that follow."

No, I will not. I cannot.

I did not answer, maintaining my study of the floor in silence.

"Go now."

The words pounded like the death sentence I had written myself on her parchment.

No, she had written it. Written it long ago.

I moved my hand toward the door, feeling her stare at my back as I did.

Mirror, mirror, on the wall.

No, I would not scurry.

With quick, but long, firm strides, I walked away from the icy shadows of a blank, but glimmering, room, the huntsman of snow that I had become.

And, with it, the hunted.

I walked into Dr. Yin's office the next day, my heart pounding.

Dr. Yin looked up with a bright smile. "Hello, Rebecca! Nice to see you."

"Hello, Dr. Yin."

Chapter 15
Of Eyes and Roses

"Your turn, Rebecca," Alex said. "And, this time, spare us the ten-page list." He grinned.

It was Thanksgiving Day. As per the family tradition, we were going around the table to enumerate upon that for which we were thankful. Last year I had opted for an extensive list that included among its highlights albino wombats, the font Monotype Corsiva, and automatically opening umbrellas.

"Says the guy who just thanked half a population of *Star Wars* characters." I offered a teasing smile.

"Yeah, well, only one insane list is permitted per year."

"And only one elongated intermission per ten years," Grandpa interjected with a wry smile. "Go ahead, Rebecca."

I cleared my throat. "Yes. I am thankful for . . ."

At that moment, I heard the sound of laughter, echoes in the distance. And I saw two figures sitting on a swing set, completely at ease, completely blissful. Completely free.

Incandescently happy.

I drew in my breath quickly, without warning.

Why now?

What other time?

". . . those I love, both near and far." I managed a small smile and returned my focus to the plate in front of me.

How easy to turn serious with a topic such as this.

My pensive wandering was interrupted by reality.

"Short but sweet." Dad looked at Mom with a grin.

"Didn't know she had it in her," Alex observed.

"Lovely," Grandpa said softly, as he prepared to pass the yams to Grandma.

"Hey, Grandpa? Have a moment?"

I stood uncertainly at the entrance to the library.

"Always." Grandpa motioned for me to come forward. I sat down and looked back up at him.

"This doesn't have anything to do with your 'thankful' list, does it?" His large, brown eyes observed me thoughtfully.

"Well, no . . . yes, but no."

"Peter?" His eyes maintained their clear focus.

"Yeah."

"He's very important to you."

"Yeah, I mean . . . it's just," I fiddled with the string on my jacket, "hard to have one of your good friends so far away. So far away, all the time."

I bit my lip. "I don't get to see Adri as often as I used

to either, but this is . . ."

"Different," Grandpa finished.

"Yes."

We sat there in silence, taking in the sound that wasn't to be heard, the silence that somehow mattered.

But it was also a difficult silence.

"Because at least Adri is in the same country," I quickly interrupted the lyrical flow of quiet. "I can see her more often."

"Logical," Grandpa said, his gaze unwavering.

"I suppose so, yes."

"I'm sure he feels the same way."

"Maybe."

Once again a silence lapsed as I stared at the shelves upon shelves of books lining the room. There was a history in each of them, but not just from the story written upon its pages.

"I mean, yeah . . . I'm sure you're right." I looked up at him again. "But . . . I actually came here to talk to you about something else."

"Go ahead, sweetheart."

"It's about my internship. I . . . don't think my mentor —Dr. Yin is her name—has the same psychological philosophy as you—or I—do. In fact, I think . . ." I paused. "I think she does not have much respect for her clients."

"I see," Grandpa said. "That is a serious problem indeed."

"Yes. It has been nagging at me for some time, when I really think about it . . . but, right before Thanksgiving break, I observed some terrible disrespect toward a client." I shivered involuntarily. "I just don't know what to think. Part of me wants to believe that my mind exaggerated the extent of the problem. She is highly respected in her field—"

"Throughout history, there have been many highly respected in their field who deserved no such honor."

"Yes, yes, you're right." I sighed. "But I just don't get it. Sometimes things seem normal. I can relate to her—she has significant knowledge and intelligence that I admire. Sometimes . . . sometimes she almost seems like a friend. It's difficult to reconcile that with . . . what I recently observed. And difficult to admit that I have felt that same sense of unease since the first email that she sent me."

There was a pause, and then Grandpa spoke.

"Knowledge can be powerful. But it can only be *beautiful* if there is more to it. If it is guided by something greater than the simple desire to enhance the potency of the mind."

I nodded.

"The desire to further explore your intellect is a noble undertaking, to be sure. But it's not all there is to it, Rebecca. Knowledge without Truth . . ."

". . . is meaningless," I said quietly.

I recalled the words of Dr. Yin from a few weeks before, and everything came full circle.

"Without it, knowledge can only be an incomplete vessel, incapable of flourishing. Let me tell you, Rebecca," Grandpa leaned against the sofa arm, "I encountered many professionals in my time in the field. Every single one of them cared about how the mind worked. Only some of them cared about the people behind the mind. That is not to say," he held up his hand as I was about to interrupt, "that all of them were corrupt. I never observed abuse of a client. But they were in the field for the wrong reasons."

I leaned forward, considering his words.

"When I was a young man—only a few years into the field—I was at the wedding of one of my clients. The first of such I had ever attended. Her mother walked up to me at the ceremony and told me that there would have been no wedding if it weren't for me—that I had saved her daughter's life." His eyes met mine. "I know that you would try to do the same, as would other colleagues and friends of mine. But could you say the same of your Dr. Yin?"

No. No, I could not.

"You are a perceptive girl, sweetheart. While none of us can see perfectly, you should still trust that."

I nodded. "Thank you, Grandpa."

"And," he paused, "if you did see something questionable, keep your eyes open. Wide open. Harming those whom you have vowed to help is a venture that should never be permitted."

Eyes wide open.

"I think I'm going to Mass tomorrow," I said.

"The Body of Christ."

My hands, open and outstretched, reached toward the greatest Eternity.

"Amen."

I walked down the aisle, eyes cast in the distance, as the temple of my soul greeted the crowned dove that lifted its voice in silent carols of silk air.

Softly, softly, but as strong, as steadfast, as the ebb and flow of the tide carrying its watery heart to the lingering shore of its hallowed sanctuary. An echo brought to fullness as it dwelled within.

An echo that became flesh.

"Thank you," I whispered, peace renewed in my heart.

With the last notes of the final song leading its

people outward, I grabbed my purse and followed suit, dodging an arm as I did. A hand outstretched toward the door, I opened it, as if repeating another time and place.

The wind cycled in airy breaths as the door came to a close.

Father D'Angelo stood, his figure bent before an abundance of roses, as he blessed the medal of a small child. He affectionately tousled her hair before waving her family goodbye. I waited throughout the encounter, taking it in like a time capsule newly discovered.

It was nice to see Fr. D'Angelo again. The priests at St. Mary's, the parish that I now attended in Los Angeles, were excellent . . . but sometimes I yearned for home.

It was nice to see the face of an old friend.

"Rebecca!" he exclaimed. "Come here, child!"

I ran, forgetting and not caring who watched, and threw my arms around him.

He squeezed my hand as we moved apart. "I was wondering if you would be back over your break, my dear girl. I'm glad to see my 'niece' again."

Before I had left, we had made official on the long-held belief that he was secretly my long-lost uncle.

I smiled. "So good to be home. I'm glad to see you."

Fr. D'Angelo searched my eyes. "You mean that, I know. But there is something else . . . What is it?"

"I . . . well, I talked to my grandpa the other day."

"Fine fellow. Always thought he would make a great priest."

I raised an eyebrow.

". . . if it weren't for the fact that you had to be born."

"Better."

I took a deep breath, the sense of good-natured fun abruptly left behind.

"I'm dealing with a difficult mentor at my

internship," I said slowly. "I don't understand half of it, but part of me does."

I quickly launched into a cursory overview of the events, narrowing them down to feelings, and words, as Fr. D'Angelo watched me carefully and listened. When I finished, he opened his mouth to speak.

"The situation—and the person—there's something about it. It's taking away my peace of mind . . . and everything that happened . . . I just don't . . ." I stopped, unable to continue.

Father D'Angelo watched me without saying a word.

"Yes," he said, "There is something wrong. Very wrong."

I paused, taken aback. I had told him no details, and yet, somehow, he understood. I had forgotten how perceptive he could be, how well he could discern a situation, and how fully he was able to see into another's heart.

Without having to see the fullness of the situation, he understood.

"And so it is," he said quietly. "I wish that this did not have to be your journey because I am your friend, your honorary 'zio.' But it is not a surprise that you would be attacked. That you, the person you are, would face a hostile force that is more than the callous words of an imperfect human. And I think I knew it would come soon, for you, as much as I wished it would not."

He paused. "Rebecca, we live in a world where darkness seems, in the minds of many, something banished to the world of fairy tales and superhero movies. How surprising it then becomes—even for those of us who believe otherwise—that it may appear in our own lives, in our own battles. To face an opponent that is more than the average 'jerk,' who has made a deadly choice, is, let us admit it, nothing that we expect to experience."

I swallowed, looking down at my feet and then back into Fr. D'Angelo's eyes.

"But it isn't the end."

My eyes wavered out of focus, and then cleared.

"There is a host of angels surrounding you, Rebecca. Not figuratively. *Literally.* With wings spread far to encompass you, protect you with their Light. Remember that they are with you—see them with your heart and soul—whenever you are forced to engage in battle with forces that seek and have become, through their own will, evil.

"This host of angels will surround you, guide you, and protect you. They will raise their arms as you raise your sword and enter into battle."

" 'There's something special about a palm woven into a rose,' " I quoted softly, taking his hand instinctively.

"Yes, there is," he said, looking deep into my eyes. "Don't lose sight of that."

I took the palm rose once again into my hand and, within it, into my heart.

Chapter 16
Of Chairs and Light Switches

A young girl with round cheeks and pigtails sat on the floor of the room. Her sister, easily identifiable in appearance, sat beside her, her hand clasped in one of her own.

"Hi, Abi and Adi!"

The two girls instantly rose as I approached them with a smile. Their eyes lit up in excitement. "Miss Veritas!"

I laughed as they threw their arms around me in an embrace. "I've missed you, too." As we drew back, I took the hand of each. "But why are you sitting on the floor alone? Where is Dr. Yin?"

"Oh." The younger twin by two minutes—Abi had told me with all the enthusiasm of an older sibling—looked down. "She should be back soon. We're just sitting here to wait."

I nodded, my eyebrows furrowing in slight confusion. "I see, girls. But . . . why don't you have a seat at the table?" I gestured to the desk ahead, where Dr. Yin often sat. In fact, without her presence, it seemed empty somehow, like it was only part of itself without her. The two were as inseparable as inanimate object and human could be.

"Dr. Yin always has us wait on the floor," Abi explained with some remorse. "She said that the desk chairs are too comfortable, now that we are in Stage 3."

"Stage 3?" I paused. "What is that?"

"Oh, how far we have gotten in school. I mean, *this* school, not writing and reading school. But we all have different things we do in each stage. Like with Adi, Stage 1 was all about getting scared of the dark."

"Oh, I see," I said. "You mean when Dr. Yin tried to help Adi become less afraid of the dark."

At its mention, Adi whimpered, her arms now held tightly about her knees. She did not look up.

"Oh, no," Abi said, her eyes wide. "I mean when Dr. Yin *made* Adi afraid of the dark."

My breath was caught in my chest, unable to reach out to the surface. "What do you mean, Abi?"

"Adi, my sister," Abi pointed to the huddled form on the floor, "she wasn't afraid of the dark until Dr. Yin did all the tests to make her scared."

Tests.

"She kept saying things, like when you repeat 3 plus 3 equals 6 over and over again. And sometimes she did scary things. She said that Adi would be better when she was afraid. But," Abi looked up at me, those big, round eyes reaching mine in earnest perplexity, "I don't think it made her better at all."

"Girls, if you will excuse me, I . . . I will be right back." I managed a smile as my head whirled, touching each child on the shoulder before I made my way to the door.

"Okay, Miss Veritas," Adi chimed in at her sister's last word, looking up with a mournful expression.

I could not leave them for long. I could not.

I tore down the hallway, as fast as I could without running, and thrust myself into the bathroom. For moments or perhaps minutes, I leaned against the counter, my chin jutted toward the mirror with my eyes cast below its surface. I swayed back and forth, my mind free of coherent thought and riddled with a collage of chaotic images and half-perceived thoughts. I did not know what I was doing, thinking, or even saying to myself. I simply stood. I simply held on, held on to the counter in hopes that it would steady me and erase what I had just heard.

That it would erase reality.

My mental slumber was halted by a different sensation, persisting in the back of my throat. I ran to the nearest stall and threw up.

My hand outstretched for the door, I slid, slowly, as if in a dream—as if in a nightmare—to the floor.

My hands fell to my lap, a lost piece of paper gliding slowly to the ground in an autumn wind.

My hands formed a seat and reached around my face as I sobbed, my entire body playing battlefield with the tears that slipped down my cheeks. And, once again, whether for moments or minutes, I sat there, lost in incoherence, clouded by the pain of a screeching lightning bolt, and broken by the silent echo of youthful innocence assailed, raided in a mindless snap.

When I returned to Dr. Yin's office, the girls were gone. My eyes shifted around the room in a wild frenzy, delirious fear wrapping itself around me as I expected the worst.

Dr. Yin stood behind her desk, watching me. "You are late, Miss Veritas."

I gulped. "I was here, but had to use the restroom. Abi and Adi . . . where are they?"

Her dark, piercing eyes watched me, even as she turned them toward her desk, as she sat down. "Yes, they were here, but I asked them to wait with Donna in the front office so that we could speak."

Reasonable. Reasonable, and perhaps true. But now it did not matter, now that I knew a greater truth.

I simply nodded and sat down in the seat before her.

Like Adi before me, my hands were now clenched together, forming what, in less of a disarray, could have been a fist. As it was, it was only a scattering of body parts, form pulled haphazardly together rather than resolutely held. But I would not be Adi today. I would sit for Adi.

"Frankly, Miss Veritas," Dr. Yin said over her spectacles, "I am a bit concerned about your progress. In addition to the resistance to my methods that you displayed . . ."

At that moment, I saw in my mind's eye another huddled figure.

"—which I could overlook, on account of it being your first attempt—I sense lack of confidence in your work. If you are to use your own methods as you suggest—" At those words, she looked up at me, her eyes expressionless.

So, she had been forwarded the email from my supervisor, stipulating that, in accordance with university guidelines, I could deviate from my mentor's methods as long as I worked collegially and cooperatively with said mentor.

"—you must achieve success in those methods. For example, I did not receive your second client report in my box this morning. I wonder at the cause of your tardiness, if you are as committed to this profession as you suggest."

I blinked, temporarily distracted from my hazed stupor. "But I turned it in, right before Thanksgiving break. Donna told me that you received it on your desk the following day."

"She said no such thing, Rebecca. I think you need to consider what you are saying."

At the sound of her words, my temper flared, breaking through the icy coldness of shocking discovery. I had had enough.

"I have considered it," I said through my teeth, tempering the anger that pulsated through me. "I know what I did. I am not," I said, looking her straight in the eye, "and have never been a liar."

"Silence is deafening" was an expression. Today it became a reality.

I waited, staring at the light switch ahead. Images of Adi once again entered my mind and I swallowed.

Staring ahead at the terror that a light switch could bring.

"Miss Veritas," Dr. Yin finally said, breaking through the silence, "I expect prompt and excellent work from you in the future. There will be no excuses and no extensions. I hope that your practicum work from here on out will likewise be first-rate. I expect your best work tomorrow with my clients."

Did she say it like a threat?

"I will be there," I said evenly.

For them, not for you. For Abi, for Adi, for Stacie, for Albert. For them.

"Good. Now, let us begin . . ."

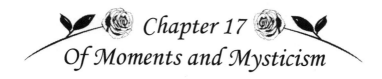

Chapter 17
Of Moments and Mysticism

My hand reached for the door hesitantly, as if it were an opposing force and not simply a quick exit. *As if the motion would somehow render me helpless.* I paused, allowing myself to catch my breath and, as I did, slipped my hand into my purse. In the midst of my lost thoughts, my hand gripped a familiar woven fabric, real and solid.

I lifted the scapular to my mouth and kissed it.

"Out we go," I whispered, slipping it over my head. With one hand, I opened the door before I could convince myself otherwise.

God before me.

St. Patrick's Breastplate hung softly in the distance, remnants of a beacon of light breaking through shifting shadows, as I approached the sidewalk.

God behind me.

I pressed the button on my key, locking the doors of my car.

God above me.

Raindrops lingered in a melody of remembrance cast from the heavens above as I myself cast aside the dryness of the present day.

God beneath me.

I stepped forward, becoming part of the motion, apart from the reality pulsing through my body and piercing my heart.

God beside me.

I looked ahead at the building before me, a building that had once filled a dramatic nightmare but had become so dramatically real.

God within me.

I touched the brown scapular around my neck.

"Jesus, I trust in You."

And onward I strode.

"Miss Veritas?"

"Yes?" I looked up from a stack of paperwork. For whatever reason, Dr. Yin was taking over most of the client sessions today. A quick study of the expression on her countenance had kept me from asking further questions, and I simply busied myself with the forms that she had left for me to fill out, occasionally glancing up to observe her work with clients. Most of the time, though, she (and her clients) were absent from the office.

Stacie stood before me, hesitation marking her slightly stooped form.

I had not noticed she was there, I realized. *She must have entered rather quietly.*

"Miss Veritas," she repeated, ". . . Rebecca, I wanted

to give you something." She felt inside her jacket pocket for a moment and then retrieved from it a small flower.

A rosebud.

"It was growing in the garden, see . . . I wanted you to have it," she repeated, "for . . . for . . ." Her words trailed off.

I let them.

"Thank you," I said quietly, staring at the rose until it was in my hand, neatly enclosed.

Stacie nodded and, for an instant, her eyes met mine, not with the conflict and nervous fluttering I was used to seeing from her.

There was something in them . . . of the Beyond.

She walked away from my desk, leaving me to continue staring silently at the rose.

An unexpected gift.

I felt for the woven fabric around my neck and pulled it toward my vision.

The scapular of the traditional brown, simple string, and written prayer.

And an image of Mary.

Mary surrounded by roses.

The rose scapular occupied my thoughts as I left the practicum building that day, but even more in the days that followed.

For, in the days that followed, roses—whether a "real" rose or in some other form—began to appear right around when things got especially difficult, when I was feeling especially discouraged or upset.

The timing was impeccable.

To some, this instance would seem coincidental, I

thought to myself. Yet I saw it as a sign of hope from God. I somehow just *knew* that it was.

And, as I lay awake, looking upward, in the nights that followed, I thought of the rose, that had always—unbeknownst to most—been special for me, but also that it was a symbol of our Lady.

Christ's mother was praying for and with me.

Chapter 18
Of Firsts and Lasts

"Hello, Miss Veritas," Dr. Yin said, as the door closed softly behind me. Diana, a tall, blonde woman with a severe aversion to heights on her list of many fears, sat opposite her at a round table in the middle of the room, a new addition to the office since I had last visited. She smiled at me in greeting.

"Hello." I sat down, nodding at both of them.

She said that the desk chairs are too comfortable, now that we are in Stage 3.

I shuddered, banishing these thoughts from my mind.

"Welcome to the first week of takeover."

My banished thoughts flew from my mind as I stared at Dr. Yin, stunned. "I was under the impression that that would be two weeks from now. I have not . . . prepared myself for this exercise."

Would she lie?

"Oh, I know that, Miss Veritas. But it seems that you are advanced enough now to move on to the next level. I also would like to end this internship as quickly as possible so that I can take on another intern before the end of the year." Dr. Yin's face was a blank slate, unreadable.

"I . . . see."

"Here is a prompt from which you can work when counseling Diana today." Dr. Yin handed me a sheet of paper. I glanced down, noticing that it was in a question and answer format.

"You may begin." Dr. Yin left the round table, returning to her desk. Her eyes remained focused on us, the careful eye of a scientist examining specimen under a microscope.

I scanned the paper quickly. *Brevity would have to do.*

"Hi, Diana."

"Hi, Miss Veritas." Diana smiled back.

I looked at the sheet for the first question. "Can you tell me any important details about the past week?"

"Yes, I definitely can! A lot of things happened. I had that recurring dream again . . . the one where I fall off a ten-story-building?"

I nodded. "I remember."

"Yeah, but this time, my husband was standing there with a baby in his arms. That was the last thing I saw before I fell."

I paused. *Dreams are dreams, but they often stem from some reality.*

"Have children been on your mind lately?"

"Not . . . more than usual."

I wanted to follow that up with another question, but something told me to wait.

Next question: What has been bothering you lately?

"Diana, what has been bothering you lately, other than the aversion to heights?"

"Fear of drowning. Fear of being poisoned. Fear of being kidnapped. Fear of being tortured. Fear of getting bitten by venomous snakes."

"I can certainly relate to that last one especially. I can't stand snakes."

"Me either."

I looked up from the Q and A. "Have you always had these fears?"

"Well . . . no. They started about two years into my marriage with Marcos. Four years ago."

"Even the fear of snakes?"

"I never liked snakes, but I didn't think about them that much."

Drowning. Poisoning. Torture. Kidnapping, potentially leading to any of the above.

"These fears you're describing," I paused, "they all seem related."

"They do?"

"I don't want to make assumptions," I said slowly, "but there is a possible connection . . . Diana, you said that these fears started to take shape about two years into your marriage?"

Diana nodded.

"Can you tell me about anything that happened around that time?"

There was a brief silence. "I had a lot of work conflict," she began, uncertainly. "My current job wasn't paying very much and my boss was difficult. I was seeking new employment."

I nodded encouragingly. "Anything else?"

"Sophia."

"Sophia?"

"My baby girl, Sophia."

I swallowed, looking into the eyes of my client. "What happened to Sophia?"

"She . . . didn't make it past her second year. Chronic chest condition."

My eyes sank into hers. "I am so sorry."

"Thank you."

Quiet wrapped itself around the small room, as I pondered over what I had just heard and what I might say next.

"Diana, I am only a counselor, but I think that, given the timing and nature of your fears, they may be linked to the death of your child."

Diana's hand flew to her mouth. "Sophia."

"They all pertain to death, or the possibility of death. Perhaps the image of you falling as you see your husband and child is about you falling into despair. Perhaps your fear is less about your own death and more about . . . the fear of losing someone you love."

Diana sat, silent.

"I know this is a hard question," I said gently, "but if I may ask . . . what did you do in reaction to Sophia's death? How did you cope?"

"I focused on my work more and more. I joined more groups and associations to fill my time with more activities, even when I wasn't working."

"You tried to forget."

"Yes . . . I think so."

"Sometimes . . . sometimes we try to avoid reality if it is painful. To us, as humans, it seems like the best thing to do." I paused. "It is good to move on with your life, to remain determined to persevere even in the face of the most horrendous of circumstances. But, if we do not allow ourselves to truly heal, it is counter-productive. It . . . hurts us more. Diana," I leaned forward, looking into her eyes, "you have suffered so much."

Diana nodded, her jaw shaking, as she attempted a smile.

"But that pain needs to be faced head-on."

A gasp left her throat, a sharp intake of air, before her body was wracked with sobs.

"Why did she have to die? Why did my baby have to die?"

I stood up, moving quickly to where she sat, before she collapsed into me.

For several moments, there was nothing but sobs, as I held her collapsed form, speaking soothing words, but mostly not talking at all.

She finally drew back, wiping tears from her eyes.

"It's okay, Diana. You are going to be okay," I whispered. "This step you made today will lead to dozens more. And . . . don't ask 'why' because that reduces a life to a question."

Diana nodded, blowing her nose with a tissue I handed her.

"Your beautiful baby girl is so much more than a question."

"Oh, Miss Veritas . . ."

"Rebecca."

"Rebecca . . . thank you so much. I don't know how I would have managed without what you just did."

"You did all the hard work," I said softly.

"All that being said, I don't think that I will ever get over this completely."

"No one ever does. No one should. It shaped who you are, and it will continue to shape who you are." I took a deep breath. "But the important part is how you choose to have it define you."

Dr. Yin cleared her throat from behind us. I had almost forgotten she was there.

"Session time is up. Please show Diana del Toro

out."

"Thank you, Dr. Yin." I stood up, escorting Diana to the door.

"If you need anything, anything at all, my contact information is on the card I gave you during our first meeting."

"Thank you, Rebecca." Diana hesitated and then pulled me again into a brief hug. "And thank you again for helping me today."

I smiled, biting my lip so that tears would not also flow from my eyes. "I'm so happy that my words helped you at all."

Diana closed the door behind her, a wad of tissues still in her hand.

It would be a while. But I think she was on the road toward being okay.

Once I closed the door, I jumped back into the room, sitting eagerly at Dr. Yin's desk.

My near tears turned to radiance. "Dr. Yin, that is why I wanted to be a psychologist! Oh, I know she has a difficult task, but I think . . . I think she's getting better. That's all I ever wanted . . ." My words trailed off as I happened to look up at my mentor.

Dr. Yin's face was impassive.

I had almost forgotten who she was.

"Miss Veritas, you did not follow the script past Question 2. That was your assigned task."

"I . . ." I fumbled through my words, "I thought that was more of a guideline. And the conversation as it went . . . with all due respect, wasn't that worth more than asking those questions specifically, as they were?"

"Let me make myself perfectly clear, Miss Veritas." Dr. Yin looked at me over her dark gray spectacles. "You are not the mentor; you are my intern. If you have problems following *my* methods as your email to the university committee attests, then you will follow standard protocol. This," she pointed to the paper still lying at the round table nearby, "is standard psychological procedure. You would be wise to follow it instead of allowing the pride of your youth to get in the way of learning something from those more experienced than you."

"Dr. Yin, I assure you those were not my intentions. Nor did I realize that I was to follow the script precisely. But I will do so in the future."

"Good. Now take a lunch."

I lightly traced the outline of a small rose petal, soft and delicate. The rose stood before the window surface in silent watch, a mixture of the passionate boldness of red and the serene quiet of white.

It was also my favorite color. For a girl, that would not seem unusual in the slightest. Yet I wondered whether there was not still some greater meaning to it.

The rose had grown since Stacie had first given it to me a week before. The bud had opened more fully, allowing a clearer view of the maze inside. Yet it was a maze unlike a labyrinth, one fully centered and clear. The stem remained the same vivid green of the day that I had received it, and, despite its light shade, the pale pink was a particularly vibrant variety.

I dropped my hand, gazing for a moment out the window, the misty horizon covering the world with a sense of enigmatic wonder.

And then I lifted my hand, touching the woven brown scapular around my neck.

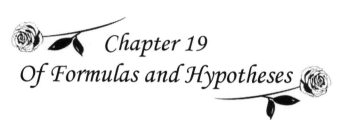

Chapter 19
Of Formulas and Hypotheses

"Stacie, can you tell me any important details from the last week?" I scanned the questionnaire, before looking up at my client.

It was the second day of the first takeover week. Yesterday I had proceeded with the other two clients of the day using the methods requested by Dr. Yin. She had made no comment, and, thus, I assumed that I was fulfilling the assigned tasks as she desired.

"Yes . . ." Stacie's voice was wobbly, yet a little more comfortable than usual.

This room must hold automatic dread for her.

I smiled encouragingly.

She offered me a hesitant smile and continued. "Well, I watered my garden this morning after breakfast as usual. Most of the flowers are not in season, but I have some radishes . . . and my new rosebush is still blooming, even though it's not the season."

The rosebush from which she had picked my rose. I wondered briefly how that was so, for it was indeed winter.

I continued with the questions, a talk show host short on time. "What has been bothering you lately?"

"Lots." Stacie sighed. "I can't seem to stop tripping over everything. Nothing I do ever seems to be enough. I work at the local movie theater, but I'm always mixing up tickets."

"How do you feel when this happens?"

"I . . . don't feel good at all."

"What are you thinking about when this happens?"

"I'm thinking about . . . my house, my job, this guy at work who will never like me because he's very handsome." Stacie heaved a great sigh. "And I think about . . . mirrors. Mirrors all around, in a room."

I caught my breath, remembering a crouched figure in front of a mirror.

That was real, too.

For once, I was glad that I had to stick to the formulaic questions.

I paused. "What do you think you can do that will help?"

"I . . . well, I don't really know. Think less? Or maybe . . . think more?"

I smiled briefly. "Why do you think that?"

"Because maybe I'll be less distracted?"

"Do you have anything else to add?"

"Solve the problem."

"How will you accomplish that?"

"By . . . not looking in the mirror."

I sat, my toes curled nervously, opposite Dr. Yin at her large, mahogany desk. Stacie and I had run through the entire set of twenty questions, as if practicing for an interview or competing in a marathon. Yet I did not feel that it was wasted time. It may have felt more restricted, but it did allow Stacie to express herself.

And expression is part of humanity . . . a part that should never be lost.

Dr. Yin studied notes from a dark spiral notebook in front of her. I tried my best not to fidget, my anxiety only increasing with the passage of time.

You did as she asked, I told myself, arguing with the irrational fears circling through my mind, *there is nothing with which to be concerned. All is well.*

For a moment, I convinced myself. And then Dr. Yin raised her head.

"Rebecca Veritas, it is important that, as a psychologist, you do not simply read from a list of questions. You must improvise, listen to your patient, and develop follow-up questions based on what is said. You may not always get through all twenty questions, or even half of them. Today you were a student, not an intern. You need to be both."

No, it had been too easy.

My heart raced. "But I thought that . . . you wanted me to follow that format exactly. I'm . . . a little confused."

"You clearly misunderstood my intent." Dr. Yin stood up, placing the spiral notebook, without a flinch or any betrayal of a change in her movement or countenance, on her desk. "Now, I have much work to do this afternoon. Please take a shorter lunch so that you may file these folders for me today before the next client arrives." She indicated the folders lying in wait next to the cabinet.

Was she lying? Could she have forgotten what she had

told me previously? Had I really misunderstood what she had said two days ago? Why had she not told me after the first session yesterday? Why wait until today? Why, when I was graded especially on my takeover . . .

I sucked in my breath.

Interns will be assessed on all aspects of their work in the practicum setting. However, the takeover month will be worth the most in the final weighing of grades and suitability for the practice. – Subsection C of Practicum Guidelines

She knew.

And I had not misunderstood.

I looked Dr. Yin straight in the eye, as she turned to collect her lunch bag and purse. "Of course, Dr. Yin. I would be delighted."

I watched from the sidelines, as Dr. Yin ran alongside her clients, a bright smile capturing her face as she waved occasionally to bystanders. It was the day of the American Psychological Association's walk-a-thon. As it took place during practicum time, it was required viewing.

And, as I stood there, my eyes affixed to the field, I suddenly came to understand that all she cared about was her reputation. That what she was doing was meaningless.

She was a woman of masks.

"Isn't that Dr. Yin?" a young woman with auburn hair whispered to her friend, drawing me away from my inner thoughts. The two stood a few feet away from me, appearing to be in their mid-thirties.

"Yes, that's her! She's making such a difference in the lives of her clients. I'd like to write a piece about her in the newspaper one day."

"Really?" The first twirled a strand of hair around her ear. "That's such a great idea! Just look at her—" she pointed, a smile widening across her face, "you can tell what a wonderful woman she is just by looking at her! How sweet it is that she is running with her clients . . ."

My stomach turned. *I couldn't hear any more.*

I stared ahead at the field, watching as Tybalt ran across with gallant strides, followed by Stacie, breathing heavily, a few laps behind him. And, as they flew by, Dr. Yin jogged ahead, the perfect image of confidence and poise. As she passed me, her eyes flickered in my direction, holding mine for a moment with the truth.

And then she jogged on, flying into the distance of adoring crowds and invisible fanfare.

They know not what they do.

I stood, the wind rippling through my hair, tearing across my shoulders, burning my cheeks.

I stood at the peak of a gray silk mountain-guardian, at an altitude that provided little moderation in climate or speed of wind.

I stood, not knowing how I had gotten there and feeling moisture, a sudden dampness, on my left cheek that I also blamed on the wind and its mountain.

I felt a hand lightly touch my shoulder and turned.

She stood, tall and graceful, elegant, yet not proud. She stood, her eyes sapphires of the morning sky, and light gauze-like robes of a like hue billowing softly about her, moving only slightly in a wind apart from that of the mountain.

The Lady in Blue.

Her eyes, large and sympathetic, spoke to me, and a single tear that I could no longer ignore fell across my cheek. She stepped forward and lightly wiped it away.

"Will you pray with me?" I asked quietly, my eyes tired and lifeless.

The Lady in Blue nodded and gently took my hand to guide me toward a nearby crook in the crevice of rock. And here we sat in silence and in word, gazing far, far above, seeking her Son, and praying from the depths of our hearts.

As the sky above us darkened in the quickening nightfall, the Lady in Blue squeezed my hand and slipped away with a quiet smile as suddenly as she had appeared.

The Lady in Blue.
The Virgin Mary.

I woke up with the light of dawn, rosary beads clasped in my hand.

I closed my eyes again for a few moments, remembering the peacefulness of the dream that had found me, before finally arising with a content heart.

Chapter 20
Of Follow-ups and Follow-downs

"Diana, it's nice to see you again." I smiled at the client across from me.

It was the first session on the third day of takeover.

"Miss Veritas . . . I *can* call you Rebecca?"

"Of course!" I responded amiably.

"Rebecca, last night," she could barely control the wide smile that swept across her face, "last night was the first night in months that I did not have a nightmare. At least, one that I remember."

I clapped my hands in delight. "That's wonderful, Diana! I'm very glad."

"Thanks. Me, too." Diana folded her hands comfortably on the table. "I also, right before I went to bed, found myself saying a prayer. I haven't prayed in such a long time."

"That's—"

Dr. Yin cleared her throat from behind me, sending a tremor down my back.

I smiled encouragingly, hoping that the message would be received by Diana.

Diana nodded, a slight inclination of the head.

I hate being watched, I thought to myself. *And it's so hard to act naturally when you feel unsupported by those who watch.*

"So, let's get to the formal inquiry," I said lightly, attempting to break from my thoughts into relaxation with hyperbolic humor.

A mixture of both formula and spontaneity. If Dr. Yin sticks to her last request, that is.

I scanned the Q & A, now slightly wrinkled from frequent use. "Can you tell me any important details from the last week?"

"I cried a lot, but it seemed to help," Diana began slowly. "It feels a little lighter in here." She touched her chest with one hand firmly pressed. "Not completely light, but better than I have felt in a long time."

"I'm so glad to hear that, Diana. Now that we're making some progress, it might be good to discuss possible next steps. What do you think might help you continue to heal?"

"Well, another thing I've been doing over the past couple of days is listening to music. When I was growing up, I listened to a lot of country music since I lived in New Mexico. There are many songs by those artists that are comforting. They deal with loss, and make me feel like I'm not alone . . . and they also remind me of home, if that makes any sense? So, I feel comforted by that, as well."

"That makes perfect sense." I jotted a few notes down in the notebook beside the Q & A sheet. With Albert absent from the client list, I planned to use Diana as the subject for my case study, in which I would discuss her journey and any progress made therein.

"And also . . ." she paused. "Could I add more?"

"Sure!"

"Well, I like painting. When I was a teen and struggling with typical adolescent woes, I did a lot of that. It helped me to express myself, get out what I was feeling."

I smiled in understanding. "I do the same with writing, poetry especially."

"Oh, do you?" Diana asked eagerly. "I didn't know that! Well, actually," she laughed, "I don't know much about you at all. But it's nice to know that you get where I'm coming from."

"Thank you! I'm glad that *you* understand, too. I guess we're kindred spirits!"

"Are you a fan of *Anne of Green Gables*, too?!" There was no mistaking the excitement inching across her face. "I used to watch it all the time as a girl! Still love it."

"Yes, huge fan." I nodded emphatically before stealing a quick glance at the clock, mindful of the time.

I did not want Dr. Yin to accuse me of carrying on off-topic conversations.

Not that getting to know your clients was a waste of time.

"So, Diana," my eyes returned to the sheet of paper, scanning down until Question 7. "Is there anything else that has been on your mind that you would like to discuss?"

"I was talking to my husband," she said after a brief pause, "about what we discussed in our last session. He was overjoyed that I was feeling better, but . . . I also realized something else. I feel terrible I didn't realize it before." Diana stared ahead into the distance. "Marcos was as devastated at the loss of Sophia as I was, but he seemed okay after a while. He put on a courageous face, and I thought that meant that he was okay, but it really meant that . . . he was just trying to be strong for me."

I nodded in understanding, encouraging her to continue, as I recalled a moment with Adriana two years before.

"But," Diana looked up, her eyes misty, "he wasn't okay. And when I told him what you said . . . that helped him, too."

One client, yet two affected. I blinked rapidly, overcome by the realization of the potential of every encounter.

Every encounter, whether in a psychologist's office or not.

"We've decided to put together a tribute for our daughter," Diana continued, "a collage of memories through photographs and written recollections." Her eyes met mine, trusting and open. "What do you think about that idea?"

"I think it's wonderful!" I said enthusiastically. "In a way, it's like your painting, but . . . it allows the two of you to do it together. To heal together. That's . . . beautiful."

"I think so, too. And we're not in a rush right now, but . . . I think we'd like to have more children. There will never be another Sophia, but I want to know what her brothers and sisters could be like. I want to hold a child in my arms again who laughs, and smiles, and dreams like she might have. I . . ." Her words trailed off, as she turned again to face a blank wall.

Yet that blank wall, once empty and nuanced, was now a blank page ready to be inscribed, the beginnings of a tapestry, woven with ancient threads of beauty, of stories, of life.

My brows creased together, my eyes alight. "God bless you both."

"You are too soft." The large gray binder dropped to the desk with a slam.

Dr. Yin offered me an impassive stare, her short hair neatly pinned, no loose stray, like the perfectly impenetrable countenance she displayed.

It was as if she hadn't, and never would have—intentionally or otherwise—dropped a binder or anything at all.

I remained silent, my stomach twisted with sudden pain. I had never had much in the way of stomach problems previously. But every day this week, it throbbed with intense cramps and eventual nausea.

"You need to be more firm with my patients. You should never get sidetracked." An inner sigh of resigned expectation broke forth with that one. "You are too mild, too nice. I don't think you really understand how to conduct a serious psychological session."

Remain calm. That is your only chance.

"I . . . have more to learn," I said, as amiably as I could manage. "Do you have any specific suggestions on how to improve my craft?"

I will not speak.

I will not move.

"You are a weak girl," she said evenly, the inflections of her voice ever constant, with no change or break in their flow. "You need to be strong."

I can oblige.

You know all.

I stared back at her, my eyes leveled with hers in inscrutable certainty. For a moment, our eyes remained engaged, unflinching and impenetrable, as the shrill, steady call of a siren ran across the street outside, mixing with the effervescent glow of traffic lights and a steady pitter-patter of pedestrian feet sauntering across the street in wakeful gait.

What is strength?

I fall to the ground
In the chaotic clashing of darting shapes
The final act of a pageantry
In which I never knew I had a role
My knee stinging
As the brightness of my costume
Bedecked in butterflies and marigolds
Turns mechanical cold
An android you would have as a toy.
I struggle against the transformation
As your words bite against my skull
My heart is torn apart in whispers
But, for them, it is much more
And so I remember them, and who I am
And suddenly a metal arm throbs and is no more
I will not be a machine
I will not be your toy
I will be human
And, with this, strength unfolds.

"I need a break, Mom."

The voice on the other end of the phone came through. "I know you do, baby."

"I am going to go insane."

"Well, you already are insane, so you don't have to worry about that.

I grinned, even though she couldn't see it.

"Runs in the family."

"True."

"I know this is weighing you down now. Someday . . . someday everything that is happening now will be very different in your mind than it is today."

"Reminds me of something I said to a client the other day."

"Brains also run in the family," Mom said teasingly.

"Too bad I can't follow my own advice then." I heaved a great sigh.

"Do your best. And call to rant to me whenever you'd like."

"I just can't believe Dr. Yin is the way she is. I can't imagine her having a future in the field, and don't know how she got where she is. I'm not just imagining it . . . she . . ."

"Rebecca, I thought you were going to report Dr. Yin to the American Psychological Association."

"Yes, I am. But now that I have more control over the situation during takeover, I decided to wait."

"Don't wait too long."

"I won't. And Mom . . ." I hesitated. "Do you still think about 1999 sometimes?"

There was a pause on the other end. "Yes, I do."

"I do, too."

"I know, baby."

"I love you, Mom."

"I love you, too."

Chapter 21
Of Heroes and Angels

It was the last day of the first week.

Tybalt, a middle-aged man from Spain with dark hair and piercing green eyes, sat before me. The name was the one he had given us, but it was an identity that he had taken himself rather than his birth name. I had worked with him previously, though not as much as some of the other clients. He had a more extreme case, with multiple personality disorder usually exhibiting itself as delusions of grandeur . . . and delusions in general.

During some sessions, he believed that he was his namesake, the villain from Shakespeare's *Romeo and Juliet.*

With the exception of Albert, who no longer attended sessions, he was the most difficult case.

I cleared my throat, preparing my first question. *Just*

because it's difficult does not mean there can be no success.

Tybalt waved his hand as if it carried a sword, his eyes intensely focused on something in the distance.

"Tybalt, it's nice to have you here today."

Tybalt said nothing, his eyes narrowing, as he carefully studied an invisible opponent at the other end of the room.

"Tybalt, is there anything you can tell me about your past week?"

Tybalt relinquished his seat, crouching to the ground as if preparing a sneak attack. For a moment, I recalled the words of Dr. Yin during our last session, and wondered if she was right. *You are too soft.*

But she wasn't right then . . . and I didn't think she was right now.

I relinquished my own seat and stood for a moment in hesitation.

If Tybalt really believed he was in battle, I would have to be careful about my reactions or face potential consequences. It might require a firm hand, but not a harsh one.

I stepped forward. "Tybalt, your family needs you back at the . . . fortress."

Tybalt cocked his head slightly, his ear bent toward me. *He had heard it.*

"Tybalt!"

"Lady, I must to battle! The womenfolk can tend to the children!" he pronounced, moving forward slowly to attack his opponent.

"But . . . what if there are . . . foes at the homefront?"

Tybalt spun around. "What is this you say? Do my enemies attack so near?" He brandished his "sword." "Do not fear, Lady! I will be on my way! They will pay dearly for this!" He began to charge in the direction of Dr. Yin, whose usual impenetrable gaze now betrayed some sense of warning in my direction.

"Um, no, kind sir! You must not!"

Tybalt faced me fully for the first time, his eyebrows scrunched in perplexity, as his dark green eyes scrutinized me. "And why not? The enemy is after my family! I must attack!"

"The enemy," I whispered, "is not what you think."

"I don't understand," he said, scanning his surroundings frenetically before finally returning to me, his eyes narrowing. "Are you a sorceress, set out to deceive me?"

From bad to worse.

"No!" I said quickly. "I am your friend, I promise! But your enemy is invisible to me."

"Invisible," he eyed me skeptically, "what do you mean? Do you not see the knight clad in the armor of a warrior ahead?" He pointed to his previous destination, where stood nothing save a wall. "And did you not say there was a worse enemy at home that I must fight to save my people?!"

"Yes, but I can only speak to you of this if you sit down." I pointed to the round table in the middle of the room. "It is an urgent matter that we must address together, in private."

Tybalt's eyes flashed between the unseen enemy ahead and my distinct form before he finally nodded, reluctantly taking a seat at the designated table.

"Tybalt," I began slowly, considering my words, "you are a great warrior."

He nodded in agreement, putting his sword back in its "sheath" at his waist, with a confident grin.

"You defeated Mercutio, sworn friend of Romeo . . . long ago," I said, recalling previous remarks by Tybalt in order to construct some sense of time placement. "But since that time, you have been under attack from within your own . . . mind."

"My own mind?"

"Yes. You see enemies that are not there."

"I . . . that is not true! I am a great warrior!"

I began again, my voice soothing. "You are still a great warrior. But . . . something happened to your mind about five years ago."

"Sorcery?"

"Not . . . exactly. But think about it like that. What would happen if someone cast a spell on you so that, half the time, you forget who you really are and see enemies that are not there?"

"If this is so, I will fight it! I can defeat anything!"

"Yes," I said eagerly, "you can."

Tybalt stood, determination evident on his countenance. He moved his hand to his "sheath." "I will find this sorcerer and force him to reverse the spell!"

"Tybalt, sit down," I said firmly, "there is more to discuss."

Tybalt remained standing for a few moments in silence before finally obeying my command.

"Think about it," I looked into his eyes, trying to get through, "if the 'spell' makes you see things that aren't there, what do you think might happen? Innocent people could get hurt."

His eyes wavered slightly, as if in conflict.

I pressed further. "And what would happen if you behaved like someone you aren't? You might be sent to the madhouse . . ."

At this he turned his eyes directly toward mine. "That must not happen."

"No, it mustn't. But, to break the spell . . . you are going to have to trust me."

"Trust you?"

"Yes."

He looked me over. "You seem like a virtuous lady. Perhaps I should trust you."

I breathed out in relief. "Good, very good." I slid a yellow file folder over to him, opening it as it landed in front of him. At the very top lay a photograph of him, depicting the ceremony in which he received a doctorate degree in microbiology.

"That is me?" He eyed the picture uncertainly. "But what is that strange item in my hand?"

"It is a trophy. You won an award for your . . . great skill."

"That sounds more like me." He nodded approvingly.

"Your real name is not Tybalt," I said quietly, my eyes penetrating his. "It is George Henderson."

"No, I . . ." he stared at the contents of the folder, containing more personal photos, birth records, and other relevant documents that I had collected from his file and put together in hopes of getting through to him, "that is not my name." For a moment, his eyes once again wavered, plagued in evident doubt, before finally addressing mine. "Is it?"

"Yes, it is," I whispered, "and one day the spell will not cause you to forget it. You will remember. I . . ." I looked up, my eyes sincere. "I believe in you."

His eyes were pools of green, swirling in the passage of time. "You are kind, Lady. I will break the spell." He put his hand on mine. "With your help, I will break the spell."

I bit my lip, trying to force back tears. "Yes, I think you will."

"How might we begin our quest?" He leaned forward, determined.

"Tell me, George Henderson, what you remember of your childhood."

The pools narrowed, conflicted. "My father . . . he beat me. He had no reason to beat me."

I glanced down at the file.

Three reported incidents of assault on a ten-year-old George Henderson by his father, renowned English professor Thomas Henderson.

Reality within fantasy.

I leaned forward, my eyes intent. "I know it is difficult to talk about, but can you tell me more?"

He nodded, his eyes now focused on mine. "I will."

I sat, my stomach once again throbbing, before Dr. Yin and her large gray binder.

God help me, I prayed silently.

The session with Tybalt had produced some progress. Tybalt was still caught in delusion, but he was willing to explore the possibility that he was wrong about some of his perceptions. As we continued to talk, he recalled moments in his life that were confirmed by his record. They were not always completely accurate—referring to a "poisoned chalice" that his father allegedly gave to his mother, resulting in his "execution," when it was really a stabbing resulting in life imprisonment—but they were based in reality.

And I grasped onto those threads of reality with all my might, tiptoeing cautiously through them with alternating gentleness and firmness, but mostly at the same time.

He was making progress. Little, but some. *And, for that,* I thought to myself as I waited for Dr. Yin's final pronouncement on my first takeover week, *I should be grateful, regardless of what is said here. For him, and for others, that the Holy Spirit has guided me toward some healing and hope.*

Dr. Yin finally snapped her pen closed, her eyes addressing mine in their usual hawk-like scrutiny. Yet, now, her lips curled slightly into a smile.

I wasn't sure what that smile meant, and I swallowed, my arms rigid.

If I did not do as well as I had hoped, it could affect the likelihood of procuring a good job at a psychological practice. But I could not focus on it.

Regardless of what transpired today, I would endure.

"Miss Veritas," Dr. Yin began, maintaining her steady gaze, "I must admit that I am surprised."

Surprise could be good. Very good.

"Given your academic record . . ." Dr. Yin took off her spectacles, in the presumption of a casual gesture that I instantly knew was put-on.

My academic record consisted of solely As. And high As, at that.

I inhaled slowly. *No, this was not good.*

". . . I would have expected better work from you." Dr. Yin looked up, her eyes once again studying mine, as if in wait, as if to observe any reaction that they might procure. "I will give you your final evaluation at the end of the semester. But I pride myself in keeping my interns appraised as to their current standing in the program. You," her eyes pierced me, cool and blank, "are not, as of now, in good standing."

The pain in my stomach intensified, crashing down in sudden anguish. It lifted higher toward my chest, reminding it gleefully of the lower capacity of my lungs.

My asthma had improved over time and was usually triggered by artificial scent, not stress.

Until now.

I swallowed again. "What do you mean good standing?"

"I think you understand." Dr. Yin stood up, closing her notebook. "Winter break begins tomorrow. When you return after one week, you will have three more weeks to observe and co-participate in psychological strategies. Those sessions will be the final recording for my assessment of your work."

"Do your best," she said, standing by the door with a small smile.

I watched the rose, petals outstretched, allowing further growth. My mind turned to Stacie's garden and the flourishing rosebush, rolling in conflict and despondency, sorrow and fear.

Can a rose survive in winter? I whispered, my eyes held, transfixed by the flower before me. *And, if it could, would it find a lotus flower?*

Would the lotus flower survive, too?

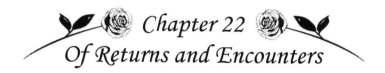

Chapter 22
Of Returns and Encounters

"Hey, you're back!" Jeffrey looked up from the cash register, offering me a wide grin, the instant the door closed with its announcing chime.

I grinned back. "Long time no see."

He moved from behind his appointed station to give me a hug. "It's been pretty boring without you."

"Aww, thanks. It's just been really . . ." I played with the zipper on my purse, "hard to find time with my internship responsibilities. I had to reduce my work schedule."

"To the one day I don't work!" Jeffrey accused me with a raised eyebrow, but I could see the twinkling barely concealed beneath.

"I've missed you, too!"

"Okay, I suppose that makes it all better." Jeffrey heaved a great sigh in the pretense of his despair. "Now

. . . get to work, young lady, before the manager accuses us of being idle!"

"Right you are!" I purposely marched toward the back of the room to deposit my belongings and punch out my time card. When I had secured my purse in its cubby (Strange how one of your first jobs could remind you of Kindergarten), I continued the routine, moving toward the cards at the center back of the room. I paused briefly, my brows furrowed in confusion.

My card was already punched out for the day.

"Jeffrey," I approached the cash register again with a slight semblance of a smile, "did you punch my card out already?"

"What? No."

"You playing with me?"

"If I had played a joke on you upon your return, it would have been a lot better than a punched-out work card."

"Okay." I shrugged. "Must have been one of the managers then. Weird."

"Yeah, weird. Now are you going to get behind this register, Madame, while I fill some orders in the back?"

"Yes, right you are again." I saluted him dramatically.

He laughed and made his way to the back.

I stood behind the register, awaiting customers. *It's strange how I have missed this*, I mused, *but not really realized that until now. I used to be impatient in slow moments like this, but now it's like a reel of nostalgia, circling in the motions of a big ol' navigator's wheel on voyaging vessel. It's a part of me, even if I never appreciated it much before.*

The door chimed again, announcing the arrival of a customer.

Well, I straightened my name tag, stretching my neck for a glimpse of the door, *as long as it doesn't bring back memories of rush week. Nostalgia can only go so far.*

A figure stepped through the door with broad, even footsteps.

My mother once told me as a child that you can tell who is coming by the mere sound of their footsteps. I remember looking at her incredulously, my short curls bouncing in agreement with my dissent. Yet, upon her departure, I heard in her footsteps the essence of *Mom*. Ever since, I would know who was approaching down the hall of our home without prior visual identification.

And the footsteps I heard at the entrance of the bookstore carried the vague echo of a memory that promised dread.

The man from the mall, donning the same gray garments I recalled from our first encounter, stood before the cash register. A smile weaved cleverly across his face.

"What a small world." He spoke in smooth, soothing tones.

I told my imagination to discontinue communication with my thoughts.

"Hello." I managed a smile. "How . . . funny to see you here."

His smile remained plastered on his face, as if painted with the mask of a clown. "Isn't it . . ." His words drawled on like a Southerner without an accent. "I'm here to purchase some materials for my . . . laboratory."

Okay, imagination, that was movie-level creepy.

"Your laboratory?" I responded, forcing an upbeat cadence. "You're a scientist . . .?"

"Of sorts." A second smile curled his lips.

"I . . . see."

"Actually," he let out a laugh that seemed so natural and pleasant as to erase the previous few minutes, "I just like to call it that. Really, I am a man of many trades and think a cursory study of your bookstore will find me the items that I wish to have."

"Right you are. I . . . do you need any help looking?"
Please say no.

The clown smile widened before returning to the tall and gallant gentleman.

"I'd be delighted."

"One moment." I forced another smile before scanning my surroundings quickly.

I'll help you if I know where Jeffrey is currently located, that is.

And, much to my relief, I did not have to search far. Jeffrey was approaching the front of the store, taking inventory with clipboard in hand. He cast an idle glance in my direction and broke into a wide grin.

"Oh, hey there!"

But he was not talking to me.

I pursed my lips. Jeffrey could not possibly know Creepy Dude.

The man responded to his greeting with a theatrical clap of the hands. "Jeffrey! I was just telling Miss Veritas here what a small world it is!"

"Yeah, man, it sure is!"

"Jeffrey," I cast a polite smile at the stranger before refocusing my attention on Jeffrey, "may I speak with you privately?"

"Of course."

He took my arm and guided me toward the center aisle.

"So, what's up?" He leaned against the bookshelves.

"I'm just . . . concerned."

"About?"

"About . . . I'm not exactly sure."

"Rebecca," he eyed me carefully, "what's goin' on?"

"Okay." I took a deep breath. "I'm just not sure about that guy who is waiting by the cash register. But

... maybe you could tell me how you know him and I'll feel a lot better."

"Oh, that's what you're worried about?" Jeffrey glanced back at the man at the register, who continued to watch our interaction with great interest.

"Yeah." I moved back so we were less visible. "I saw him at the mall twice, just . . . watching me. Staring at me in this weird, creepy way. I don't know why he's doing that, and it sort of freaks me out that he now knows where I work. Or . . . even the possibility that . . ."

No, he couldn't be following me. That's ridiculous, I reminded myself, *especially since he appears to have two reliable contacts.*

"Well, I don't really know him all that well. We just run in some of the same circles."

I paused before deciding against asking what those circles were.

"But I get why you're worried. I'll stick around while you're dealing with the guy." He bent down, searching my eyes. "Does that make you feel better?"

"Yeah, it really does." I smiled faintly. "It's probably just my imagination anyway, but . . . it's good to play it safe."

"I agree." Jeffrey pointed ahead, escorting me back to the register.

The man stood silently, waiting.

"So, did you decide upon anything?" I said pleasantly.

Of course he didn't. Too busy watching our conversation.

The man spoke lightly, as if having adjusted from his native patterns of speech. "I was about to look around, but remembered that I bought a new set of . . . items just the other day. How . . . forgetful of me." His eyes sunk into mine, their blue almost too light.

I cleared my thoughts. "Well, I hope you have a nice

evening . . ."

Jeffrey shook his hand. "Nice to see you again, sir."

" 'Man' is better," he slipped eloquently from formality to casual streetwear. "Makes us seem almost like . . ." he cast a final look at me, his lips curling, "friends."

I shuddered involuntarily, covering the motion with a quick jog to the front of the register. "Goodnight."

"Goodnight, Rebecca." He tipped his hat, returning to the formality. As he left, I looked up and saw a cold hunger beneath his translucent blue eyes.

"Well, now that that's over . . ." Jeffrey drummed his hands on the counter. "Let's get back to work."

"Let's," I said, my eye still on the door.

I wiped the windows of the bookstore, the light fading beyond. It was finally closing time.

The distinctive sound of a vacuum purred through the room.

Great, I have trash duty then, I thought to myself in self-deprecated resignation.

After a few minutes, the trash was collected, materializing into two large trash bags. I heaved them over the side into the garbage bins.

"See ya." I waved at Jeffrey, who saluted me with his free hand.

The night was wrapped in still hush as if in wait as I made my way to the back parking lot where the outside bins were kept.

I scooted them into their appropriate positions, and, as I did, I heard a faint sound from behind me.

I spun around quickly, my eyes scanning the vicinity with the nervous skittishness of a frightened animal.

The night did not answer, leaving behind any echo of sound in its still surrender.

My heart beat wildly in my chest. *I know I heard something.*

With a shaky hand, I moved my hand to my pocket.

The phone rang a few times, stopping my breathing with each moment.

Jeffrey answered.

"Jeffrey—"

A faint rustling, closer this time, heightened my panic.

"—please come out right now."

It did not take long before I saw the familiar figure of my co-worker hurriedly walking toward my position.

"Rebecca, I came as fast as I could. You sounded completely freaked out. What's going on?" he searched my eyes with concern.

"I heard a sound." I tried to calm the tremor in my voice, as Jeffrey cast a look quickly about the area. "It seemed more . . . paced than that of an animal."

"I'll walk you back," he said simply.

With one last, furtive glance behind me, I turned to follow my co-worker back to the store.

I knew the cadence of those footsteps.

Chapter 23
Of Picnics and Parachutes

"Would you care for a turkey sandwich?" Amelia asked politely, playing the role of a restaurant host.

"I would be delighted," I responded amiably. "Thank you for asking."

"My pleasure, Miss Veritas."

Teresa looked at the two of us and smiled, shaking her head. "Well, you two certainly hit it off."

"That's because your friends are cooler than you are, Teresa." Amelia smiled widely, blinking her eyes innocently.

"Hey, knock it off, Amelia." I nudged her arm playfully. "You know your sister's awesome."

"She's . . . all right," Amelia said slowly, as if making a life-altering decision, "I suppose."

Teresa threw a pillow at her.

"Hey, Amelia, what happened to that sandwich?"

I interjected with mock disapproval. "Your restaurant service isn't very efficient."

Amelia tossed the sandwich at me. "Speedy delivery!"

I looked down at the sandwich in my hands. "Um, thanks."

Teresa eyed Amelia authoritatively. "If that tomato-filled sandwich had fallen on the floor, you would have had a big clean-up job. And another sandwich to make."

"I pride myself on the number of tomatoes in my sandwiches," Amelia said, her eyes beaming. "It's like that episode you were showing me the other day, Rebecca, from that old show—"

"*Avonlea*," I said. "When Felicity had a pie thrown in her face after enumerating upon the many cherries in her pie. Probably not something you'd want to re-enact."

Amelia grinned.

"Also, *Avonlea* is not old. It was made in the '90s."

"That is *so* old. Like, practically ancient. Kinda like you."

I grabbed the pillow that was now on the floor and held it up teasingly. "I am not old."

"Children, come to the table," Teresa announced. "The table is set."

"Your sister throws sandwiches, and we're going to eat them in a dignified manner? You're a good role model, Teresa," I said, grinning from ear to ear.

"Yeah, I know," Teresa said, suppressing a smile. "Have a seat." She indicated the entrance of the dining room with one hand.

We sat down, biting eagerly into our sandwiches after saying a spontaneous version of Grace.

"So, Rebecca," Teresa said, putting her glass of milk down. "How's the bookstore work going?"

"Pretty good." I dabbed at my lips with a napkin. "Same ol', same ol'. Some interesting customers. Lots of shelving. Random fun moments with employees."

"Oh, yeah, I think I met one of them when I went to the bookstore last. You weren't there, but I remember you mentioning the name . . . Jeffrey, I think."

"Yep!" I replied, glancing at Amelia, who was listening to the conversation with keen interest and without her usual effervescent interruptions. "He's awesome. Kinda like a big brother with a little of the crazy next door neighbor complex thrown in."

Teresa laughed. Amelia finally spoke, looking up at me with a grin. "That's totally awesome. I always wanted a brother."

And I always wanted a sister.

"Do you ever see him at church service?"

Mass, I corrected mentally, but smiled inwardly. *I don't need to correct everything all at once.*

"Nah, he doesn't go to my church."

"Maybe he goes to mine!"

"Probably not, actually. He's Jewish," I explained. "He goes to a temple."

There was a long, awkward silence. Amelia finally broke through the quiet, exclaiming, "But you can't be friends with someone who's Jewish!"

"Why not?" I asked, blinking. "It's not like he's telling me to go to his house of worship. We're just friends."

"That's not true!" Amelia stood up, her voice more agitated than I had ever heard before. "Not like this."

"Amelia!" Teresa said severely. "Sit down and *calm* down."

"Like what?" I asked, attempting to keep the calm in my own voice. "I'm not sure what you mean."

"Like . . . you can be an acquaintance with people

who aren't Christian," Amelia said, finally sitting down with a little more tranquility. "Do school projects with them, talk to them. But you can't be that close to them! You can't adopt them as honorary brothers!"

"I don't see why not."

Amelia stared at me, as if she were seeing a stranger or maybe another species. "What is wrong with you?"

"Amelia Anderson!"

Amelia ignored her sister, looking at me one last time before turning away. "You just can't."

"Amelia," I said quietly, "maybe we disagree on this. But, while Jeffrey and I don't agree on many things, we're still friends."

"But he's not a Christian!"

"No," I said, looking her squarely in the eye. "But he is a human being."

The silence of before deadened, and, almost as a more intense replay of earlier events, Amelia stood up. She walked to the doorway, looking back at me.

"You're not a Christian," she said, her voice breaking as she almost yelled out the words, "and I can't stand you." Without another word, she ran out of the room, a glimmer of tears shining on her face in her flight.

I stood up. "I think I should go."

"I'm so sorry," Teresa looked at me with sympathy. "Amelia—"

"It's okay," I brushed it away dismissively. "Do you remember where I put my coat?"

"Yeah, it's over here!" Teresa grabbed my coat from the closet by the front door. "I'll walk you out."

The air was cool, almost brisk, a stark contrast to the feverish heat of the last several minutes. Teresa and I walked in silence, not saying a word until we reached my car.

"I'm sorry," she said again, looking at me almost

pleadingly. "Amelia's thoughts aren't my own. I don't feel the same way she does and, even if I did, she was still completely out of line. She should know better."

"She's a teenager. You don't have to explain."

"That's no excuse." Teresa put one hand on the hood of the car and looked back at me. "She just listens too much to what some of the more extreme pastors say. Soaks it up like a sponge. It's not the way we were raised, and not the way I think at—"

"Teresa," I interrupted, "I said it's okay." I forced a smile, opening my arms to give her a hug. "See you next week?"

"Yeah," Teresa said with a slight smile, though I could tell that she wasn't completely convinced. "See you then."

I smiled again, this time more earnestly, as I sat down in the driver's seat. *I couldn't take the look on my friend's face.* "Have a good weekend."

"You, too."

I drove away, visions of laughing children in fields of sunflowers playing in my mind.

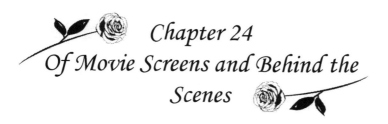

Chapter 24
Of Movie Screens and Behind the Scenes

"So, are we on for tomorrow?"

The familiar voice of my co-worker Jeffrey, relaxed and casual, came through the phone.

We had made plans for a Saturday outing, a wel-come change from my schedule in any scenario, but more welcome now than ever. I was hoping that it would take my mind off my internship . . . and the latest turn of events.

"Of course! Can't wait. This movie looks to be great. And it will be fun to hang out of course!"

"Good. Should I pick you up, or are we meeting there?"

I hesitated. *Picking up sounded too much like a date.* I did not think that Jeffrey harbored any delusions about our relationship; we seemed to view it in a similar light.

Yet it still seemed prudent to err on the side of caution.

"We can meet there like ten minutes before the movie starts if that sounds good to you."

"Awesome . . . yes, that would be perfect."

"See you then."

"See you then!"

Parking complexes are like modern-day dungeons.

I settled the Silver Rider into a space in the dim light of the public garage, and switched off the car. With my purse in one hand and keys in the other, I emerged from my vehicle.

I stood for a moment, surveying my surroundings. Cars were planted like medieval prisoners in an underground complex covered with the darkness of night.

Yep, still a dungeon.

Even if, I thought with a smile, *the level of drama it embraces is not all that bad.*

When I crossed the street, arriving shortly at the ticket booth outside of the theater, I scanned the area in search of my friend.

Odd. Jeffrey was nowhere to be found, as far as I could tell.

After a few more minutes of unsuccessful searching, I pulled my cell phone out of my purse and dialed his number.

It rang for only a few seconds before he answered.

"Hey Rebecca!" came his cheerful voice. "You there yet?"

"Yep, I'm standing right here," I said, once again glancing about for any sign of his presence, "right at the ticket booth."

"Oh, sorry, girl! I'm here, too, but I'm actually sitting at a table on the other side of the food court. Was here a bit early, and thought I might get a bite to eat in the meantime. I'm still waiting for my order . . . But I can meet you there—"

"That's okay," I interrupted quickly. "I just got here and there are only a couple of people ahead of me. I'll meet you there."

"Okay, if you're sure!"

"Might want to get something myself. Where are you at?"

"Cinnabon."

"Okay, I'm definitely on my way."

He laughed. "See you in a few."

I snapped my phone shut, tossing it back in my purse, and headed in the direction of the food court. It was just around the corner and, if memory served me correctly, Cinnabon was one of the stores closest to the entrance.

As I walked comfortably across the sidewalk, taking in the light breeze and slight hint of ocean air uncharacteristically present in an incongruous setting, a stabbing pain accosted my stomach.

Ouch. I paused for a moment, leaning against the wall, in order to regain myself.

There wasn't anything unusual that I ate today, I reasoned to myself, *wonder why that randomly happened.*

Ah, well, who knows, I said, finally pushing away from the wall, the pain subsiding slightly. *And it seems to be fleeting.*

I entered the food court, shutting the large double doors behind me, with a content and carefree heart.

Jeffrey sat at the front table, deep in conversation with two other young men who appeared to be about his age. When I arrived, they turned around, following

Jeffrey's lead of waving me over.

"Hey girlie!" Jeffrey jumped up to give me a quick hug. "I hope you don't mind that I brought some friends."

"Oh, no, of course not—" I glanced down, the pulsing throb in my stomach reasserting itself in one wide swoop.

Directly across from Jeffrey sat a young man with sandy blond hair, his eyes a flash of hazel. Large tubed earrings were scattered across his ears, running to a small piercing in his nose. His eyes took me in, settling comfortably on everything below my face.

"Hey," he said, his eyes constant and unmoving, until they reached mine with a predatorial gaze.

Once, long ago, I had faced the objectification of a common fool in a common college bookstore. He was the unfortunate result of a pattern in society, never to be accepted, but never to be unexpected.

As I looked away briefly, searching instead the face of Jeffrey, I realized that this man and his consistent stare were *beneath* that society.

"Nice to meet you," another voice intoned, causing me to return my attention to the other side of the table.

He sat to the right of his pierced companion, bearded and significantly older, yet no more than thirty-five. He wore a flesh-colored tank top, revealing a large muscular structure. With the exception of a single tattoo on his right shoulder, he was a blank canvas when compared to the young man beside him. Yet he watched me with the aged knowledge that accelerated the patterns of that same man.

If it had not been for the presence of Jeffrey, I would not have felt safe.

I forced a smile. "Uh, nice to meet you, too. Shall we . . ." My eyes returned to Jeffrey, as I gestured toward the exit.

"Sure, girlie! Let's go, man." He turned toward his friends, who quickly relinquished their positions at the table and followed behind me.

I moved ahead quickly, yet with the uncomfortable knowledge that their stares were still directed behind me.

Jeffrey glanced over at me from the other side. "Having a nice day, Rebecca?"

"Uh huh," I said pleasantly, smiling slightly. "Got a little writing done on a story today. I haven't written that much in ages . . . well, other than psych papers."

"Oh yeah? That's pretty sweet. What's it about? Or," he said teasingly, "is that classified information?"

The quiet tapping of feet behind me pounded in my ears.

"It's . . . actually a bit different from my usual. More of a mystery."

"Ah, so not romance, you mean?"

I laughed, my stiff body relaxing. "Hey, I only write romance as part of genres that are not specifically romance! Like fantasy. But, yes, I'm obsessed."

Jeffrey nodded, rounding the corner with long strides. I quickened my pace in order to keep up with him. Judging from the sound behind me that was more distinctive than it should have been, the two other men followed suit.

We arrived at the ticket booth, Jeffrey taking his place in line. I moved to his side quickly.

"Hey, I never gave you my name." The goateed man moved up so that he was standing to my left. "I'm Bill."

I turned to him, flinching slightly at the way he watched me. "I'm Rebecca."

The bleach blond walked up beside him. "Hey, Rebecca."

"Hi."

I turned my attention to the ticket booth, uneasiness shifting through me.

"Hey Jeffrey," Bill waved a hand at my co-worker, who turned back to him. "I'm going to grab one of those informational booklets at the post office really quick. My niece is coming in from out of state and would like to see it, I think."

"Okay, bro. You know where it is?"

"Uh, sort of, but," his eyes once again fell on me, "maybe I could use a guide."

"Hey, Rebecca," Jeffrey's eyes flickered over me briefly, "you worked there a few years back, right? Mind pointing Bill in the right direction?"

Yes.

"Not at all," I said tentatively.

"Great! I'll keep our place in line."

I left the line, waiting for Bill to reach me. As we set off in the direction of the post office, his bleach blond friend called out.

"Hey, wait up!" He walked quickly in our direction. He offered me a wide smile. "I'll come."

Discomfort swept through my chest as I plundered into the distance, the cool air strengthening, gusts blowing across my face.

I pushed a lock of hair irritably away from my eye, maintaining my steady pace.

I did not want to slow down.

When we reached a narrow alley about a yard away from the post office, a small, nondescript, gray-and-white office, relatively unbothered by the flow of traffic scattered throughout the surrounding area, I felt a light, directed sensation at my back. I turned swiftly around, coming face to face with Bill, his eyes leisurely measuring my form with slow, liberal strokes. His friend chewed on what appeared to be gum, smiling broadly.

I took a step back, pointing to the building ahead. "It's best that we move along before the movie starts—"

"Oh, I don't know." Bill smiled widely, moving closer. "I think we might want to have a little fun before the show. Don't you think, Kaiden?" He winked at his companion.

Kaiden grinned, the earring in his nose accented by the subsequent widening of the nose, and approached me from the other side. "I think so, too."

Bill inched forward, pulling me against the wall, before lowering his eyes and moving his hands closer. "You look nice."

The subsequent trickling cackle from his friend sent shivers down my spine as he too moved closer, pressure soon felt firmly directed below my back. I kicked furiously, aiming with precision at his knee, and elbowed Bill hard in the face. Bill winced, his friend bending briefly in pain. With the two momentarily disabled, I dashed across the remaining space between post office and theater, the space of the last few moments suddenly rushing by in a single instant as I rushed into the ticket line.

Jeffrey turned around, his eyebrows creased together in perplexity. "Hey, Rebecca . . . are you all ready?" He cast a furtive glance about. "Where are—"

"Jeffrey, you should know that your friends just tried to touch me," I glared at him, anger pulsing through me, "and, in fact, succeeded to some extent. They are in an alley somewhere, momentarily disabled due to sound reflexes. And you should know—"

"Rebecca, what are you talking about? I'm sure you're overreacting . . ."

"Overreacting?" My eyes flashed. "Your 'friends' . . ."

"Look, I didn't mean to—Rebecca, I've never seen

you this mad . . ."

"I don't really care what you meant to do, or how you think I act. Whatever it was was not in the best interest of anything that should have been! And," I repositioned my purse spastically as it attempted to fall, "it should be clear by now, but, just in case you didn't figure it out earlier, I'm leaving!"

I tore across the last remaining space, between that world and the one that held my car, held my home and my life. Jeffrey's voice called into the background, but it was only a receding sound as I sped away toward the parking garage.

When faced with a choice between them and me, he would always pick them.

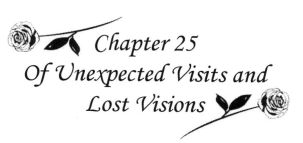

Chapter 25
Of Unexpected Visits and
Lost Visions

I pulled up to the driveway, glancing through the side mirror briefly.

What in the world . . .

Alexander stood, leaning against the front door of my apartment, the pitiful image of a hitchhiker desperate for a ride.

As I approached, Alexander tipped his head slightly. "Check your phone much?" he said cheerfully.

I glanced down at the cell phone in my right hand to observe that there were three missed calls from the past few hours.

"Sorry about that. Did you call last night?"

"Nope, wanted to surprise you."

"Take notes from Adriana?" I raised an eyebrow.

Alexander scrunched his own eyebrows

inquisitively.

Eyebrow communication: Fail.

"Never mind. Come on in." I felt for my keys in my purse.

At the last moment, I glanced back at him, sighing in exasperation before I could contain myself. "Another male."

"Um . . . nice to see you, too?"

"Sorry," I winced apologetically as I opened the door to my apartment. "I've just had a weird day."

I gestured to the small coffee table and then sank into a chair on the opposite end. Alexander followed suit, taking the seat closest to the door.

"So, your weird day?" he prompted.

"Yeah. Well . . . I went to the movies with a co-worker—Jeffrey, I've mentioned him before. But . . . he brought a couple of friends from a seemingly less savory background . . . and I felt unsafe. As it turns out, they bothered me . . . and, well, I left. So, I'm not particular happy at three members of your gender at the moment, and I'm sorry that you had to pay the brunt of it." I paused to catch my breath, eyeing the basket filled with fresh blueberry muffins at the center of the table.

Appeasement.

I offered him the basket.

His eyes lit up. "Fresh?"

"Of course."

I couldn't help but smile through my frustration. My brother loved blueberry muffins to the point where he transformed into an eager little boy whenever they graced him with their presence.

"Anyway," I continued, as he bit into his Aquiles' heel, "sorry for being a grouch, dude. I'm glad you're here."

"Yeah, I would have liked to have been at the movies.

Those guys and I would have had a nice chat."

"Thanks."

He glanced up. "Hey, I know you would have rather had Peter there, but . . ."

Okay, that's it . . .

"Why in the world does everyone keep talking about Peter?!" I exclaimed, waving my hands in exasperation as I moved quickly to my feet. "First Grandpa at Thanksgiving, now you . . . yes, he is my friend, but this is getting to be ridiculous!"

"People are pointing out what they see."

"What they see?!" I spun around, eyeing him in irritation.

"Yeah, it's as plain as . . ."

Rebecca, just . . . chill.

I took a deep breath.

"I don't need a man to define me," I said evenly.

"No, you don't. You never have. But you need Peter."

Slowly, slowly, spinning. Out of presence, out of control.

I gripped the chair in front of me tightly. "Wouldn't matter if I did."

"Look, sis, I'm not really one for serious conversations . . ." I felt the air shift around me as Alexander moved closer, but I refused to turn around to meet my brother's eyes.

I couldn't. I just couldn't.

"This is out of character, so I'd better stop before I ruin my reputation. But . . . this is out of character for you, too, and I think you need to face that and understand what it means."

I gripped the chair tightly, too tightly.

"It's been two years, Rebecca . . ."

Two and a half, I mentally corrected.

". . . it's okay if you allow yourself—"

"To hurt?" I finally looked up, biting my lip. Our

eyes met and, for a moment, he held it.

It was a gaze that held the comfort of familiarity. There was no mystery, no enigmatic depth, but unrestrained length, the length of years—the laughter of childhood games and Christmas carols of home—lining its pathways with simple, yet easily overlooked, understanding.

And in that was something reassuring.

"Thanks," I muttered.

"Let's go eat some more muffins," he said bluntly.

I raised an eyebrow, and we both fell into laughter.

For hours or minutes, we ate and talked about nothing serious, yet everything important, stopping from time to time to play a new round of Crazy 8s. When it came time for him to go, I was reminded of the smallness of my apartment.

A home without family.

"Hey," I said, after giving Alex a farewell hug, "thanks for what you said earlier."

"No problem." he glanced back, his hand on the doorknob. "It was Mom's idea. As a woman, she knows these things." A grin broke across his face, and then he walked into the night.

I watched the door in silence for several moments after he left.

A young boy, his fiery red hair tumbling in layers of haphazard rebellion, surfaced in my vision.

Oh, how we have grown.

I turned on my laptop, not really knowing what I expected or hoped.

Last night, after my brother had left, I composed a message to Peter. It didn't say much, but it allowed me to reach out. Peter and I had remained in communication, but most of our conversation was restricted to quick

Facebook messages and emails.

And this was still a quick message, but it was a quick message given with a new presence of mind.

I clicked on the small red number notifying me of a single message.

> *Hey Peter!*
>
> *Just thought I'd check to see how you're doing. :) What's new?*
>
> *Rebecca*

~

> *Hey Rebecca,*
>
> *I'm doing well, thanks! I'm rushing out right now so I can't talk too much.*
>
> *Peter*

I guess I had hoped for more than that.

I leaned forward, resting my hand against my forehead, and breathed in deeply.

He was busy. This I understood. But I couldn't help but wonder what place I now held in his life.

Two years could change so much under the facade of changing nothing at all.

I paused, recalling a saying. *People make time for what is important to them.*

Would this be the norm of things when things were less busy? Had our relationship changed? Was he—

"I thought we were kindred spirits," I said to the computer screen.

It did not respond. Of course it didn't. I couldn't make it act contrary to its nature, just like I couldn't . . .

I turned away. *He was gone.*

All this time, I had thought his departure would only be a physical one. That nothing could ever possibly change. That his new setting, new experiences, new relationships, would in no way alter his perception of old ones that he had left behind.

I clicked out of Facebook and stared ahead.

I knew he would always care about me. I could never be so caught up in disillusion to think his sentiments were so fleeting or shallow. That wasn't Peter. And I knew Peter.

But maybe he could still be Peter and not be as close to me as he was before. Maybe I could be Rebecca, that friend he met in California, a friend who he would talk to from time to time, but not hold an active part in his life.

I didn't want to be that Rebecca.

I wanted to be so much more.

When you lose, it comes in bundles
Packages delivered, never hoped to be opened
When you lose, it knows no moderation.
But pours out like a flood . . .

Chapter 26
Of Music Boxes and Melodies

I opened the music box, a dainty thing of pink floral designs. Its winsome tune trickled throughout my small apartment.

I wonder if she would have liked pink, too.

I picked up my purse, pulling it over my shoulder.

I am going to go to work. Work is all I can do.

When I arrived at the bookstore, Jeffery looked up, guilt tainting his countenance.

I lowered my head and headed toward the back.

"Rebecca."

I reluctantly turned back, meeting his gaze. Jeffrey's face was contorted with remorse.

"I'm sorry, Rebecca. I really am."

"I know."

"It wasn't okay, what happened back there. And I

take responsibility for the circumstances."

I paused. "You walk in two worlds."

"Yes. I'm sorry."

I nodded and turned to resume my walk toward the back and its time card.

"We're still friends, right?"

When faced with a choice between them and me, he would always pick them.

But I couldn't afford to lose our friendship.

"Yes." I finally met his eyes. "I'm not in a habit of throwing away friends. I just wish . . . things were different."

"I'll try my best. I wish I could promise."

"Yes, I know."

That would have to be enough.

Yet there were limits to such a coexistence.

As I finally turned away, I realized that that would also mean limits to our friendship.

A work friend.

Yes, that is what he would be.

The luminescent flow of a sunbathed garden— illuminating the shifting colors of its inhabitants— echoed in my memory as I opened the antique bookstore door in the shaft of window light.

The books, like the flowers of the garden, awaited me with the thrill of a new mystery.

Tara stood among the shelves of books, organizing them with the speed and efficacy that I was now accustomed to witnessing in her presence.

"Hey, Tara!" I greeted her with a smile, as I entered.

"Rebecca!" She came forward with a warm beam on her countenance reminiscent of that same sunbathed world. "I'm so glad to see you again! How may I help you?"

"I was hoping to finally purchase that rare edition of *Sense and Sensibility*. From when I left too early last time . . . ?"

"Ah, yes, I remember. You came with your young friend. Just one moment, and I will find it for you." Efficiency once again her friend, she hurried into the maze of bookshelves in search of the correct item.

The unspoken rule of a bookstore visit: One must never simply arrive with the intent of purchasing a given item, but also partake in the delightful pastime of browsing.

I walked around the store, scanning the shelves for intriguing titles and covers, picking up a book from time to time when it piqued my interest.

I bent down, looking at the bottom shelf of a section on the far end of the store.

A large, crimson book without a title on the spine attracted my attention.

I picked it up, shifting the weight of the book for a moment as I examined the cover.

No title on the front either.

How bizarre.

The pages were stark white, indicating a very new edition of the book. Yet the spine and cover were bent out of shape and recognition.

I moved my hand to open the book, curiosity overtaking me.

The crash of descending glass filled my ears, causing me to jump. I turned around quickly.

Tara stood, bewilderment filling her eyes with animalistic instinct. A flowered glass vase lay in pieces on the bookstore floor.

"That book should not be there," she said in slow, paced breaths. After a moment's deliberation, she quickly rushed forward, taking the book from my hands.

"It was a mistake," she mumbled, as she walked away.

I took a step back, stunned by the urgency in her voice and action.

What book could this possibly be?

I examined Tara's face again as she turned back from the counter, behind which she had placed the book. Her eyes were sifting between pain and panic.

Was it fear or loss?

I could not tell.

Hypotheses formed in my mind of possible reasons for her despair. An inappropriate book that scandalized her?

No, I thought, as Tara returned with the copy of *Sense and Sensibility* in her hand, *she did not blush or show any sign of embarrassment.*

A personal connection to the book then? One that caused her pain.

Plausible.

Tara handed me the faded blue copy of Jane Austen's classic novel. "Look it over, and then I'll ring you up if you're still interested," she said in calm, measured tones that were too deliberate to be mistaken for nonchalance.

I absentmindedly turned it over in my hands, opening the book to examine its pages. It was a beautiful book made more beautiful by the passage of time. It was a piece of timelessness itself.

Yet any examination was superficial, for I could not focus at all, caught up in the mystery of recently transpired events.

"Looks great," I said through the blur of swirling thoughts, following Tara to the counter. "How much is it?"

Tara named the price, and I nodded, reaching for my

purse in order to take out my wallet.

She rang up the order, placing the book neatly in a bag when she was done.

"Will that be all?"

I eyed the book behind the register.

Curiosity may be your downfall, Rebecca Veritas. Let it go.

"Yes, that will be all." I cleared my throat, taking the bag.

Tara offered me a forced smile as I turned to leave the store.

The mysterious crimson volume, a broken vase, and the hopeless expression in a storekeeper's eyes remained with me the entire way home.

"Okay," my voice shook, "I've had dreams that have verged on the absurd lately. But this isn't a dream . . . and it's not absurd. And—"

"Stress manifests itself in interesting ways." He shrugged. "At least it was vaguely amusing at the beginning."

A tear cascaded down my cheek. "Rebecca, I'm sorry, I didn't mean to make light of it."

"Oh, no, you didn't! I didn't mean . . ." My voice trailed off. I looked at the floor.

"It may seem cliché, but I know that you will get through this." Jeffrey's eyes met mine reassuringly.

Cliché. Oh, that was reassuring in a way that he couldn't know.

I smiled. *If only . . .*

"I don't get it. How do you sift through coincidental events and the real thing?" Jeffrey posed, leaning against the bookstore counter.

"Because," I said quietly,"

Coincidence feels like just that
. . . coincidence.

But, when it's the real thing, it comes over with the
fullness of its truth.

Sometimes as a whisper, other times, like a roar, but always
with this certainty.

With this knowing that you know."

"Like falling in love." Jeffrey took on a thoughtful expression.

"Not just like falling in love. Falling in love again and again."

With Beauty. With Truth.

Chapter 27
Of Roses and Swords

I climbed into bed and quickly snuggled against the covers like a little girl desiring to be instantly comfortable. My limbs sank against the mattress. *I had no idea I was this tired,* I thought to myself, staring pensively at the ceiling as a kaleidoscope of images flashed through my mind. *Didn't I get eight hours of sleep for once last night?*

I closed my eyes, pulling the quilt up higher in the sudden crashing entrance of icy cold . . .

When my eyes fluttered open, I felt the distinct sensation of many small animals crawling over the surface of my body. They moved sporadically, trampling across my chest in search of my back . . . and then, all at once, they were on both simultaneously, as if they had never moved at all. I swatted at invisible assailants as my body played catch with hot and cold.

There were no assailants. It only felt as if there were.

It only *felt* as if they existed.

I slowly pulled myself out of bed, a wave of dizziness overwhelming me. I held onto the wall, steadying myself, before walking down the hall.

Never—in the heat of summer or my greatest illness—had I ever felt that hot.

"Rebecca? Rebecca, are you okay?"

My mom approached, her brow furrowed in a line of worry, as I entered the family room.

I shook my head. "I feel so hot . . . and cold . . . and . . ."

"Sit down." She guided me toward the table, holding my hand. When I was finally seated, she put her hand on my forehead.

Her eyes flashed with concern and alarm as she said, "Let me get the thermometer."

I sat, trying to remember what it was like to have a normal body temperature.

I closed my eyes again, not to welcome sleep but to remove myself from my surroundings. *Open, close. Open, close.* After what seemed like an endless minute—so long yet barely distinguishable as such through the fog that had penetrated my brain—my mother reappeared, a small, gray thermometer in hand.

"Hi," I said weakly, through the haze.

"Hi," she said. "Open your mouth."

I obeyed, allowing her to place the thermometer inside.

She usually didn't wait until it read my temperature. But today she did.

I didn't want to think about what that meant.

But, before I could attempt to think further, the device beeped, delivering its answer.

I took it out and looked at the number displayed on the small screen.

104.8 degrees.

I took a deep breath. *That couldn't be accurate . . .*

Battle: Hot.

"Rebecca, what does it say?"

I handed it to her without a word.

Battle: Cold.

Her face turned white. "This can't be . . . Francis . . ." She walked to the next room, calling my father over. He arrived, standing in the doorway. "What's . . ." he paused, seeing my mother's face, "wrong?" he finished. He surveyed the room before his eyes finally fell upon me, thermometer in hand.

"104.8," I said, my hand lifting to feel my head again.

"Take it again, hun," he said confidently. "Probably an inaccurate reading."

Once again, I obeyed, lifting the small device to my mouth.

It beeped within a few minutes.

104.8.

Mom froze, and then burst to action. She grabbed a glass and pressed a button on the ice maker. The sound of water trickling lightly was momentarily comforting, though I had no idea why.

Perhaps it reminded me of . . .

I squeezed my eyes shut. *My head hurt too much to think.*

"Here, drink this slowly." My mom handed me the glass, now filled with water.

I took it without a word and began to sip.

Once upon a time.

I kept drinking, burning up . . .

There was a girl whose hair was as dark as ebony.

. . . hoping to put out the fire.

Her tale is long, and you know it well.

I put down the water to take a breath, before

plunging my head forward.

But the moment of note today was the one in which our fair maiden . . .

I could not cool down. I could not cool down. I bit my lip, trying to hold back tears, as minutes raced by.

. . . ate a plump apple as red as a ruby-engraved ring . . .

Oh, God, help me, please.

. . . from a woman called to be a guardian . . .

I poured the water onto my face, to no avail . . .

From a woman known as a mentor.

As I put down the glass of water, now empty, half an hour later, the only coherent thought that crossed my mind was this:

I feel like I'm dying.

I looked up to observe my mom looking back at me.

At the beginning of the last half hour—or was it 45 minutes?—she had given me medicine to keep down the fever. I did not notice any difference. It could take time, but somehow that was no comfort.

I was scared.

"Mom," I said quietly.

"Rebecca dear," she said gently, "Dad bought a new thermometer while you were drinking—"

I hadn't even noticed he had left.

"—just in case the old one is broken. Not that it doesn't seem like . . ."

They were scared, too.

"Are we going to the—"

"If you are not better soon, yes," she said softly. "But the medicine usually takes a little time to take effect. We'll see how you are in a few minutes."

"Okay," I said. "By the way, I think I'm dying."

Mom paused. "No, you're not. You'll either be fine here, now, or you'll be fine at the . . . Keep drinking."

I lifted the glass, refilled by my mother in the lull of

conversation, to my lips in what had become a pattern, a routine.

A routine that I did not wish to continue.
She returned, the new thermometer in hand.
Another routine.
I took it in my hand . . .
104.7.
The temperature was as real as it had felt.
And all I could do was drink water.

Away in the manger,
No crib for His bed
The little Lord Jesus
Laid down His sweet head.

Away in the shadows
Thousands of years since
A girl tosses and turns, fever-spent
As the world awaits the birth
Of its King.

Let it be done according to Thy—

She clicked on the message, wiping sweat from her brow as she allowed herself to sink into the seat.

Peter's words of sympathy filled the page, and she allowed herself to smile through her tears.

Patricia Veritas turned off the computer in the dead of night, taking one last look at a small photograph on the piano, and left the room.

Chapter 28

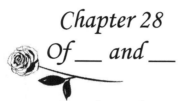 ## Of __ and __

The door opened gently, as if aware of how I felt.

"Hey," I said.

A figure emerged, transforming into my mother. "Hey." She sat down on the edge of the bed and took my hand. "How are you feeling?"

"Better. Still woozy and sleepy, but . . . oh, it's such a relief to feel cool again." I let out a huge sigh. "I'll never take normal body temperature for granted again."

Mom smiled through the lines of worry. "Nor will I."

I stretched my neck, straining to see what she held in her hands. "Did you bring something?"

"Yes." She bent to open up the folded paper in her hand. "I sent out some prayer requests earlier tonight. Adri's came in a little bit ago—she was very upset she had not seen it earlier—and Peter . . . his came in about a minute after I sent it." Her eyes met mine.

Oh.

I looked down with a quiet smile, shaking my head. "Sounds like . . . *him.* There was a time when . . . I was convinced that there was an automatic notification system on his cell phone that alerted him to these things, even if he insisted that there was not."

"When it comes to you, it sure seems like there is."

There was a pause. I ran my hand through my hair absentmindedly, as Mom sat silently beside me.

I finally spoke. "Did they send something in particular that you wanted to share?"

"Yes . . . I printed it out. Would you like me to read them now?"

"Yes, please."

Mom held the paper in front of her for easier viewing and then began to read:

> *Oh my gosh!!!! WHY DID I NOT SEE THIS EARLIER?!?!? Stupid, stupid drama practice. Mrs. Veritas, is she ok?! I mean, I know you said that she was a bit better, but . . . ok, will you send a message on to her for me? Thank you SO much!*

I couldn't help but smile, even though I wished that my friend had had no need to give to such alarm. The message was just so Adriana-esque.

Mom continued reading:

> *Hey DUDE,*
> *So, I heard that you have been feeling rather poorly. Dude, I am just so incredibly sorry to hear that! I wish I could be over*

there right now to cheer you up with random insanity, but, as you know, I'm with family in Arkansas at the moment. Soooo . . . I hope that this message will at least cheer you up a little bit.

DUDE, you are super mega epic, and you need to get better ASAP so that we can go on the swings and act like little kids! What will I do without my partner in random insanity??? I have no idea. So, GET BETTER.

In all seriousness, please, please feel better. I'm praying for you like crazy.

Love you. <3

Adri

She turned to the next page . . .

Mrs. Veritas,

Thank you for letting me know. Please understand that Rebecca is in my thoughts and prayers. I pray as I write this, and my intentions in the rosary tonight will be focused on her. Could you please relay the following message?

Thank you.

Sincerely,

Peter Joseph Asturian

I smiled at the formality of his message. So *Peter-*esque.

Rebecca,

Please get well soon. We need you.

Peter

A tear slipped down my cheek.

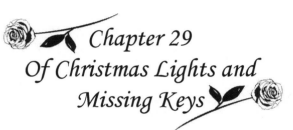

Chapter 29
Of Christmas Lights and Missing Keys

"We wish you a merry Christmas, we miss you a merry Christmas, we wish you a merry Christmas and a Happy New Year!"

"Miss you a merry Christmas?" I grinned, looking down at my nineteen-year-old cousin Sarah. "Changing the lyrics, are we?"

Sarah protested, "I miss Christmas already!"

Her older brother shook his head with mock exasperation. "Gosh, way to cover up a mistake, Sarah Katara!"

Sarah Katara was an old nickname that had developed when her brother Stephen mispronounced her name at the age of four.

I smiled. *Some inside jokes never fade.*

"Well, hello, I like Christmas music all year long! What makes you think it *was* a mistake?! Furthermore..."

My gaze fell across the room as the sibling argument became an echo of background space. It rested on the Christmas tree before me, decorated brightly with ornaments and garland. Tinsel danced sporadically across its wide branches and held my attention.

Perhaps, I thought, looking at my cousins laughing and joking, *those events . . .*

"Rebecca!" My inner thoughts were interrupted. I looked up to observe "Sarah Katara," who had apparently moved on from her discussion with her brother.

Her eyes were earnest. "I've been meaning to tell you . . . I'm so glad you're okay. I didn't know until after the worst was over, but . . . oh, gosh, I'm just glad you're alive!" She threw her arms around me in a spontaneous hug that could only be defined as definitively and wonderfully cousin-ly.

"Aw, thanks, cuz. I'm glad, too. After all," I continued with a mischievous grin, "Who else will throw wrapping paper at you?!"

I picked up a pile of the used wrapping and began to throw it at her, refilling with new material in quick succession.

"Hey! No, you don't!"

The entire room erupted into beautiful chaos as Sarah, and then Stephen, and then aunt, uncle, and grandparents alike began to throw festive missiles at each other.

*Perhaps those "anomalous" events in ordinary family rooms that come from time to time, that we may view as "random," are really little bits of brilliant tinsel that swirl around and around inside of us, whether joyful, bittersweet, or anxiety-causing, always returning to rejoin the others, always entirely **human**.*

And, then, perhaps, the word "little" is only an

illusion.

"Nothing like the Christmas spirit!" Dad proclaimed as he launched a Santa-covered piece with renewed vigor.

"Okay, okay." Grandma smiled, lifting a finger in apparent reprimand. "Enough for now."

She moved toward the doorway, and the rest of us followed suit.

The table was laden with all key elements of an Italian Christmas feast. Delicate pillows of manicotti, filled generously with ricotta, mozzarella, and meat—covered with tomato sauce—simmered deliciously beneath foil at the center, framed at the left by skewers of spiedini and on the right by the steaming platters with round layers of braciole.

"Mangia," Grandpa said.

We said grace, thanking our Father for his plentiful gifts, and eagerly awaited as my mother passed out portions of the manicotti.

Dad arrived late with a puzzled expression. "I wonder where my keys are. I couldn't open the car door to put in the presents."

Mom's brow furrowed in concern. "We'll take a look. For now, just use mine. Or, at least," a smile tiptoed across her face, "when you have finished eating."

Dad's face lit up at the food before him and he quickly dashed to the kitchen to wash his hands and murmur a belated "grace."

"So, Sarah, what are you learning about in your history courses?" Grandpa turned his head toward my cousin.

Sarah was new to the college scene, nearly prepared to finish her first semester of coursework. As of now, she planned to be a history professor.

"I'm preparing my thesis on World War II," Sarah

remarked. "Specifically the causes and effects."

"Ah, yes." Grandpa nodded. "You said that over the phone."

I smiled. It seemed that both Sarah and I had been affected by Grandpa in our career choices. While I pursued psychology, Sarah was driven to uncover the stories of time, like the family histories she was accustomed to hearing at the dinner table.

"Yeah, it's really fascinating."

"Did you know," Grandpa said with a wry smile, "that I was at the Battle of the Bulge?"

That question was the epitome of rhetorical questions.

In the Veritas family, it simply meant that Grandpa was about to launch into one of his stories of the past.

And so he did.

The family leaned forward eagerly. There was nothing like Grandpa's storytelling, even if we had heard some of the stories countless times before. It never got old.

After a personal account of the Battle of the Bulge, Grandpa recalled the time that he went hiking with Grandma and ran into a baby black bear who thought they were its parents.

We laughed and continued to devoir the banquet before us.

After some time, the supply of spiedini was depleted.

A grave occasion at an Italian feast.

Without an Italian grandmother, that is.

"Stephen, would you get the other platter of spiedini from the oven?" Grandma asked her grandson.

"Sure thing, Nonna."

He left his seat and headed toward the kitchen.

The conversation turned to politics, and I covered

my ears with the resounding dissenting opinions that broke forth.

"I don't know about you," I said loudly, when the debate reached an especially heated moment, "but I for one am excited about the new *Cinderella* movie."

They stared at me like I was a conqueror descending upon a desolate village.

"Never mind," I mumbled.

Stephen reappeared at the entry to the dining room, a puzzled yet amused expression on his face. In one hand, he held the sheet of spiedini; in the other lay a set of car keys covered in breadcrumbs and seasoning.

"Is this what you were looking for?" he asked my father with a wry smile. "Found it in the oven."

The entire table looked back and forth between the spiedini and the decorated keys before bursting into rousing laughter.

Dad wiped moisture from his brow. "I guess I was a bit too anxious to get some spiedini in my stomach."

A piece of parchment played with the zephyrs of winds. It glided elegantly, closer, closer, until it became a moment of yesterday . . .

I was one of those people who loved to listen to Christmas music all year long. Whether it was "Sleigh Ride" or "Silent Night," it embodied the Christmas spirit that I wished to carry with me through every season. It was a special sense of joy that further brightened even the most festive of days.

December 11, 2011

The Christmas season has an interesting way of sneaking up on you when you least expect it. About two months ago, when

I walked home, it just felt like Christmas. I couldn't explain why, but it just did. From what I remember, it was not even particularly cold. Thus, "winter" weather could not explain away this anomalous feeling. Nor could the date provide an explanation. It was closer to Halloween and Thanksgiving than Christmas. When I told my brother Alexander about it, he took the opportunity, as he often does, to burst into song.

A few weeks ago, I walked into the student union building. Upon my arrival, I was greeted by the sound of Christmas music. *A Christmas Story*, a movie I had not seen but heard about, was playing on the TV. Once again, I felt like it was Christmas. Of course, it was December and, thus, much closer to Christmas. Yet not every day in December feels like that. It wasn't just the nice entrance song, either . . . it was a feeling in the air.

Foreshadowing is an interesting literary device, isn't it? But what about when it happens in real life?

Such "foreshadowing" can be like ecstatic raindrops bouncing up and down, anticipating the sublime moment when they will faintly linger on delicate rose petals, seemingly brighter than before, in a new world of cool freshness that delights the traveler. Yet such foreshadowing may also be like a flashing light of doom on the computer tower and the accompanying inner (or outer) scream when the computer laughs maliciously from its luxurious vacation spot. Thoughts cross your mind . . . is the computer coming back, did it leave my files in the airport or only some of them . . . or is it simply taunting me for an instant and I, worrying needlessly? And sometimes it is a scrumptious and bright ruby-red slice of the mysterious maze of a tomato carefully concealed within a roll-up . . . it does not look like foreshadowing at all, yet there is always the hope that it may be.

A feeling, a song.
I smiled upon recalling an old journal entry I had written during my undergraduate days of college. It

was so exuberant in its thrill and drama.

I was even crazier then, I noted, as I followed my parents, brother, and extended family out of the car.

Or not.

We closed the door and stood for a moment before the church, peaceful and still.

Mass had not begun, yet Christmas hymns once again played faintly in the background, likely a last minute choir practice. But I realized that, clichés aside, it was also "something in the air" that caused me to feel that way.

As I held the large double doors open for my younger cousin, it also dawned upon me that no Christmas feeling was like celebrating the Christmas Mass.

It was not only joyous. It was filled with *holiness*.

I took my seat at a pew as the opening notes of "Joy to the World" began.

I took my place to join the feast with my family in Heaven and on Earth, with all the saints and angels who took their place beside us in mystical reverence as we sang out the triumphant glory of the birth of our King.

I took in the church, luminous and bright, leading to the altar where our Lord dwelled.

I closed my eyes, a serene smile covering my countenance.

The First Noel.

After Mass ended, I made a beeline for the Nativity set display that Fr. D'Angelo had brought back from Italy several years before. It was a large, detailed work to the left of the altar, and, ever since I was a little girl, it was a tradition of mine to join the Three Wise Men in their journey to visit the Holy Family.

I made the Sign of the Cross and knelt before the

scene, Sarah close behind.

"Adoro te devote," I said softly, gazing lovingly at the image of the Christ Child.

My eyes turned then to Our Blessed Mother, who knelt to the side of the Christ Child. She wore garments of gold and white—a counterpart to the veil over her head—and a dusty pink shawl hung from her arms. Her gaze was directed attentively toward her Son, wrapped in swaddling clothes. St. Joseph, a brown cloak over the simple white shift of a villager—stood to her right, bent toward the child.

I bent forward to note with awe the detail of the third Wise Man—while his face was sculpted with delightful precision, the ornate decoration of his multi-colored robe—layered underneath with midnight blue and adorned at the edge with intricate golden design—was particularly striking.

"Beautiful, isn't it?" my cousin asked from behind.

"Yes," I said, touching the dark red petal of one of the poinsettias placed in the background of the scene. "Yes, it is."

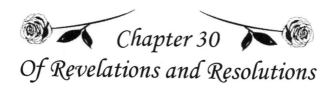

Chapter 30
Of Revelations and Resolutions

I stood in the receptionist area, unable to sit on the accommodating cushions.

They were too comfortable for how I felt, and I did not seek their comfort.

I wrapped my light pink jacket around me, and waited.

Waiting rooms were a staple of society so common as to be overlooked. Patients and interviewees, waiters and teachers, gathered there as if it were a commonplace occurrence, often occupied with their electronic devices or reading materials, occasionally intermixing with the diverse company that they held. For a moment, perhaps an hour, they would wait, wait for something, and when that waiting was over, it was simply dismissed, goodbyes stated, reading materials closed, a momentary pause in the day that did not hold up to whatever came next.

Waiting was often a resented gift, imparted to those who accepted it grudgingly in the hopes that something better would come along when the gift was tossed aside, boxed away for the next recipient.

Yet I did not know why I was waiting now.

I did not know why I was here.

Sounds shifted into movement, and then a word, as the door swiftly swung open, revealing a new inhabitant of the waiting room.

She stood, her cheeks flushed, exhilarated as to what might await her when the waiting period was over. Long strands of medium brown hair were neatly brushed, yet wisps flickered out of their arrangement, tempered by the wind, and perhaps her enthusiasm. Bright eyes peeked out from under the threshold of the door.

It was Teresa.

In a single, measured bound, I approached my friend, causing her to halt in her progress toward me.

"Rebecca," she said, her eyes bewildered by my urgency, "what's wrong?"

I shook my head, unable to speak, feeling the eyes of the secretary following our meeting.

And yet it would not matter. I could not speak at all.

I looked imploringly into my friend's eyes. "Go," I whispered.

She faltered, taking a step back, conflict arising in them.

She worked so hard for this. She had to wait a semester . . . and I would have her wait longer?

Even if she were re-assigned, that would cause a delay.

But it was a delay that she needed, needed more than anything in her life right now.

"Go," I repeated again, looking pointedly at her.

Her eyes focused on mine, emerald green meeting hazelnut brown, and then she withdrew, confused understanding on her face.

"I will go," she said quietly, turning to leave.

In that instant, the door to the long hall that led to Dr. Yin's office opened, and a figure emerged.

Dr. Yin stood at her own threshold, a small yet imposing figure, instantaneously eyeing the two of us.

"Well, Rebecca," Teresa cleared her throat, "I'll be going now . . ."

Her sharp, precise voice cut through the girl's words. "Aren't you my new intern?"

"Yes, I was . . . assigned to you for the next semester . . . but plans have changed. It is a pleasure to meet you again." Teresa moved hurriedly in the direction of the door, and soon a swift brush of air pressured through the room as she closed it. There was a low thud, and then nothing.

Dr. Yin's hawk-like eyes remained on me, unwavering.

She knew.

I did not need to pretend.

"Rebecca, will you follow me down the hall?" Her words were icy, disconnected from her person yet immeasurably a part of it.

I nodded, following her through the door, my breath quickening. I moved deliberately, each step distinct in sound as it pounded through my ears, translating in my mind from its auditory reception to a visual image, a dark imprint upon a snowy ground.

The second door closed with a thud as I let it fall behind me.

"Dr. Yin," I said, my voice shaking, "I know what you did."

And she knew. She knew what my memory held.

"I don't know what you're referring to." She plastered on a smile as she closed a portfolio on her desk.

"You created their fears."

She turned slightly; her quickening pace slowed.

"And you fed the ones that already existed, filling them to the point of near break."

There was a pause, a silence, that I knew could not last much longer. When she finally spoke, her words were detached, isolated from any human form or bearing save one lost from existence.

"You are a foolish girl," she said.

"I can't let you do this anymore," I managed to say, my words shaking as they left my thoughts. "I can't let you hurt any more Adi and Abis."

"And what would you expect to do, dear child?" Her words surfaced, as if mere glimpses of speech.

"I . . . I will do anything in my power to protect them."

Protect them using any method necessary.

Dr. Yin stood, her eyes expressionless. "You would be wise to reconsider."

I had not intended to reveal so much, but she saw past my barriers, to a weak place that few could see and only she would abuse.

My heart beat wildly in my chest, but it was steady, like the answer resounding within it.

"I cannot," I said quietly.

"Then," she said, the monotony of her speech gaining an edge, "you have lost a semester of work."

The words rushed out in an instant before I could contain them; my heart stilled. "You . . . can't do that," I said helplessly. "I already completed . . . all my work . . . it can't be discounted . . ."

"It can."

My words retreated, lost in another place, a place that was not here. I stood, motionless, as I watched Dr. Yin, a sardonic smile on her face as she shook her head in half-measured pity.

"You made your choice. But I knew from the beginning that you would. Girls like you always do. Oh, yes, I know the type." She laughed, a hollow, empty laugh. "So eager to make an impression, to 'help out.' " She spat the words out in disgust. "Young and naïve. Sickeningly sweet compassion. *Innocent.* A girl locked in a tower with no life experience. But, you know, Rebecca," Dr. Yin leaned forward, her eyes blank yet cold at the same time, extracting the contents of my heart and soul with a narrow gaze, "this isn't a fairy tale. Your tower will never protect you from the darkness outside."

"And your tower will always be a prison," I said softly.

Dr. Yin's eyes flashed for the first time with anger. In that moment was perhaps found a vulnerability, but her tower could allow no vulnerability. She recovered with a measured stare.

"I see," she said icily, "Perhaps this meeting requires a climax, Miss Veritas. You do like fairy tales, *don't you,*" she said, leaning over to reach a gray handbag lying to the right of her desk. "It's about time to find your fairy tale ending . . ."

When I saw what she held in her hand, my breath was caught in my chest, panic beating with wild abandon.

I did not need certain knowledge to understand what she was about to do.

In her hand was a crucifix, the figure of Our Lord nailed to the Cross.

"Dr. Yin, what are you—" Panic accosted me with its knowledge, creeping through my breath.

"What am I doing?" Dr. Yin lifted a mocking

eyebrow. "I'm doing what should be done to lotus flowers and their wooden gods."

The crucifix fell to the ground, as if through the idle drop of a distracted hand.

"Smashing it to bits," she said.

And, before I could cry out, she lifted her foot.

The sound of screeching brokenness was more than I could have known, as I heard the sound of metal shattering into fragments of distant recoil.

Fragments of faded vision.

I watched helplessly, tears streaming down my face.

My Lord Jesus, I am so sorry.

She lifted her foot again.

"Stop!" I lunged myself toward her, pulling her to the floor. For a moment we struggled, but, then, with a flicker of movement, I was thrown from the site, my knee stinging.

Dr. Yin stood before me, a cruel smile twisting its way across her face. "Now watch."

And, with an evenly-paced measure, she lifted her foot, again and again, until it was a scattering of nothing more than broken pieces.

No, it was much more.

Dr. Yin bent down to retrieve a piece from the wreckage, strangely tainted with pink and yellow. She held it before me, cocking her head with pleasure.

A lotus flower in the center of the cross.

"Killing two birds with one stone," she said softly.

And, with that, she walked slowly to the door, the sound of her footsteps deafening my ears.

She closed the door with barely a sound.

I reached for the broken pieces that held all that I was.

Like candlelight flickering, away, away, lost.

And I fell to the ground, weeping.

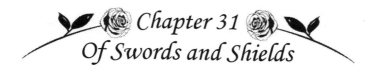

Chapter 31
Of Swords and Shields

"Please fill out this form, Miss Veritas."

My eyes took in the sheet of paper that Donna, Dr. Yin's secretary, had placed before me. At the very top read the words, "Mentor evaluation."

I looked up, briefly puzzled.

"It's from the university," she explained in practiced routine. "They sent it for you to return upon the completion of your internship."

My internship, which was due to end three weeks later.

I took a deep breath. But this would afford me an opportunity.

With a quick movement, I eagerly took the pen that she set before me and began to write. Moments passed in silence broken only by the soft pulsing of the grandfather clock throughout the room.

I finally put the cap on my pen, my hand aching

from the rapid flurry of movement across the page.

It was done.

I folded the paper neatly in thirds, placing it inside the accompanying envelope, already addressed, and offered it to the receptionist.

She took the envelope, her eyes resting on me in a brief, precise measure, before opening it.

My heart spun around, doing summersaults of anxiety in my chest. "That's private."

She ignored me, her sharp blue eyes scanning the sheet. With one quick movement like all her others, she reached for a corner of the page and slowly ripped it.

"What are you doing?" I reached for the paper urgently, attempting to pull it back. But it was already shreds in the wastebasket before I had touched a single inch.

She offered me a patronizing look. "That will not reach your university. It contains inaccurate data."

I shook my head, a sickeningly sweet scent filling my mind in the touch of a memory. "You have no right."

The secretary ignored me once again, returning her eyes to the computer positioned on her desk.

Somehow I doubted that her business on the computer had anything to do with the standard practices of a psychological institution.

I moved my hand to the purse wrapped around my shoulder, searching for my cell phone. As I did, a slight flurry of sound brought an unknown item from that location to the floor.

I reached for the floor, grasping for another small envelope that had floated downward.

The secretary stood up, as if notified on her mechanical device of the envelope's departure, and reached it first.

It was the only envelope in my purse, and I did not

have to examine it closely to know what it was. Earlier that afternoon, I had written a report to the American Psychological Association stipulating Dr. Yin's immoral practices.

The secretary glanced only at the address before ripping it to shreds like the other testimony, tossing it lightly into the wastebasket with the offhand flicker of the sprinkling of table salt.

"Please note," she said, her eyes fixed upon me with an icy glare, "that any further attempts of communication with the psychological association will be blocked using any means necessary."

Out of the corner of my eye, I saw a stout, middle-aged man pass through the halls, his eyes meeting those of the secretary with a smile. He wore a badge with the Emerson Psychological Center insignia, a black-and-white symbol similar to the design of the fountain in Dr. Yin's office.

A new employee?

But my mind had no capacity for this knowledge.

The thought was dismissed, scurrying away as if it had never existed.

I inched toward the door, my body moving automatically through the motions. When I closed the door, my steps halted, bringing me to the coolness of the building walls. For several minutes, I stood there, wrapped in the vaporous shroud of poisonous mist that I suspected Dr. Yin's patients felt all the time.

How tragic.

And how lost I had now become.

Tears trickled down my cheeks. *I had always been secure in who I was, even as a child.* But right now . . . right now I wasn't even sure of who I was. The Rebecca I knew was lost in the haze that had enveloped her. She had been squashed, demoralized, defeated.

I gazed at the deep azure of the heavens, a sight that so often gave me peace. It conveyed a hope that I could never deny, yet all I could do now was weep.

"Rebecca?"

I felt a hand on my shoulder and turned around.

Adriana's eyes were filled with concern. "What happened? I didn't see you out front, so I tried the back."

I had almost forgotten our plans for the evening. A belated celebratory dinner dance at a local dance hall in honor of the new year.

Celebratory.

"Sorry."

"Don't apologize. Just tell me what's wrong."

And so I did, explaining the harsh truth, the newest stage in a backstabbing reality without truth. The malpractice. The lies. The cold world of politics that doomed to failure those who wanted nothing of it. How a cold, unfeeling psycho psychologist was trying to, no melodrama intended, ruin my future.

Adriana listened quietly, touching my shoulder every once in a while in sympathy. When I finished, however, her eyes were clouded with anger.

"They can't do that!" she exclaimed, pacing back and forth in a rage. "That woman is sick. They can't blame you, let alone *fail* you, for their incompetence!"

"But that's exactly what they're doing, Adri," I said softly.

"Did you file for malpractice?"

"Yes. The secretary had me fill out a form and then ripped it up right in front of my face. The entire office is filled with her spies, Adri. Dr. Everson's grandfather must be rolling over in his grave."

Adriana turned swiftly. "No matter what they say, I know that you will be the best psychologist of the century."

"Thanks, Adri." Her warmth, her humanity, a humanity that I had witnessed little in this part of the city, got to me. A sob burst forth that could not be contained, and Adri leaned forward to squeeze my shoulders. "We're not giving up. We're in this together . . . as always. Just as you have always been for me."

"Rebecca?!"

That voice.

I looked up to observe a distinct figure coming from the opposite direction.

Closer, closer, into focus, into presence.

The final haze broke free, blurred lines cleared and placed into reality. Peter sped across the remaining territory in what seemed like a single leap, and, in an instant, his arms were wrapped around me.

Peter.

I stared at his shoulder, my eyes glued to its form. "You're here. I . . . I don't understand . . . our monthly phone call, your internship . . . you . . ."

"I knew I would be here over Christmas vacation," he said softly into my ear. "There was a lot of planning to be done, in addition to my work. As for our monthly call . . ." I could hear the smile in his voice. "It would seem to be redundant."

I caught my breath. *How could I have been so foolish?*

But now the present moment called for more than this.

He looked up at Adriana, a question in his eyes. He listened intently as she repeated my story, holding me close and stroking my hair soothingly. I closed my eyes, leaning my head against his chest in defeat. I tried to ignore the re-telling of the story; hearing it spoken aloud again was like a fresh stab to the heart.

In this strange world between reality and disconnection, my ears finally detected a deep and tangible silence.

I looked up. Adriana was paused in thought, as if frozen in the middle of a battle plan. Peter still had one arm around me, but the other was at his side. His eyes were lost in the distance, a thoughtful expression filling his countenance, as he too was frozen in time.

I buried my face in his chest urgently, not caring how pathetic I seemed. He responded, moving his arms more tightly about me, encircling me in a warm embrace. I had a sudden desire for him to pick me up and carry me away off somewhere, anywhere.

I blinked, trying to clear my mind with that brief movement. *I'm not thinking straight*, I told myself.

But that didn't make me move back. Instead, I moved my head higher, into the crook of his neck. His sweet breath covered me, warming my face, a face that had been frozen in the icy coldness of defeat and terror. I closed my eyes again.

Adriana cleared her throat. I perked my ears, but didn't move an inch.

"So, I have a plan!"

The excitement in her voice made me finally turn around.

I groaned. Adriana's eyes were filled with a glimmer of adventure mixed with a glint of mischief. I knew that look all too well.

"What's my major, Rebecca dear?"

"You have *got* to be kidding!" I shook my head in disbelief. "I appreciate your support, Adri, really, I do . . . but this time you've gone too far."

"I like it," Peter, who had been silent up to this

point, finally spoke. "Let's do it!"

Adriana's self-assured smile widened. "Two against one."

I groaned. "I guess there's no harm in trying."

"Exactly." Adriana moved to the front of us, as if she were a military commander leading an army into battle. "Let's go!"

Peter turned to me with a grin. "One for all!"

"And all for one," I muttered, trying to ignore the smile that was beginning to inch its way across my face.

It was like he had never left.

The photograph dropped before her eyes with a slam. The secretary, her face outlined with snake-like tendrils, looked up in confusion.

Adriana stood before the front desk at the Everson Psychological Center, her hands on her hips and her eyes burning with fury. "That's my uncle."

"Very nice, I'm sure." The secretary blinked for a moment in uncertainty before nodding pleasantly, a clown's smile plastered on her face. "May I help you?"

Adriana ignored her question and leaned over the desk, the dark hair framing her face staring ominously. "Do you know who my uncle is?"

"No," the secretary's phone voice bubbled over the room.

"He," Adriana glared fiercely, "is the head of the local newspaper, and *he* will denounce you all for malpractice, poor treatment of your interns, and overall injustice."

The secretary blinked innocently. "I'm sure I don't know what you mean."

Adriana looked at her squarely in the eye. "Oh? Well,

I thought you would say as much. That is why I brought a witness." She urged me forward with a dramatic wave of the hand, and I took my cue and stepped up. "This poor, innocent young woman has seen firsthand the terrors of your master's regime."

I groaned inwardly. *Oh brother.* I looked up, expecting to observe a carefully concealed smirk on Donna's face, but saw instead, complete and total bewilderment.

Okay, maybe the plan wasn't that bad.

Adriana continued. "Not only has she witnessed the intimidation and general ill-treatment of your clients, but she has herself fallen victim to the whims of your psycho psychologist. Look at this face!" Adriana pointed to me tragically. "Brimming with youthfulness, a recent graduate eager to pursue the career of her dreams! And she has been told that, if she does not imitate Dr. Yin's insane practices, she will lose an entire semester of work! Is that just, I ask you? Is it?!"

"Dr. Yin is a well-respected professional," the secretary replied coolly, having recovered from her former bewilderment. "I assure you that she would never be involved in any actions of a questionable nature as you suggest."

Adriana glanced quickly at me, her eyes burning with fury, before re-asserting her imposing stare at the occupant of the front desk. The gesture was brief, but it conveyed exactly what I was thinking: *The place is thick with Dr. Yin's drones, mindless drones or conscious, calculating spies as disturbed as she is.*

"Don't forget my uncle," Adriana growled, pounding on the desk with one hand. "We like to call him Darth Vader!"

The secretary yawned, glancing at the clock with the pretense of boredom. "As I said, Dr. Yin is every bit of a professional. Your accusations are wildly false, little girl."

Adriana's eyes flashed at the secretary's last words, but an anger boiled inside of me that burst forth before Adriana had a chance to say anything.

"You lie." I spoke slowly and softly, yet the power of the words tingled throughout my entire body, providing a strength that could not be ignored. "I have seen the damage that Dr. Yin has done to her clients and it is nothing short of tragic. I care deeply for these people, and all she gives them is hate. And, whenever I work with them, I am degraded by her afterwards in the lowest manner possible. She tries to make me feel utterly worthless, but she has not succeeded. And she never will. Not her or anyone like her. Because I will never live in a world as cold as Dr. Yin and her brainless minions. If that," my voice rose, "is a professional in your world, then your professionals are cold automatons who have lost their humanity."

I stepped back from the desk, an orator who had just finished her speech. But this was much more than a speech to me. It was life.

The secretary was silent.

Adriana smiled approvingly at me before turning back to Donna, stepping forward to occupy the position previously filled by me. "There you have it," she said smoothly.

"I'm not afraid of two little girls." The secretary tried to speak with confidence, but I detected her fear.

"The world is filled with little girls who need to stand up to bullies like you," I said softly.

Adriana was staring furiously at Donna, a lioness ready to pounce. "Little girls?!"

Caution: Danger ahead. Do not refer to Adriana as little in regards to either her age or stature. If you happen to disregard this most basic of laws, approach with caution. *Much, much caution.*

"You're all going to Hell!" she yelled.

There you go. I put my face in my hands. *Note to self: Do not incite Adri when she is already fired up.*

And that was when Peter walked through the door.

"Sir, may I help you?" the secretary eagerly addressed the new individual in the room.

Peter stepped forward gallantly, assuming a tourist look as he scrupulously examined his surroundings with notebook and pen in hand. "I'm visiting from Canada and am doing a study on psychological practice in the United States. I thought that this establishment might inform my study." He surveyed Donna with a wide smile.

"Excellent timing!" Adriana strode forth to shake his hand. "Hi, I'm Adriana Hanson. I was just denouncing this establishment for malpractice."

"Indeed?" Peter's eyebrow rose curiously in a way that almost made me laugh. "How utterly fascinating! I must make note of this!" He quickly snapped his pen, opening to a new page in his notebook.

"Sir, I assure you that no allegations have been proven yet!" Donna broke in with a feigned laugh.

"No matter!" Peter waved a dismissive hand. "I simply must hear all. Who is the young lady to your right?" he asked Adriana, jabbing a finger in my direction.

"An eyewitness." Adriana turned to the secretary and smiled brilliantly.

"The drama heightens! My colleagues will be most intrigued!"

"Colleagues?!" The secretary's eyes widened. "Sir, might I suggest that you come back another day . . . ?"

"Alas, my time in this country will be short." Peter

shook his head tragically. "I must finish my study at this institution today."

"Mental institution," I whispered to Adriana, laughing quietly.

"I heard that!" Donna glared at us, the pretense of the perfect secretary fading quickly. However, upon one look at the raised eyebrow of Peter the Tourist, she closed her mouth, muttering half of an apology.

"Sir, I assure you that their allegations are far from the truth," she quickly asserted. "Perhaps you will find it to be more prudent to interview the staff rather than," she cast a hateful look in our direction, "a couple of unprofessional young women."

"Hmm," Peter paused as if deep in thought. "Perhaps I will conduct my interviews of the staff here first, and then move on to the lovely young ladies here." He winked heroically, and Adriana feigned a rosy blush.

"Yes, perhaps you will even find an interview beyond the staff to be irrelevant, especially given your limited time!" the secretary said eagerly.

"No, no." Peter tapped his pen open and shut. "I'm afraid both sides of the story must be heard for a balanced picture to be procured. However, I may start with the staff as you have suggested. Is Dr. Yin in?"

"Not at the moment," the secretary said quickly, "but her lunch hour will be over within the half hour!"

"Ah, the Devil is taking a hiatus!" Adriana proclaimed.

"Adriana dear," I cleared my throat, "Perhaps it would be best if we left—what was your name again?" I turned to Peter.

"Mr. Asturian at your service!" Peter bowed graciously.

"Yes, well, if we left Mr. Asturian to the interviews of Miss Donna for now."

"Right you are!" Adriana waved her hand, the concluding paragraph of an essay. "We will depart," she cast a mischievous look at the bewildered secretary, "for now!"

"Farewell, ladies." Peter saluted us.

"Farewell!"

As we reached the door, Adriana turned back for an instant, her eyes luminous. "I'll pray for your soul!" she called as the door slammed shut.

I shook my head, grinning. "Was that last part really necessary?"

"Why not?" Adriana sat down on the planter outside of the psychological center with a satisfied sigh. "If we're planning an ambush, we might as well go for all the gusto!"

"Yes, well, I suppose the question would then be why an ambush would be necessary."

"Ah, well, it worked, didn't it?"

"Perhaps, perhaps."

We sat for a few minutes again in silence, each of us satisfied in our own way. I lifted my gaze to the heavens once again. Understanding—to the degree that I could comprehend—would have to come later. But I knew that it existed. *And that was enough.*

My meditation was interrupted by the sound of a door coming lightly to a close. I looked back at the front of the psychological office to observe Peter's exit, triumph evident on his countenance. I glanced at my watch. Nearly half an hour had passed since Adriana and I had left the office, although the time had seemed much shorter.

"Intimidation a success!"

"Was intimidation our goal?" I asked dryly, biting my lip to avoid smiling.

"Not really. Just justice," Peter responded with a

grin.

"Truth, justice, and the American Way!" Adriana proclaimed.

"Something like that." Peter grinned. "Although, I don't have much claim to the American part."

"Truth?" I raised an eyebrow. "What was that part about colleagues?"

"Hey, that was true!" Peter protested with a grin. "I have several friends studying psychology in Alberta, and they always keep me up to date on their studies, as I find it to be fascinating. Now *I* have some material to give *them*!"

"Ha, ha. Well, okay then."

Adriana eyed me significantly, waving what appeared to be an imaginary weapon in front of my face, as Peter watched us in amusement.

I cleared my throat, my eyes suddenly bright with the days of old. "But of course."

When we were young, Adriana and I would often have swordfights, pretending that we were adventurers of old. It was my idea, always having been in love with the glory and romance of medieval times. We would also knight our comrades . . . or, rather, my brother, who was dragged outside one day while he was attempting to build a small spacecraft. It didn't fly, but our imaginations did.

Even now, our unspoken codes and inside jokes from days bygone were understood.

I forgot that I was supposed to be the one keeping everyone in order as a mischievous smile swept across my face. I took the imaginary sword from Adriana's hands, who curtsied deeply, and then turned to Peter with a wry grin. "Kneel." Peter obediently knelt with a small smile, but said nothing.

I gently placed the imaginary sword over his head. "Dost thou vow to serve our country with honor and truth, to always honor the code of chivalry?"

Peter bowed his head dramatically. "I do."

"Sir Peter," I pronounced, waving the imaginary sword above Peter's head, "I dub thee an honorary knight of the United States of America. Arise, sir knight."

"Thank you." Peter bowed his head graciously as he finally stood. "I will forever honor this . . . highest of honors."

"You'd better." My guard was now completely let down, and I was grinning unreservedly, unable to stop. Peter's eyes met mine for a single instant, a moment in which the brilliant beam of sun and moon met.

"Well, courageous comrades," Adriana asserted, "this is where we make our exit! To our original destination . . . Confetti Way!"

"Lead the way!" Peter and I proclaimed simultaneously.

As Adriana stepped forward with all the assumption of a military march, Peter fell behind to stand beside me.

"That was really brave . . . what you did back there." Peter squeezed my hand.

"Knighting a non-citizen? You're welcome."

Peter chucked. "You know that's not what I meant."

True.

"Attempting to impose a monarchy on a democratic society?"

Peter heaved a dramatic, rather put-on sigh before shaking his head with a smile. "The mission?"

"What did I do?" I asked, halting momentarily in confusion. "This was Adriana's march."

"No, I don't think so." Peter's eyes met mine again, but this time for a long moment. "I think that this was Rebecca's March."

"You're crazy." I shook my head with a smile.

" 'If that is a professional in your world, then your

professionals are cold automatons who have lost their humanity.' "

"Wait," I paused, now truly confused, "how did you hear that? You weren't even in the room at the time."

Peter cleared his throat, looking at his feet for a moment with all the embarrassment of a ten year old who has been caught spying. "I may or may not have been listening in during part of the speech."

"May or may not have?" I raised an eyebrow.

"Well, I had to know when to come in!" Peter protested.

I laughed. "I suppose." I took his hand hesitantly before quickly dropping it. "Thank you."

Peter smiled that smile of his. "No problem."

Chapter 32
Of Old and New

"So, Adriana knew?" I lifted an accusing eyebrow, as Peter and I stood in the middle of the banquet hall, music playing softly in the background.

He laughed, a cup of coffee in one hand. "Yeah. We talked about a month ago, and she was adamant that I keep it quiet until the—how did she put it?—the *reveal*."

I sipped from my own glass of water. "I should keep a better eye on Adriana. She shows no restraint with her surprises."

"Perhaps not," he said, "but I was all too eager to surprise you myself." He looked at me. "As long as silence would not be interpreted as . . . distance."

How little he had to see to know.

I nodded and turned to put down my glass. He followed suit, as the music began to move slowly to the foreground, growing more and more distinct until it surrounded us in lavish swells.

He took my hand and gently twirled me around. I twirled out farther, unaware of my surroundings, blissfully free and ridiculously content. When I returned, taking Peter's hand again, a smile began to form, inching slowly from the corner of his lips. There was also an unreadable look in his eyes.

Strange. By now, I would have thought that I could dissect him completely, facial expression by facial expression. But I had never seen this look in his eyes before.

So, I would focus on the expression that I did know.

I cleared my throat. "What?" I demanded, my voice lifting in mock accusation.

"What?" he repeated back to me, the former expression in his eyes now replaced by a teasing glance that I knew all too well.

"Are you trying to say that I'm a freak?" I raised an eyebrow.

"I have said and have yet to say . . . nothing."

"But you meant it! And," I ran one hand through my hair with a haughty twist, "I'll have you know that I am *not* a freak. I'm . . . a freak-dork-nerd-geek!"

Peter burst into laughter. "A 'freak-dork-nerd-geek'?"

"Yes. You'll note that it has rhythm. In fact, I'm composing the theme song for it as we speak."

"You would."

I looked up with a smile. "Yes."

The last song, a vibrant pop anthem, had finished. I listened as the music shifted to a quieter piano melody.

Peter moved closer, taking my hand once again. "May I have the honor of this dance, Freak-Dork-Nerd-Geek?"

"You may."

It wasn't a slow dance . . . or relatively fast like the last one. It just *was*.

I did not know what steps I danced or how quickly I danced them. I scarcely remembered the song past the beginning of its melody, and yet, at the same time, it was like it would never leave my mind. Half the time I was lost in another world, and, during the other half, my eyes shifted their focus to Peter, as if he were an important part of that world.

It is one of those dances that you can only have with a close friend, I thought. I had never heard about them before, but now I knew.

Peter squeezed my hand, and I suddenly became aware that silence had ensued. The music had stopped.

At least to the outside.

"Thanks for this dance," I said quietly.

"Anytime."

In that instant, I felt compelled to turn, and, sure enough, Adriana was walking not too far away, seemingly absorbed in some sort of undercover pursuit. She finally found us, waving from a distance. I dropped Peter's hand and met her. I sensed him following close behind.

"Hey, dude, sorry; I got sidetracked by the sign by the lemonade. That symbol seriously looks like the Jedi insignia. I told the workers there, but they didn't believe me. Ridiculous, right? Anyway." Adriana broke from her rant to eye us. "What have you two been up to?"

"Oh, we were just dancing," I said offhandedly.

"Oh, right." Adriana surveyed her surroundings as if rediscovering that she was in a dance hall.

My eyes met Peter's, and we both grinned.

There's something about a friend acting so entirely like herself that boosts your spirits in an inexplicable way.

The atmosphere changed, seemingly with our mood,

to bring forth a vibrant salsa beat.

"Well, Adriana—" Peter cleared his throat.

"—since you missed our earlier dancing endeavors," I interjected.

"—would you care to join us now?" Peter finished, his eager, boyish side showing in his face.

"Dude," Adriana grinned, "the party has just started."

I stood in the middle, taking her hand in one and Peter's in the other. "Let's do this."

We stepped to the left, center, right.

We glided around in a circle, an airy laughter filling our spirits.

We moved apart, dancing the salsa steps from which we had deviated.

We spun around, hands apart, but together.

I looked at my two friends and smiled.

One for all, and all for one.

I looked at the painting before me. The Virgin Mary stood, gazing into the distance, a cloak wrapped around her in colors of the sea. Golden fabric reached her hair, outlining her face. There was a pensive look in her eyes, as if she were not really in the present place or time, but cast in the Beyond. And, yet, in her arms, lay a child that centered that present. Asleep, he clung to his mother, his tiny arm cast into that sea. *Symbolic*, I thought to myself.

The background was misty, shrouded in soft, almost blurred gray hues, nearly indistinct in their light strokes. It was evidently stone, and, yet, it reminded me most of the expression on Mary's face. Of the Beyond.

Of her Son, the Christ child, in her arms.

I turned at the familiar cadence of footsteps behind

me.

Peter approached, standing behind me quietly. He had spent the rest of the day with Adriana and me, playing board games and charades in the recreation room of my apartment complex. We had laughed through the early hours of the night, once again together as the first real trio I had ever known. I bit my lip, trying to keep the smile from materializing on my face, at the way he was always discreet and sensitive to my state of mind. He knew that I was caught in a moment of contemplation and did not wish to disturb me.

He knew *me*.

But he also knew that I would eventually want to talk about it.

I finally spoke, still gazing at the painting. "Madonna of the Streets. My favorite Marian portrait."

"Mine, as well," he said quietly from behind me.

"It . . . evokes something in me. There's just so much love in the scene. And, yet, it isn't confined to the present scene or world. It *transcends* it. Perhaps that is what love does . . . transcend reality, I mean." I took a deep breath. "But love can also transform this world. St. Catherine of Siena once said, 'If you are what you should be, you will set the whole world ablaze.' But," I turned to him urgently, "how can I even light a single candle if someone blocks off the first step?"

"You will," he said simply.

"How can you be so sure?"

Peter smiled and said nothing.

I considered issuing some sort of protest on his gender's inability to communicate thoughts in plain English. Or some sort of demand that this particular individual convey some sense of his inner thoughts.

But I didn't.

And I was glad for it.

For the next moments in time, frozen yet never more alive, we contemplated the Madonna and her Child above in silence, while, beyond, luminous stars set fire to the night sky.

A young woman wearing a nun's habit stood, holding a basket. Her round, sweet face, with quiet, tender eyes, was turned slightly to another figure, who was bent forward on her right.

The majesty of the rose garden was a silent song that weaved its way softly through the wiry vines and densely formed bushes that it held. The taller woman handed a plump red rose to her younger companion, who then delicately placed it into the basket that already held a small bundle of the flowers.

She closed her eyes, smiling, as she put the last rose in the basket, its maze of shrouded understanding capturing her heart as it once did on Earth. Yet, here, she understood it better.

It was simple, this rose, despite its complications.

"Mother," she said, "thank you for allowing me to help you in your garden."

The woman, her serene blue eyes smiling joyfully at her assistant, simply nodded and said, "It is my Son's garden, but He has allowed me to keep it so that others may better understand."

The small nun nodded, looking again at the bundle in her arms with pure love. "I will deliver these now."

"Thank you, Thérèse."

I smiled through my sleep.

The image of the Blessed Mother handing a rose from a Heavenly garden to The Little Flower, who would deliver them to the world, would remain with me for the rest of my days.

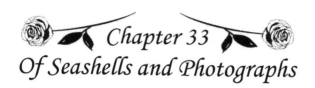

Chapter 33
Of Seashells and Photographs

"Coming!" I dabbed my lips slightly, removing any remaining toothpaste, before dashing to the apartment door.

Peter stood, eternally formal and tall, his countenance marked with a subtle smile.

He was wearing a T-shirt with the words Alberta Youth sprayed across, as he bent over to halt the mad dash of a trash can that I had accidentally set into motion.

I smiled. Oh, how this reminded me of two years ago, when he visited our house in Cedar Heights. Only, last time, I had expected him and ran outside before he had had the chance to ring the doorbell.

I opened my mouth to greet him, but his words came first.

"So, what are we doing today?" He leaned against the door in a gesture that still seemed somehow to impart formality.

My mouth opened wide before finally shutting.

"So, what do you do for fun?" a tall, thoughtful young man with hazel eyes posed without further preamble at the back of the church.

I raised an eyebrow, suppressing a grin. "Did we have plans today, Peter?"

"Yes. Well . . . no. But I thought that we would."

I moved forward, leaving the threshold of the door so that I was standing with one foot outside. "And what plans are those?"

"I think," a wry grin spread across his face from its subtle beginning, "that we may be headed to the beach. At least," he unshouldered a large bag, "that's what I assumed when I packed this."

He was insane.

I grinned.

"Peter, did you happen to notice the weather?"

Peter surveyed his surroundings with a cursory glance. "It's a bit cool."

"It's . . . *freezing*, Peter. This is what we Americans generally refer to as 'winter.' "

"You'd never survive as a Canadian."

"Okay, fine, Peter."

"Fine what?"

My eyes met his in the rambunctious giddiness of a child coupled with the subtle nuance of an adult. "Let's go to the beach."

I threw the toothpaste tube that I had not realized was still in my hands into Peter's somehow expectant arms, and ran back into the apartment to change my clothes.

Wisps of an ancient breeze sifted through the salt air, bringing it to life. Beyond, turquoise waves—tamed slightly by a dove's lullaby—hummed the first notes of a ballad, splashing its visitors with a quick spray of light as they strolled along its shore.

"Peter." I sat down, letting tiny bits of sand fall between my toes.

He followed suit, sitting down beside me.

I gazed ahead, watching the waves tumble down with ecstasy, yet serenity, of spirit, and sighed deeply.

"What is it, Rebecca?" He leaned forward, his eyes intent. The motion returned my eyes to his.

"I um . . . you know when you told me about Little Dan?"

Peter nodded, his gaze unwavering yet now more somber in aspect.

"I never told you . . . something. And right then . . . I wouldn't have. God knows I wouldn't have." I closed my eyes, remembering the moment in the religious education classroom when Peter told me of the accident that had robbed his little brother of his mobility. "I couldn't think of anything but that. And it's . . . a different matter. But later . . . I did. And I've been wanting to tell you about it for so long, but I guess I figured that it would be better said in person."

Peter said nothing, waiting silently with the same expectant, unobtrusive gaze.

"When I was really little . . ." I took a deep breath. "I . . ."

Silence followed, broken only by the lull of seagull and wind-thrown sea.

I sighed again. "And I thought this might happen, so," I reached into my jacket pocket, "I also wrote it down."

I handed him the small piece of paper and turned

my eyes back to the sea.

The waves continued in a cycle of eternity, never fading, never leaving, never stopping. *A cycle of forever.*

After a minute or perhaps a dozen, I felt a gentle hand on my shoulder.

His eyes, large and full, reflected in mine.

"Rebecca . . . I am so sorry. For you. For all of you."

"Some may not understand. The impact or the significance. How I would be affected."

"They should."

Somehow the mere impartment of knowledge to one trusted can bring a relief with effects that can never truly be measured.

I nodded, holding his gaze. For moments longer still, we sat there, communicating words that could never be spoken in the same way aloud.

Yet, like a weary traveler by the name of Antonio, the icy temperature required a change in quest . . . or, more accurately, *movement.*

I shivered, breaking the gaze. "I'm going to run."

I ran toward the sea, while Peter remained behind, watching.

No, I did not see him. But I knew.

I stopped a few inches from the shore, my body warmed by the exercise, and looked down at my feet.

A small object, too open and fragile to be a rock, lay near.

I bent down to inspect, reaching with a hand to pick it up.

A seashell.

I held it up in pure delight, cradling it as if it were the rarest of opals, a creamy mirror of every present shade and mingled tone of God's landscape. "¡Una concha de mar!"

I jogged back to where Peter remained seated, a

quiet smile marking his countenance.

"Do you remember . . . the poem I wrote for you?"

"Aye, I should say so." He leaned back on his haunches. "I read it every Saturday."

"You do?"

"Yes."

My face warmed.

"Why every Saturday?" I continued, ignoring the flush in my cheeks that still remained. "Because it's the end of the week?"

"That and . . ." he turned briefly, looking into the distance of sea and shore. "It's the day I left for Alberta. The day I left here."

The soft caress of a sea breeze lingered, wrapping around us in indulgent simplicity.

"They say," I said slowly, "that, if you put a shell up to your ear, you can hear the waves, even if you're far away from the sea." I held it to my ear for a moment before handing it to him. "You should . . . you should keep it."

"Thank you." He held the shell to his ear, as if awaiting what it might tell him.

"Esta concha de mar vive en un mar de lejos. Pero se acerca a la orilla cuando respiran las olas. De risa o llanto. De sol o lluvia. O nada en particular," he quoted softly.

The waves called the seashell, filling it with their song as if they had heard his words—and my own.

He knew it. He knew it by heart.

I looked down, unable to speak.

Yet I lifted my head only a moment later, an impulse of convenience surfacing.

"Peter, would you care to inspect that rock formation with me?" I quickly pointed ahead at the long, irregular formation that jutted into the ocean some distance from us on the right.

"Sure."

I stood up, waiting, as he unzipped his shoulder bag. *Rebecca, stop being curious.*

He pulled out a smaller inner bag that was still too large and bulky to betray any sense of shape. It reminded me of those dolls I was fascinated by as a child; within each doll was one more until reaching the smallest of all.

I cleared my throat. "Ready?"

"Yeah." He shouldered the new bag, dropping the old one on one of the beach towels we had brought. "Let's go."

When Peter left for Alberta, I often thought of how I missed our exchange of conversation, how I missed the way he communicated to me with his eyes, how large yet almost understated his grin could be. As we walked toward the rock formation, I realized that I had forgotten how much I missed *this*, how much I just missed walking next to him in companionable silence.

I carefully ascended, balancing with each arm positioned outward. While I was not one for daring heights, this vantage point was perfect while still maintaining enough security for my liking.

Well, I thought to myself, as I almost tripped over a less even portion beneath my feet, *a more adventurous sort of security*.

I paused. Peter's long, steady footsteps were nowhere to be heard.

"Peter?" I cautiously turned around, making sure to watch my step.

He remained beneath the formation, a large, old-fashioned camera wrapped around his neck and pointed directly at me. The camera case—as well as the concealing inner bag—lay near his feet.

"What are you doing?" I squinted at his figure

below, shielding my face.

I was not particularly camera-phobic, but I wanted to know the nature of these covert operations first.

"What does it look like?"

"Why are you sneaking around to take a photo of me?"

"Maybe because I wanted a candid shot?" he called back with a grin.

I rolled my eyes, suppressing a smile. "And I'm the freak-dork-nerd-geek?"

"Speaking of," Peter returned the focus of the camera to me, "now that my candid shot will no longer be possible, would you mind striking a dramatic pose?"

What in the world had gotten into him? This was unusual, even for Peter.

"A dramatic pose?" I raised an eyebrow.

"Yeah. Like you're queen of the mountain or something."

I snorted. "You are a freak. But, fine . . . I'll do it only because I *am* Queen of the Mountain."

I took on a conceited stare, leaning slightly backward with all the air of a royal heir.

"You know, you're lucky I know you. Otherwise I might think you're the paparazzi stalking me."

"Duly noted, Your Royal Highness."

"Does that work? Regal enough?"

"Yes, indeed."

"I don't look like a poser, do I?"

"As in, someone who is posing?"

"Peter Joseph Asturian, you know perfectly well what I'm referring to!"

"No, Rebecca, you don't look like a *fake* poser."

"As compared to a real poser?"

"Yes. Now, as much as I enjoy our banter . . . may I

take the photo now?"

I paused, as if deep in thought, before a grin finally broke forth. "Well, I suppose."

"Good."

Peter repositioned the camera, adjusting various knobs and levers.

"Didn't you bring your iPhone today?" I squinted at Peter from my position on the rock. "It has a camera."

"Too modern."

I smiled. *I had suspected as much.*

"Ready?"

"Yep!"

"Say . . . *Intermission.*"

I laughed. "Intermission."

"Say it again without breaking your regal stare?"

I steadied my facial expressions, pretending that my life depended upon it. "Intermission."

"Actually, just say nothing."

I said nothing.

And he took the photo.

"So . . ." I moved to a more natural position, "what are you going to do with the photo?"

Really, Rebecca? Of all the most ridiculous questions . . . What do you suppose he'll do? Toss it in the ocean, perhaps, along with the camera?

He put the camera back in its case before looking up, his eyes once again resting on me.

"I'll put it with the poem," he said.

Kindred spirits are a special kind
A deeper breadth, no measured height
A friendship that knows no boundaries
To the understanding that it concentrates.

It ebbs and flows with sun and tide
It mingles in seas of carousels
It becomes the past and knows it not.
It dreams without un-awakening.
But the Saturday kindred spirits
The Saturday kindred spirits
Are the very best of all.

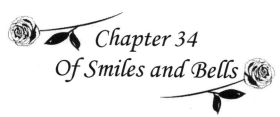

Chapter 34
Of Smiles and Bells

"It's . . . quite something," Peter studied the structure of St. Vitus Catholic Church, where he had once served as an usher, "to be back."

"I can imagine." I followed his gaze. "Even for me, it's a feeling that is hard to put into words. And it has been only a short time for me, comparably."

"I'm glad."

I waited for him to explain further, but he did not. So, instead, I turned toward him, a question in my eyes. He nodded and followed me into the church, holding the door for me as I stepped inside.

Adoro te devote, latens Deitas.

My hand flew to my mouth.

Quae sub his figuris vere latitas.

"Peter," I whispered, motionless, as the soft murmurs of the choir lifted into the air.

"Yes, it's beautiful. I love Gregorian chant."

"No, I meant . . ." My words trailed off.

Oh, how an association may develop without recognition. I had forgotten that Peter would not know the song that I would always associate with a particular adoration chapel visit. He could not be expected to read my mind.

*Well, at least not **all** the time.*

I opened my mouth to explain, as the priest and altar servers made their way toward the back of the church for the procession.

Mass was about to begin.

"Let's find a seat," I mouthed.

He nodded, and we moved forward.

There were several seats on the right side, and Peter stepped aside to allow my entrance.

When it came time for the Offertory, I could not control the smile that slipped across my lips, finally alighting my face. I turned to Peter just when the basket reached our aisle. His face held the same recognition, and we could barely contain ourselves.

A young usher who I instantly identified as Tom, our co-conspirator in the preparation of the Family Day event two years prior, offered us a wide grin as he waited by the aisle.

We returned the nonverbal greeting and handed him back the basket.

I had never sat next to Peter during Mass, I realized, as the music returned. He had always been present, yet never like this.

And I realized that there was something in his presence here that established companionable silence even more than our walks together in solitude.

For that, I was grateful in a way that, like those walks, I could not completely express.

At the end of Mass, I genuflected, waiting for Peter,

who was immersed in the readings.

I watched as he read, so completely absorbed and attentive, as if life poured through those pages.

I grinned. *Of course Peter would be one to re-read the readings at the end of Mass.*

He stood up to leave, catching the expression on my face.

"What?"

"Never mind." I waved his words aside. "In other news, I think we have someone to visit."

Peter's eyes lit up. "Yes, let's see if Cedric is here! He's still an usher, right?"

"As far as I know, yes." I paused. "I didn't see him on Christmas, or over Thanksgiving break when I attended Mass during the week. But he may not have been scheduled then."

Peter nodded. "I cannot imagine Cedric leaving. This is who he is."

Somehow, when Peter said those words, I knew them to be true. As we neared the back of the church, my breath held in anticipation, I expected with no doubt that the elderly usher would be there.

I distractedly ran a hand through my hair as we walked, the motion throwing me back in time.

Cedric, Fred, the sea captain. Three people, yet one. A guide, standing watching quietly in the background, following us through that spring both in reality and fantasy, through the stories we wrote with our actions and those we wrote with our pen.

When I had come face to face with Cedric that Palm Sunday, realizing who he truly was, I had also come face-to-face with the reality that I could never truly know who he was.

My breath accelerated, as if I were walking through a dream that had occurred of my own imagining.

But it had not. It had not.

Cedric, wisps of gray and white hair lessened with the passage of time, was bent over the small table in the usher's closet, a stack of papers sifting through his hands. When he looked up, his dark gray eyes focused steadily, a smile weaving its way across his face.

"Peter," he said, instantly leaving the stack to greet his former co-usher and dear friend. "Welcome back."

There was warmth in his eyes and joy in his voice, yet I detected no surprise in either.

Peter clapped him on the back, and the two embraced.

The old seaman, if he were such in this land, finally met my gaze. "I am glad to see you, as well, Rebecca."

"As am I." I hesitated before moving forward, impulsively throwing my arms around him.

Cedric smiled, as I drew back. "What brings you two to St. Vitus? I heard that you were working in L.A." He nodded toward me.

"Yes, I am, but I'm visiting family at the moment."

"Christmas vacation still?"

"Mine ended earlier, but," I jabbed a finger in the direction of Peter, "his break started about a week ago."

Cedric's eyes returned to Peter, approving. "I'm glad you took this time to come back to see old friends."

"I am, too," Peter said fervently.

For one guarded and quiet, Peter's sincerity was one of the characteristics that defined him the most. As I watched the exchange between my old friends, I was reminded of that, once again unable to resist smiling.

"Hey, Cedric," Peter took out a piece of paper, "I imagine you're not a fan of email . . ."

More a fan of notes in Offertory baskets.

". . . but do you have an address? I'd like to keep in touch."

Cedric nodded. "I do." He motioned for Peter to hand him the piece of paper and slowly took a pen from his white dress shirt pocket.

He could not hide the fact that his agility was fading. As he wrote down the information for Peter, my eyes were drawn once again to his face, now taking in more detail. The light wisps of hair forever imprinted on my mind remained, but they had lessened, revealing more the shine of his head.

I did not know how old he was, just as I could not hazard a guess as to the age of the old sea captain.

But perhaps even the seemingly ageless cannot cheat the passage of time.

As Cedric handed Peter his contact information, his eyes clear and penetrating, another thought also passed through my mind:

And so too in that is dignity.

I watched the energetic conversation between the two, awaiting my turn without anticipation, and allowed the song of the past to sift over me, once again bringing a smile to my lips.

Chapter 35
Farewell, fare well

"So, I guess this is it."

Peter stood, suitcase in one hand, at the airport entrance.

I nodded, clearing my throat. "Yeah."

"I'm glad I got to see you again before Christmas break ended, Rebecca." His eyes met mine.

"Yeah. Yeah, me, too," I managed to say.

I looked at him, and, in that moment, I was no longer at the airport. I was no longer twenty-two, almost twenty-three.

I was twenty again.

Another moment, another time . . . time repeating itself.

I took a deep breath, a wave of bittersweet melancholy filling my entire being.

Another goodbye.

The same goodbye.

We both rushed forward and caught each other in a hug. I felt moisture in my eyes as I was taken back to an old classroom the day before Easter. To a first embrace. To the hardest goodbye I had ever experienced.

And now I was experiencing it again.

He was my rock, and a rock was not meant to leave.

Peter squeezed my shoulder as we finally broke apart. "I'll miss you, California girl."

I laughed. "Did you seriously just call me that?"

"Yes, yes, I did."

I shook my head with no attempt to conceal my amusement. "I'm hardly the stereotypical California girl, I'll have you know."

"You're hardly the stereotypical anything."

I bit my lip, trying not to let the emotion overtake me. "I'll miss you, mi concha de mar."

Mi concha de mar. A poem I had written for him seemingly so long ago.

He picked up his suitcase. "Adios, loquita. Try not to write too many crazy stories in my absence."

"Adios, loquito. Say hi to Fred for me."

Farewell.

Chapter 36
Of Dresses and Stars

I walked down the sidewalk, my thoughts wrapped in my last encounter at Teresa's house.

It was nearly ten o'clock. Teresa had requested that I drop off the internship evaluation packet, as she had lost her own and was soon to begin her own internship. I had sensed the hesitation in her voice, echoes of the previous visit.

Did I want to see —

I did not know.

I continued walking, focusing on the branches of greenery surrounding the small block, quiet in the lateness of night.

As I briefly halted in my walk, staring absentmindedly at a large Redwood tree, shadows flickered across its surface.

And, with it, a scream.

I moved slowly, my body shaking, peering over the forestry that had shielded me from thought.

In the middle of the street, a young girl, wearing a sparkly, rhinestone-lit magenta dress, was struggling against a masked man, a flash of silver against her throat.

My hand flew to my mouth. *Amelia.*

The figure turned briefly toward the other end of the street.

Without a second thought, I flew upon the scene.

I stood in front of Amelia, blocking her narrow frame with my own. "You're going to have to get through me first."

God, please help me.

A silent plea.

For her sake, I showed no fear. But, in reality, I was terrified.

The man before me stared, about to open his mouth, the knife still raised. I stretched my arms around Amelia, fingering in my pocket for the correct form and shape. *Please let this work. Please.*

I pressed the Panic button on my car key, and a loud, blaring sound immediately echoed across the field and surrounding area. The man looked at us for a second, hesitated, and then quickly took off, tearing across the parking lot until his form was a small line in the distance.

I knelt beside Amelia, who had thrown herself on the ground, sobbing. "It's okay, Amelia. It's okay."

She looked up, and I moved closer, wrapping my arms around her. "It's okay," I said again, in a whisper.

"Rebecca."

It was a question, but a statement at the same time.

"Yes, Amelia?"

"Why did you help me?" she said, her eyes filling with tears as she looked up at me again. "Why did you risk your life for *me*?"

"Because," I said, my voice shaking, "you're Teresa's little sister. And maybe," I said finally, "maybe you're my little sister, too."

The tears that had started in her eyes came steadily now, like rain on a clear-casted day. "Oh."

"And because," I continued, my eyes now, too, wet, "you're—"

"A human being?" she said quietly.

"Yes."

We looked up at the stars that glittered across the night sky, filling the void in our hearts with their song, until the day chased them away.

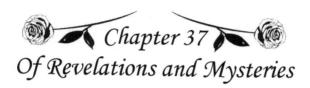

Chapter 37
Of Revelations and Mysteries

I opened my eyes, stretching my arms half-heartedly in the dim light of the room that was gradually becoming more pronounced.

The morning sun spilled its welcoming greeting, a golden shaft delicately spun at the window's edge.

As I sat up groggily, my eyes took in my surroundings. It was a small room, decorated prettily with pink floral accents, much like my own apartment. There was a small chair before a wooden desk to the right of the bed in which I now sat. It was as if I were looking at a consolidated, miniature version of my own apartment.

I looked down at the covers of the bed, a yellow-and-blue pattern depicting SpongeBob SquarePants.

Or not.

Within the safe confines of her home, Amelia had

explained sheepishly that she had sneaked out to go to a school dance that her parents had explicitly forbidden her from attending. Her friends, already sixteen, had picked her up but were unable to drop her off back home. Since the school was within walking distance, Amelia was determined to walk home before her parents noticed her absence. Within a block of her house, she was suddenly grabbed from behind. With a guilty look in the direction of her parents, she mouthed a "sorry."

"I know," she had admitted, her eyes downcast. "I shouldn't have been there."

After that incident, Amelia had begged me to stay the night. Her parents, wrapping their arms around their youngest daughter, their eyes filled with gratitude in the wake of a fear that only they could truly fathom, agreed, insisting that I stay. As I studied my young friend, I wondered for a moment if she wanted the security of my presence due to the horror of that night.

Yet, while that may have played a role, I realized that her motives were distinctive from those of her parents.

She wanted me to stay not because of what had happened that night, but because of what had happened three weeks earlier.

And so I agreed, taking Amelia's old childhood room since the guest room was in the process of being renovated. Teresa had come in from a late-night shift at the local coffee shop, and, for a few hours, we sat, going over the events that had recently transpired. I watched as her lower lip trembled at the risk that her little sister had met. Even though the two sisters never got along, it was still her little sister. She shook her head in disbelief before departing, thanking God that I had been there, and with presence of mind.

I threw off the covers spontaneously, sliding quickly out of bed. The recollections of the previous night had completed the awakening process.

And there was something that I had to do.

I walked down the stairs of the Anderson home, wrapped in a fluffy, hot pink robe that Amelia's parents had left hanging on the door.

The tantalizing scent of pancakes emerging from their warm slumber increased my pace.

Amelia sat at the dining room table, closing her eyes blissfully as she ate the pancakes with relish.

I grinned. It was another childlike moment that the fourteen year old would never have allowed her peers to witness, yet which was so entirely, completely, and lovably *her*.

"Hey, Amelia!"

Amelia jumped slightly, and then, as her vision took in the new presence, her eyes lit up. "Rebecca!"

She jumped up and threw her arms around me in an embrace. "This is an awesome morning! We are totally going to have breakfast together like it's a sleepover party . . ."

". . . only not," I finished, laughing. "Yes, it's completely epic."

Amelia grinned unreservedly. "Go get some pancakes from the stove. It's the secret family recipe and you're going to love it."

I smiled, taking a small, white plate from the table and bringing it to the kitchen. I filled up my plate liberally as my stomach growled and then returned to the hall.

"Secret family recipe?" I teased, upon reaching the table. "So, I won't know what's in it?"

"Oh, well, you can know," Amelia replied between mouthfuls of pancake, "because you're family."

A knot wove its way across my forehead, creasing the space between my eyebrows.

"Amelia, there's . . . something I want to tell you."

Amelia looked up at the subdued indecision in my voice. "What?"

I sat down across from her, the pancakes momentarily forgotten. "You know how I said that you're not just my friend's little sister, but my little sister, too?"

Amelia nodded emphatically. "And I feel the same way! You're totally my big sister, and I'm sorry for the way that I acted earlier—"

I shook my head. "It's not that, sweetie. But I do appreciate your apology."

Amelia nodded, her fork with a bit of pancake frozen in the air as she waited for me to speak.

"I've always wanted a little sister," I finally continued, "ever since I was little myself. Don't get me wrong, I love my brother Alexander very much. But he's an older brother, and that's different. I . . . always wished that I could know what it meant to have a little sister."

"Aww, that's very sweet." Amelia sniffed slightly, betraying her status as a non-sap.

"But it's more than that." I took a deep breath. "I almost had . . . I *did* have a little sister. My mom . . . when I was six years old, my mom announced to the family that she was pregnant again. I remember how excited I was." I closed my eyes briefly, recalling the moment. "I remember putting my hand against my mommy's tummy, thrilling at the movement of my little baby sister's arms and feet. I giggled and smiled, unable to stop doing either. I could hardly wait for the moment in which I would hold my baby sister in my arms. Of how I would show her the world of fairy tales, of princesses and princes, of daring escapes and sunlit balls. Of how we would share sisterly confidence."

Amelia nodded, her back rigid as her eyes drew closer together, focused on me intently.

"But the baby didn't make it. Four months in, my mom miscarried. We still don't know why exactly; my dad suspected that the stress of her job as an ER nurse — she switched to teaching later — may have been partly to blame. But, ultimately we don't know. All I know is . . . that moment when I sat, small and close to my mother, in the doctor's office. And how the doctor revealed to her the news."

I bit my lip, tears inching forward. "I'll never forget that moment, as long as I live. It's imprinted here," I touched my chest before dropping my hand to my side. "Mom would have never brought me if she had known. But she didn't. She didn't have any warning signs like other women who miscarried did. She really . . . she really had no idea."

The tears that I had attempted to abate flowed freely now, streaming down my face.

I let them.

"There were two other siblings that I never met, not even through the unseen beauty of their inner home in my mother's womb. They died two and four years before Alex was born. We don't know what gender they were. I often," I paused, pressing my lips together, "think of what they might have been like."

I breathed deeply. "I often wonder if they ever look down on me at Earth and wish that they could hug me, too. If they want to talk to me as much as I want to talk to them. If . . ." my voice broke, "I'll one day see them in Heaven."

A sob burst forth, and I could no longer speak. I heard the squeaking of a chair and rapid movement, and Amelia's arms were wrapped around me.

"Oh, Rebecca."

I turned, wrapping my arms around her.

"It's okay," Amelia whispered. "I'll be your little sister for all eternity."

The sweet cherubic face
Of the young nun-saint
She smiled with her eyes and held out her hand
A shower of roses spilling to the ground in glorious flight
Do not fear, dearest one.
"Believe that I shall be your true little sister for all eternity."
For it is true.
And the scarlet red of roses, shifting in the autumn light, returned home.

I held onto the rail, walking down the front steps of the Anderson home.

Amelia and I had spent the early morning laughing, talking, and commiserating about every varied thing that came to mind, from her school troubles to silly stories of my youth, from television shows to favorite music. When it finally came time to go, I stood, not wishing to leave, and squeezed my new little sister one last time before waving goodbye, as she herself left for school.

I absentmindedly scanned the street for my vehicle.

The Silver Rider, a sleek Honda accord, announced its presence as it caught the sun's rays.

I moved forward, adjusting my purse strap as it

attempted to organize an escape route, my cell phone in the other hand.

As I pressed the "unlock" button, my hand already reaching for the driver's door, a small image fell into my peripheral vision, and I froze.

On the left mirror was affixed a small, folded piece of paper. "Rebecca" was sprawled across its surface in broad, even strokes. A memory flitted through my mind of a small note in an Offertory basket, the word "Intermission" contained inside.

But I knew, as I lifted my hand to take the piece of paper, that this was no Intermission.

Hi, Rebecca. Last night wasn't about the little girl. See you soon.

With my heart pounding, I picked up the phone. "Hello? Yes, I'd like to file a report . . ."

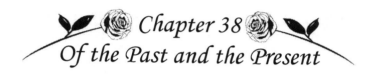

Chapter 38
Of the Past and the Present

A young girl peeked around the corner, her eyes timid yet enthralled, as she soaked it all in, droplets of a story she was formulating in her mind.

I'm really a princess from another land, she whispered to herself without uttering a word, as the buzz of traffic enveloped the scene of the station in a chaotic roar, **but they found me here, so I had to speak to the officials. They are going to find a new home for me before I am whisked away back to my real home.**

After I meet Prince Charming, of course. He will be devastated upon my departure. Maybe I'll come back for him in Book 2. As long as I can get away from the dragon . . .

Her thoughts were interrupted by the sudden departure of the incessant tapping of a pen at close proximity to her ear. She turned around as a figure rounded the corner and stood squarely in her path.

A tall man with dark brown hair and a pleasing demeanor stood before her, smiling kindly at her. He wore the traditional garb of a policeman and, judging from his movements, had recently left a small office that contained at least one hyperactive pen.

"Hello," she stuttered, casting her eyes downward in embarrassment. **Oh, I hope he didn't hear what I was saying.**

"Hello! Did you get lost, sweetheart? Mrs. Harding's class has moved on to the interrogation room."

"Oh." She blushed. "I did lose my way. You see, we were given a few moments' pause and . . . well, I got lost in my thoughts and lost my group all at the same time."

The corners of his lips moved, and he broke into a good-natured chuckle, a booming laugh that absorbed all the droplets of her story and made them somehow more complete. "You have an interesting way of wording things, little girl. I like it."

"Thank you." She offered him a shy smile. "Can you help me find the interrogation room?"

He offered her his arm, leading her toward a small room a few yards to the right. "Of course."

I sat at the same desk that the policeman I had met those fifteen years before had once occupied. Since that field trip in second grade, I had had no reason to find myself in a police station, except through the imaginative wanderings spurned by Adriana's tales of her father, a retired police officer.

I never found out his name. I wonder, I mused to myself, momentarily distracted from my fears and qualms, *if he would recognize me or I him.*

But I did not have long to answer my insatiable curiosity, for the shuffling of feet brought my attention upward, focusing on a figure that moved swiftly in the direction of where I sat. His hair was tempered slightly by threads of gray and white weaving their way into the brown, but it was the same tall policeman whom I had met as a young girl.

Only, I thought to myself with amusement, *he's not quite as tall as he appeared to me then.*

He sat down before me, offering a generous smile. "You must be Rebecca."

It reminded me of introductions given at a party, standing in great contrast with the seriousness of the situation that I myself had attempted to brush away from my mind. Yet the standard of civility was perhaps best kept in these circumstances if any at all.

"Yes." I attempted a smile.

"Well, Rebecca, I know you must have had quite a fright . . ."

I nodded. "Yeah, I pretty much thought that this kind of situation would be restricted to film and TV as far as my life was concerned." I offered a nervous laugh.

He laughed, the same deep-throated chuckle that spoke to all that he was in a single sound. "Yes, we do tend to think that way, don't we?"

I smiled slightly, and then it withdrew, reality overtaking its gleeful sprint.

His own smile faded, and he opened his mouth again to speak. "And I'm very sorry for it. But I can assure you that my police force will do its very best and protect you from any possible threat. You have ID'd the man to the best of your ability—though I understand that he was masked—which should still help considerably. We have also outlined a map of related scenes of the incident involved and hope to catch whoever is responsible for this as soon as possible."

"Thank you."

He leaned forward. "I hope you believe that. Nowadays it seems that . . . the police are not always held in the greatest regard."

I looked up to meet his eyes, recalling again Adriana's family and the way that they all gathered together at Mass every Sunday, the way that a little girl told her best friend with wide, serious eyes of how her father sometimes got home after she was asleep because he "had a very, very important job."

"My best friend's father used to be on the force. I understand the dedication—and hardship—that you face."

"Oh? Was your friend's father local? Perhaps I know the fellow!"

"Mr. Hanson. He retired about seven years ago."

His face lit up, accentuating its crease lines. "Officer Hanson! He was my mentor back in the day. I have nothing but the utmost respect for him. My, my, how circles cross these days!"

"Yes indeed."

"Rebecca, again, I need you to not be afraid. You will be safe."

"I . . . truly appreciate it."

"Let's discuss the arrangements I have scheduled . . ."

As I walked to my car, shielded on either side by uniformed men in blue, a sense of comfort weaved its way across me.

I was frightened and uncertain. Yet the kind, easy manners of Chief Nelson had distilled some of that fear, replacing it with some semblance of security.

And for that I was grateful.

One of the police officers, a young man with short, light brown hair, opened the door for me, a polite gesture that somehow increased my sense of security. I lowered my head and entered.

"Miss Veritas," the other police officer spoke, a young man of about the same age as his colleague, "we will be following your car closely behind, as the chief told you. If you run into any problems, just flash your brake lights three times. But I suspect that there will be no need for that. We will be closely watching."

I nodded. "Thank you."

When the police officers left, some of that sense of security withdrew with it.

I took a deep breath. *Be strong, Rebecca.*

I made the Sign of the Cross and put the keys in the ignition.

I had arrived at my apartment without incident. The police car nevertheless remained overnight, parked outside under the mask of night, wrapping its own mask of a blanket around the building.

I stood at the window, looking out quietly at the car that stood watch in my name. I wondered briefly what my neighbors would think but decided not to care. Safety was of more importance that the wandering eyes of others.

I yawned and flicked the switch of my lamp, swirling in shades of pink . . .

The phone rang, jolting me from my slumber, after the second night of police protection.

I jumped up, my heart beating wildly in anticipation,

snatching my phone from its place by my bed.

"Hello?"

"Hello! This is Chief Nelson. Am I speaking to Rebecca?"

"Yes, you are. Do you have news?"

"We do indeed. Please walk around to the front of your apartment. I have asked one of my officers to escort you back to the station. I understand it is early, but I thought that you would be more interested in getting answers than anything else."

I cast a brief glance at the clock, which read 5:14 AM, before absentmindedly dismissing it. *He was right. For once in my life, that did not matter.*

"I'll be right around."

"Very good, Rebecca, very good."

"Well, Rebecca, the resolution of a case is much more immediate when you have a confession." Chief Nelson smiled wryly, before sliding a piece of paper over to my side.

On it was pictured a young man with a buzz cut and different levels of earring cascaded across his earlobe. He wore a white T-shirt and looked to be in his twenties.

I blinked in near disbelief.

It was Kaiden, one of my attackers from the movie outing. Only apparently he had updated his hair.

"Well-known street thief," he said, answering what he supposed was my unspoken question, as I looked up, "*known* in particular for his trademark of leaving notes to scare potential victims of the crime. We were quite fortunate to have caught him after all this time. He is a suspect in multiple open burglary and theft cases. Your situation tipped us off to his location. Several witnesses confirmed his motive; his ego got in the way, and he boasted about his plans in public. Apparently he scours Waltring Street, as it is a nice neighborhood, looking for unsuspecting young people that he might rob. We were able to make a deal with one of his associates for a shorter prison sentence, as well, which led us to that specific area." The corners of his lips moved slightly. "Turns out he was not as courageous under the eyes of the law as behind his mask of a thief. He confessed to attempted robbery in our first round in the interrogation room. He is now safely behind bars."

I breathed out deeply, my chest lightening with each word. "Wow, I'm so glad to hear that. You have no idea how relieved I am."

"I think I do." He offered me another kind smile. "By the way, Rebecca, this will sound sort of funny. But you look a bit familiar . . . I can't quite place it."

A wide—and real—grin broke across my face. "About that . . ."

"Hey, Mom, so I haven't told you what happened over the past few days . . ."

After a reel of a lecture, I heard a brief pause on the other line. My mom finally spoke. "I'm so glad you're okay."

"Me, too. I've been eating ice cream all evening."

I had never known how long two days could be until this week.

"You are insane."

"Probably." I laughed, its lightness washing over me.

The case was dropped, and, with it, the ever-present weight in my chest.

With strawberry ice cream
And merry-go-rounds
I lifted across the ice
Of my mind.

Chapter 39
Of Elevators and Secrets

I pressed the large red button to the right of the elevator, listening to the low hum of background music as I waited for the elevator to descend. It was a rendition of Beethoven's Fifth, and, when the door finally slid open, the strength of its melody continued, as if it too waited for an entrance, or exit.

And, with this particular slide of exits and entrances, I nearly jumped backwards in surprise.

In the elevator stood Christy, the former secretary at Dr. Yin's office, a distracted look upon her face.

A few months ago—yet seemingly much longer— we had met under similar circumstances. As the two of us stood there silently, I was overwhelmed by how markedly different those two encounters were, even if presented under nearly identical settings.

I had arrived a young and eager intern; she was a cheerful secretary. And, as I continued to observe her, I realized that the lightness of spirit had been treaded upon as much on her as on me.

Christy's eyes flitted about, darting from one section of the mall to the next, before finally holding out her hand urgently. "Rebecca, step in."

I quickly obeyed, nearly leaping into the elevator before it closed. It had seemed that we had observed each other in stunned shock for several moments, when, in fact, it had probably only been a few. Yet those few seconds had communicated enough for three hours.

"Christy, it's been so long!" I began uncertainly, attempting a small smile despite the feeling warping inside of my stomach.

"Yes, it has," Christy forced a smile in return. "It's nice to see you."

The mechanic energy of the elevator' ascension wrapped its way into my mind, a reminder that this was no time for pleasantries.

It was time to cut to the chase.

"If you don't mind me asking," I hesitated, "why did you leave Dr. Yin's office?"

There was a resigned look in her eyes at that moment, the resignation that occurs when the inevitable and the expected happens, even when it is not desired.

She heaved a great sigh, staring for a moment at the floor of the elevator before looking back up. "Rebecca, you have no idea what you have gotten yourself into. Or," she offered me a probing look, "perhaps you do. Rebecca," she said slowly, "I was fired from Dr. Yin's office."

Dr. Yin was corrupt, that much had become clear to me over the past few months. But why Christy? What possible threat could she serve? She was pleasant and accommodating.

She was harmless.

I nodded for her to continue, questions circling in my mind.

"I knew for a while what Dr. Yin was doing." She cast her eyes downward, but not before I could see the evident guilt. "And it bothered me; it did. But I became very good at pretending. I would hear a cry, a scream, from her office and ignore it, as if it had never happened. But something happened, Rebecca," her eyes turned to me, searching them desperately, "the day that I danced with you and Albert. Something clicked in my brain that I could no longer ignore. I don't know why or how, but," she took a deep breath, her words rushing out before she could express them coherently, "but it did. And I could no longer stand by and allow that injustice to occur. Not anymore. So, the next time I heard a scream, I rushed over to that woman's office and pulled her client away from her."

"Stacie," I said quietly, my mind emptied of all save a single memory.

"Yes. Rebecca," the words broke out, "she was hitting her."

I sighed, staring ahead as a jolt stabbed at my heart. *It was incomprehensible to me.*

"But clients signed an agreement at the beginning to tell no one of Dr. Yin's methods, of what occurred there . . . even the little twins, who knew nothing of what it meant; she did not ask their parents." Christy laughed an empty, hollow laugh.

"And Stacie was too afraid of Yin to do so."

Large eyes, bewildered and frightened.

"And the mirror at the entrance of the center?"

I nodded for her to continue, my chest throbbing.

"It's there so that Stacie and the others . . . view themselves as she sees them as soon as they enter the facility. So that they see themselves as worthless."

I was a student in psychology. I could write pages upon pages about the motivations and psychological makeup of individuals who chose actively to critically wound others.

But I would still never be able to understand the abuse that I had just heard.

It did not matter if I could comprehend. I would never understand.

"I promised that I would report her," she continued, her eyes flashing between anger and resignation. "A day later, I received a pink slip, notifying me of my imminent dismissal. And attached to this slip was a psychological report, a psychological report of me."

I sucked in my breath, knowledge surfacing in my mind before she communicated it.

"She claimed, from her position as a psychological expert, that I was unstable and in need of intervention."

Blackmail.

"And I knew that it was a threat to send that falsified report to the authorities should I attempt to report her. So, I . . ." her words broke off, as she turned away, her face in her hands.

"I am so sorry," I finally said, unable to say anything more. "I am so sorry."

Descending, down, down . . .

"Be careful, Rebecca," her eyes bore into mine with intensity, as the elevator clicked brightly, reaching the bottom floor, "she is not to be trusted."

"I will," I managed, before stepping outside of the elevator.

Christy remained in the elevator, the hollow emptiness in her eyes with me as I made my way through the mall, in search of Adriana.

So, it was all true. And worse than I had ever expected.

When Adriana came up from behind me, I barely noticed, still staring aimlessly ahead.

"Dude," she said, peering at me in concern as I finally turned around. "Are you okay?"

"Yeah, I'm fine," I said, brushing away my troubled thoughts. "Let's go."

Adriana and I sauntered across the mall, finally breaking into our usual, easy conversation and laughter, occasionally stopping at a shop to browse.

"So, where's this epic bookstore you've been talking about?" Adriana asked, as she held up an electronic Darth Maul toothbrush at a centered display with clear distaste.

"It's . . ." I craned my neck for a better look out the window, "on the other side of this complex, if I'm not mistaken."

"Okay," she put down the toothbrush with relish, "let's go."

The vintage bookstore was as I had left it a few weeks before, its pleasant mint green exterior met by a white-washed door only slightly diminished by a small scratching of the paint on the bottom right corner.

As Adriana opened the door and I followed her in, I realized how bizarre it was that I even noticed the scratch.

Yet somehow it stood out, the one blemish on an otherwise immaculate white surface.

"Wow," Adriana said in awe as she gazed around at her surroundings. "You weren't exaggerating. This is like an underground cavern of literary delight."

I followed her gaze, once again caught in recollection of my first visit there. The way that the shelves and racks—alternating in shape and size—circled around in seemingly haphazard design actually contained an order, a pattern, that reminded me of the layers upon layers of an enigmatic floral composition.

Of the rose, petals circling in a delicate dance upon my kitchen counter.

For several minutes, we became absorbed in the literary realm, quietly taking up book after book, curious as to what world it held. As I put back a mere travel guide to Indonesia written in that language, yet still fascinating in its ornately designed cover and elegantly spun with golden-edged pages, I stole a glance at the cash register. Either Tara was on her lunch break or she was in the back. My eyes lowered, drawn in by the crimson volume behind the register.

It was still there.

"So, dude, what are you looking at?" Adriana had put down her latest literary venture and moved next to me. "That's an intense stare."

I glanced at Adriana, motioning with my eyes that she direct her attention at the book behind the counter.

"What's that?" she whispered. "And what's with the covert communication?"

"I don't know," I whispered back. "It's just that . . ."

In the impeccable timing worthy of a cinematic event, Tara emerged from the jungle of book and thorn brushed aside at the back of the store.

"Oh, sorry, girls; I didn't realize anyone was there!" Tara walked quickly in our direction.

"Hey Tara!"

"Hi, Rebecca! Another friend of yours?" Tara motioned in Adriana's direction.

"Yes, my best friend since we were nine, actually." I laughed, my eyes still pulled in the direction of the register.

Rebecca to Eyes: Stay where you are.

Adriana gave a convincing laugh that I instantly recognized as the theatrical measure that she put on during one of her play performances. "Yes, it's been so long! Hard to believe! Now, if I may forego the usual introductions and ask you a pertinent question?" She glanced briefly in my direction before returning to Tara with a contagious smile.

What in the world was Adriana doing now?

"Yes, I'd be happy to help!"

"Well, you see, I'm a theater arts major and . . . I could always use new material for my work! Now, Rebecca here tells me that you have plenty of very old material. I was wondering, might you have any early versions of the Greek tragedies?"

"How exciting! As a matter of fact, I do have some old copies of *Antigone*, with translations in about five different languages! Should I get them for you to peruse?"

"Oh, splendid!" Adriana's face lit up excitedly in a way that made me almost roll my eyes. "And I would be delighted!"

"Adriana Hanson," I whispered, moving closer once Tara left for the tangled web of pages and shelves, "what are you plotting—"

"To get the book, of course," Adriana said matter-of-factly. "Once, of course," she turned back to me, "you tell me more about it."

Of course.

"I actually don't know," I said thoughtfully, eyeing the book again as my reprimanding tone instantly disintegrated in the wake of its mystery. "But I was about to open it when Tara appeared and grabbed it from me, muttering something about how it wasn't supposed to be there. She looked . . . extremely distraught, and broke a vase in her shock that I held it."

"That," Adriana said, "is a puzzling mystery that must be solved."

She moved forward.

"Adriana," I whispered loudly, "we can't do that! It's not ours . . ."

"We will only take a look," she said firmly, taking another step in the direction of the register. "No one will be worse for the wear."

Curiosity was one of my faults. But, for Adriana, that fault was amplified beyond any semblance of control.

"What if it's personal?" I implored. "It may not be for our eyes."

"If it looks like the bookkeeper's diary got mixed up in her books for sale, I will put it right back," Adriana promised, taking a step toward the register.

"Adriana!" I pulled my friend back as Tara emerged, her hands bedecked with a rather large stack of books.

"Sorry it took so long, girls," Tara said apologetically, as she set the pile on a small stool near the shelves in front of which we stood. "I brought back some other classic plays, as well, just in case. I wanted to make sure that your friend . . ."

"Adriana," that mischievous midget-ly friend of mine responded cordially, "and thank you so much!"

Adriana winked in my direction, cocking her head slightly in the direction of the cash register.

I shook my head.

No, Adriana, I am not doing it.

Adriana sighed.

"Something wrong?" Tara asked, eyeing my friend's bizarre facial expressions that culminated in a sigh.

"I was just . . . sighing at how beautiful all these books are!" Adriana proclaimed jubilantly.

I coughed, suppressing a laugh.

". . . they could almost *distract* me from the studies for which I hope to use them." Adriana gave me a significant look.

Oh, fine. I glared at her. *I will distract, nothing more.*

Adriana beamed, taking a book from the top of the stack. "Rebecca, look at this one! It's a very old copy of one of Shakespeare's plays!"

I moved forward instantly, eager to view a vintage copy of the great playwright's work.

When I was twelve years old, I had accidentally been stung by a bee because, in my great desire to use a pink kickboard, I had forgotten that the perilous insect was taking a nap upon its very surface.

Into the bee's trap I went.

". . . and you know how much more you like Shakespeare than *me.* I would prefer to use my free time in . . . other endeavors."

Right. I stopped in front of Adriana, Tara, and the huge stack of books. *The mission.*

Adriana coughed. "Literary endeavors, I mean."

I had one second to come up with a distraction.

Books. Bookstore. Rebecca.

A smile curled at the corner of my lips. *Of course.* It was the oldest trick in the book, but . . . it was also my specialty.

"Might I see it?" I moved forward quickly, without any regard for my surroundings.

The stack of books tumbled to the floor in disordered disarray.

Specialty #1: Rebecca the Klutz.

"Oh, my!" Tara said, bending down to pick up the books. I followed suit, dashing in front of Adriana just as she sped behind the register.

She tripped, holding onto the counter to maintain her balance, before falling, tumbling to the ground.

And Adriana wasn't even a natural klutz.

"You know," I said, clearing my throat loudly. "This is rather interesting."

"What is?" Tara said, still picking up books.

"Could you put those books back down for just a moment?" I implored, as if their landing on that surface would result in vital scientific findings.

"Um, okay . . ." Tara put the books down hesitantly.

"Well, study the pattern of these books, as they are." I stole a daring look upward. Adriana was walking slowly behind the register with a slight limp.

Specialty #2: Rambling.

"Yes?" Tara's eyebrows scrunched together in confusion as she examined the display of fallen books.

"Well, it's just fascinating to me that the books are spread out like this! They're books after all . . . and books have to do with . . . um . . . imagination! And creativity! And I was just thinking that this arrangement right here, just thrown around like this, is the personification of a writer's mind!"

Adriana picked up the book, quickly hiding it behind her back.

"Does that not blow your mind?!" I exclaimed loudly.

Adriana, her hands behind her back, made slow, deliberate steps from behind the register.

"I um. . . yes, that makes sense." She paused, her eyebrows still scrunched together. "Now, should we pick up the books?"

"Yes, absolutely yes!"

She must think I am insane.

I probably am.

I picked up a few books, helping her place them back in a stack on the small stool.

Adriana approached, her hands empty, bending down quickly to retrieve the last copy. "And there you are!"

Tara offered her a cursory glance, absentmindedly

returning to place it on the stool. "Thank you."

She did not appear to have noticed her absence.

Whew.

Adriana offered me a look of triumph. "I think we'll take a look through this now."

"Sure thing! Let me know if you have any questions." Tara waved and moved toward the register, a baffled expression still on her countenance.

Toward the register.

Adriana looked at me in horror, clearly thinking the same thing. "Tara!"

Tara turned around. "Yes?"

"I actually did have a question. You see . . ."

Adriana quickly handed the crimson book to me behind my back as Tara approached. I took it, moving toward the center of the rose, in the pretense of examining more books on the shelves. Adriana's conversation with Tara receded to the background, as I sat down behind a tall arrangement of shelves.

I opened the book, my heart beating wildly.

On the title page were written the words:

China: A History of Recent Court Cases
(1990-2010).

I blinked. *What could possibly upset or disturb Tara about a book on Chinese history?*

I skimmed through the book quickly; it was a rather large volume, and I did not know how much time I would have. As I began to turn the seventy-seventh page, a photo on the bottom left-hand corner stole my breath.

I turned back, my heart in my throat.

It was a picture of a middle-aged woman, probably in her mid-thirties. She stood, wearing the typical clothes of a prisoner, among two of her fellows— identically clad—almost becoming merely another face in the crowd. Yet her hair was pinned up too neatly, and her eyes held a mechanical emptiness that I could never mistake.

Dr. Yin.

I stared at the photo in disbelief despite my certainty, my eyes finally shifting to the caption below.

Dr. Yen Yeung, a psychologist in the city of Beijing, was imprisoned for proven allegations of malpractice and abuse in July of 2005. She escaped two months later, forming one of the most puzzling cases in recent Chinese history, as no identifiable cause for her jailbreak was found. While it is now a cold case, it remains under light investigation. Yin was last seen in Canada in 2007 and continues to elude the authorities.

Yen Yeung. A different name, but the same woman. Ten years younger, but it was her. *Oh, it was her.* I stared at the photo, unable to look away.

My mentor was an escaped convict.

As I was once again lost in my thoughts and absence thereof, I heard the quiet thud of footsteps and turned.

Adriana, clearly trying to dance around the possibility of nearing my current position, and Tara rounded the corner.

Panic accosted me as I rapidly took out my cell phone, my hand shaking. I snapped a shot of the page with the photo before tossing the book under the nearest shelf.

"Oh, there you are, Rebecca! Getting lost in books again?" Tara asked as they reached me.

"Yes . . . something like that." I caught Adriana's eye, and she narrowed hers.

"Well, I thought I would give you the copy of *Twelfth Night* that you were so anxious to pick up."

Was she suspicious?

Adriana interjected, smiling. "So easily distracted by another book."

I laughed, which quickly turned into a cough.

"Um," Adriana turned toward Tara, edging at the same time closer to me. "I'm ready to ring these up once Rebecca is ready."

I looked toward Adriana and nodded, quickly bending down in the pretense of examining the bottom shelf in front of me. I cautiously lifted one hand behind me, reaching for the crimson book. I straightened, handing it off to Adriana again behind our backs, as Tara momentarily studied the stack in her hands.

That was close.

We followed Tara to the register, Adriana managing to dart quickly behind to throw the book in its proper location as I distracted the bookstore keeper with talk of Shakespeare. As Tara rang up our rather long order, I took advantage of the opportunity, guiding Adriana to the front display of books for further "study."

I couldn't handle waiting any longer.

"What was it?" Adriana asked, casting a superficial glance at the books in front of her.

I took a deep breath. "Yin," I whispered.

"Yin?! Your mentor? What does she have to do with the book?"

"She's . . . oh, Adriana, I don't know what we've gotten ourselves into. That book is a record of recent court cases in China. It's in English, but published there . . . and . . . Yin . . . she's a criminal." My words were segmented, broken in the stunned shock that still enveloped me.

Adriana's eyes widened. "What?!"

I motioned fervently for her to quiet down.

She lowered her voice. "She didn't . . . kill someone, did she?"

"No . . . not as far as I know. She escaped ten years ago from a prison in Beijing. But apparently they were pretty serious charges of abuse." I glanced around, noting that Tara was almost finished completing the order. "I will tell you more in the car. I'm really . . . yeah."

Adriana nodded, touching my shoulder briefly. We returned to the register, both lost in our own thoughts (and fears).

Oh, how quickly the lighthearted can turn to serious.

When we left the store, all I could see were mirrors and crashed vases.

"What are you going to do?" Adriana squeaked as soon as we entered the car. I had told her of the picture I had taken as we approached the vehicle.

"What I should have done long ago," I said. "Report her."

Chapter 40
Of Returns and Rewinds

"Rebecca, I heard that you came to see me." Officer Nelson sat down again, reminiscent of a visit seemingly so long ago that I wished to forget. His eyes flickered toward me inquisitively.

"Yes. I unfortunately . . . have another matter to report."

The confusion in his eyes turned to concern. "Were you threatened again?"

"No . . . it's a completely different case. I have reason to believe that a certain individual may be dangerous."

He waited, watching me quietly.

"And," I took a deep breath, "this may sound crazy, but I'm pretty sure that person is also an escaped convict from China." I didn't look up, not wanting to be affected by any incredulity on his part before I could finish my piece. "I work as an intern at Everson Psychological

Center. Or, at least . . . I used to. My mentor, Dr. Yin, has been abusing her clients under my observation. I recently came across evidence in, um, a bookstore, implying that she . . . well, making it clear that . . . she abused clients in her own country to the extent that she was jailed and later escaped." I cringed, aware of how far-fetched that all sounded.

Of how far-fetched the truth can seem.

"And where did you find this evidence?"

"In, um, a book at the mall."

Chief Nelson cleared his throat. "I understand that the recent situation may have had you a bit unnerved. Sometimes, in situations like that, we see things that aren't there—"

"No," I shook my head wildly, insistently forcing the words out, "I know this for certain . . . and I have a photo to prove it."

I pulled out my cell phone, pressed a few buttons, and handed it to him.

"That is a photograph of Dr. Yin from ten years ago," I said, as he looked at the surface of my phone. "You can confirm that it is the same woman if you just slide to the previous photo, one I took of a photo in her office earlier on in the semester for an academic slideshow."

He did so, sliding his finger to the right.

"Oh, golly." He whistled. "They do bear a strong resemblance."

I nodded fervently.

"Rebecca," he looked up at me, "Dr. Yin is known as a highly respected professional in the area even by someone like myself who has no involvement in the field. It is also difficult to prove from this photograph, even though there is a similarity." He raised a hand as I began to open my mouth to protest. "It is too faint in this photograph to be certain. But it is enough to take a look into the matter."

I settled back into my chair with relief.

"Given her reputation, it will be that much more difficult. But, if she is a criminal, then ultimately that will not matter, as far as our police department is concerned. We will look into the truth."

"Thank you."

"I would also like to take your statement." He reached for a stack in a line of cubbyholes against the wall. "Please fill it out with as many details as you can recall from your personal observations of her abuse. We will keep your identity confidential." He finally took a breath, breathing out with the same heaviness to which I could relate.

"I'm so sorry that you have had to deal with this whole mess. Sometimes difficulties come in groups."

I nodded, taking a form that he gave me from the stack. "Thanks again for all your assistance. And there's another related matter . . ."

"Please, by all means . . ."

"If you use the evidence of the photograph, there may be someone who needs protection." I paused. "As I said, I found the photo in a mall bookstore . . . and the owner seemed flustered, even frightened, when she found me with it. I don't believe her to be malicious, so my assumption is that she may be under some sort of blackmail or threat . . ."

He grabbed a piece of paper quickly. "Her name?"

"Tara. It's the antique bookstore toward the front of the local mall . . ."

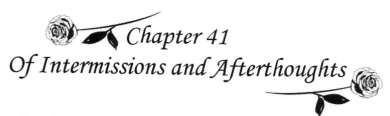

Chapter 41
Of Intermissions and Afterthoughts

"I still can't believe how lucky I was to get away from all that."

Teresa sat at the foot of my bed, shaking her head in disbelief, as I finished telling her the entire story of Yin, from beginning to end.

"No," I said quietly, "not lucky. *Blessed.*"

She nodded, her eyes serious. "Yes. And . . . you were blessed, too." She played with the pink-and-white quilt underneath her. "Those people . . . if you had not been there, where would they be now? Would they have survived to another semester? And, even if they did . . ." She shook her head again, a tear lingering in her eye, "would I have been strong enough to fight it?"

"Yes, you would have."

"I don't know. I really don't." She sighed. "Sometimes I'm such a pushover."

"That is absolutely incorrect!" I jumped up from my place on the bed in indignation. "You are no such thing!"

Teresa smiled slightly. "You're a funny girl, you know. After all you've been through, after you just collapsed on your bed and only then could tell me the story of the hell you've been living through over the past few months, you jump up just to defend the honor of a friend *to* that friend."

I returned to my former position at the foot of the bed. "I'm serious," I said quietly. "In fact, if anything . . . you're a model of what I want to be. You're . . . well, what I would call 'gentle, yet firm.' "

She laughed airily, a quiet trickle. "I like it. And thanks. And that's really funny because . . . I feel like I've become more that way because of my friendship with you."

"Oh . . . wow. That is . . . yeah, wow."

"The writer loses all coherence of word."

"That seems to happen a lot."

Trickles of laughter reached their peak, and down they cascaded in a waterfall of stress-relieving hysteria. I wiped the moisture from my brow at its finale.

Oh, how I had needed that laugh.

"So," I said, "not to return to that earlier subject, but . . . what are your plans for your internship now?"

"Oh, well, I sent an email to Dr. Everson the day after I went to Dr. Yin's office—I was too flustered to send it that exact day—and told him that, due to extenuating circumstances, I would need a new placement. I knew that that was incessantly vague and it probably would invite more questions—the answers to which I did not yet know—but," Teresa absentmindedly twirled a strand of hair behind one ear, "surprisingly, Dr. Everson just wrote back with a simple message, stating that he would look into a new placement."

"That's great!"

"Yep! I thought so. He did mention that it might take some time to find a replacement, but I don't think it matters too much. There are more than a few psychological practices in this city, and I wouldn't be opposed to going outside of it either. And . . . the time will be worth it." She looked up, meeting my eyes. "Much, much better than the alternative."

I nodded. "That's true."

"So, what about you, Rebecca? What are your plans?"

I paused briefly, considering. *What are plans to me now?*

"I don't know," I said finally. "I really hope it will all be resolved soon, now that the police are involved. They have evidence, even if it will take time to get through all that red tape, given Dr. Yin's reputation and the official confirmation of the photograph identification. Maybe they would even have to contact the Chinese authorities . . . I would suspect that she would be shipped there after spending some jail time here in the meantime. I . . . I really hope it all works out. I just don't know much of anything anymore, to be honest. And . . . sorry for rambling." I forced a laugh.

Teresa shook her head. "No. Rambling is one of the key necessities of life."

I laughed again, allowing it to fill me up. "I could go with that. In other news, have you seen the new trailer for . . ."

And so we moved on to other subjects and dialogues, other entrances and exits, like silly schoolgirls who, at the moment, wanted to be nothing else, until the day broke quietly into night.

Chapter 42
Of Speeches and Steps

"Do you ever wish that men—guys—spoke more openly?" I asked, as Adriana and I walked across the field to the tall university building standing in the distance.

Even though Adriana and I were in completely different fields, we were each supposed to attend one lecture on the psychology behind performance arts. Upon realizing this requirement, we eagerly planned to attend the same event, a talk entitled, "Theater: The Psychology Behind the Mask" at a university in downtown L.A.

"Maybe," Adriana said, looking ahead with the sun's laughter in her eyes, "but you don't."

"Why would you say that?" I paused briefly before catching up with her longer strides.

"Oh c'mon, Rebecca." Adriana shook my shoulder

playfully. "It's like you said when we were in high school." She mimicked an exaggerated version of my voice, dramatically waving one hand. " 'I can't really see myself going for a guy who is . . . well, *obvious.*' "

"I was fifteen!" I protested.

"So?" Adriana finally stopped for a moment and glanced back at me. "Has that really changed?"

"Well," I said, after brief consideration. "Maybe not."

"So, stop complaining." She grinned. "You know just as well as I do that you enjoy the thought of speaking a boy's mind before he has the chance to say it himself." She took on another theatrical accent. "You like your men . . . *mysterious.*" She feigned a faint, reminiscent of a march seemingly long ago.

"You'd better be careful, Adri," I warned with a smile. "If you keep pretending to be a hopeless romantic, you may one day become one."

"Fat chance." Adriana snorted, a trickle of laughter beginning to fill the field. "That'll happen on the day when you pick the man who says more over the man who says less."

Little did I know that those words would one day . . .

I blinked, as if hearing an echo of time.

"But, maybe," I pondered aloud, as we reached the door to the auditorium, "they could tell us plainly *once* in a while."

"Maybe," she grinned, "but don't count on it."

We continued through the door, scanning one end of the hall to the next in search of the designated room, #225.

"Hello!" Adriana called out to a fellow passenger of the hall.

The young man, wearing dark-framed glasses and a thinly spiraling mustache, paused in his walk and turned around. "Yes?"

"Do you know where Room #225 is?"

He pointed to the right side of the hall, and we thanked him, hurrying on our way.

"What's so wrong with an *obvious* man?" I continued, ignoring Adriana mouthing 'one-track mind.' "

"Again, nothing." She mounted the stairs. "Just . . . not for you."

"I don't know." I followed her. "Maybe the mysterious ones are more trouble than they're worth." I paused, recalling, but continued before her mouth opened in a question. "I mean, remember that guy I had a crush on in middle school? The *mysterious* one? He was *vexing*."

"Then I guess," she said, "you like to be vexed."

The standard frame of a door stood before us, labeled "225." We entered, closing the door quietly behind us in respect for the fact that we were a few minutes late.

A thin, wiry man who appeared to be in his forties turned from his position at the whiteboard as we entered. His hand, holding a dry-erase marker, was in mid-air, as if frozen into that position.

I cast a quick glance around the room. No one else was there.

"Are you here for the psychological talk on theater?" he asked, coming forward.

We nodded on key.

"The location was actually changed last minute. The lecturer had hoped for a larger hall in which to give the talk, but it was unavailable until earlier this morning when play practice was cancelled. You'll find them in the auditorium downstairs, to the right of the mess hall."

"Thank you!" we called out, rushing to the door.

"So much for going upstairs," Adriana grumbled,

hurrying to keep up with my famed power walk. "Will you slow down? We won't get there any faster if I die before reaching the appointed hall."

I slowed down grudgingly. "Okay, okay."

We reached the familiar set of stairs and began to descend. Adriana hopped along, taking two steps at a time, while I now lagged behind.

"Do you sense the hypocrisy in your actions?" I called out to her from behind, as she was two steps away from full descent.

A wry grin twirled across her face, as she jumped down the final step. "This is *my* madness."

I feigned an exasperated sigh and moved down the remaining steps.

Adriana was waiting by the stairwell as I finally stepped down, reaching the base floor.

"Let's go, dude!" She pointed ahead to the auditorium, where the incessant buzz of chatter was suddenly dulling to a mere trickle with the tapping of a microphone.

We both dashed in its direction, forgetting our individual idiosyncrasies in the pace of a hurried rush.

I opened the door, handing it to my friend as she entered behind me.

The speaker stood at the podium, his eyes cast nervously at the notes in front of him. He looked to be fresh out of college.

Poor guy, I mouthed to Adriana, who nodded in agreement. He probably had no prior experience.

Or just hated public speaking, like me.

"Hello!" The overly cheerful cadence of a practiced speaker strummed its way into my eardrum, breaking me from my intermission of thoughts. I turned for what seemed to be the seventy-seventh time that day to observe a young woman with short red hair and an enthused expression marking her countenance.

"Hello!" I greeted her pleasantly, as Adriana's eyes continued to flit about the room, as if in search for the latest addition to the Ewok army.

"Hello!" She handed me a newspaper, her broad grin remaining in the same spectrum of light. "We will be using the newspaper of the day for some practice in theater today."

"Thank you," I responded automatically, elbowing Adriana, who finally turned around.

The Eternal Smiler strode forth, handing her one, as well. I considered the psychology behind her smile and formed the conclusion that, despite its obvious coating of pleasantry, it was an understandable psychological decision.

"Enjoy the show!" she called back, the usher at a theater about to present the next play.

"Thank you!"

Adriana made a wide, sweeping gesture with one hand, encompassing the entire hall, which was rather large in scope for a university. "While you were talking, I made a precise analysis of the seating arrangements, and came to the conclusion that there is absolutely no space."

"Oh, fun. I guess we'll just stand here in the back then."

"Okay."

I glanced down at the newspaper in front of me, and, as I did, my breath sharply withdrew, leaving me in the cadence of a half-measured walk.

On the front page of the daily newspaper, a headline blared out at me in the calm of its gray surface.

Below was an image of a slender young woman, her dirty blonde hair disheveled as she lay on the grated surface near a backyard swimming pool, her body unnaturally placed. Her eyes were lifeless.

> Young heiress of the Cornell estate found drowned in own swimming pool in ruled suicide.

I read it again and again, a sick feeling coming over my stomach.

It was Christy.

I stared at the newspaper front cover without lifting my eyes, unable to turn away. The speaker began his talk, his quiet lull of a voice filtering through the room, but I could hear nothing.

Adriana tapped me on the shoulder, eyeing me with concern.

I shook my head, refusing to meet her gaze.

She had been so full of light. So full of light and potential. I closed my eyes, remembering how she had been, stealing a glance at a novel in her free time during lunch, always greeting me with the most authentic and kind smile when I arrived at the office.

Always herself, even within the confines of a formal role.

And she had given up on her life in the wake of a throb of darkness that spilled across her light.

I shook my head, tears paused in their wake. *I had seen her only a week before.* She had seemed so lost in a shadow, and yet all I retrieved was knowledge. Could I have done anything to distill her pain, temper her weakness and confusion?

Could I have helped save her?

I turned away from the scene, walking from the back of the auditorium to the door as if I were pacing alone in my own home, unwatched by any other eyes save my own and God.

And that was when I saw a distinct figure leaning against the opposite door with familiarity.

My eyes popped open in dismal cartoon hyperbole.

"Adriana," I mouthed, returning to the back of the room in a measured heartbeat.

I moved my head slightly in the direction of the door before which stood the man with cool blue eyes. She followed my gaze, turning back to me in recognition.

She had never met or seen the man. But she had heard enough to know who it was.

And, with her foreign recognition came a firm decision at the back of my mind, instinct weighing against instinct.

"At the intermission," I whispered, "we must leave."

She nodded, touching my shoulder briefly in a conveyance of comfort.

I did not hear the talk, as it split into syllables and then letters, phonics fragmenting its contingency in a chaotic throw of alphabet soup. Approximately every few minutes, I glanced at the door where an opposing force stood, frozen in a casual battle statement. He did not appear to see me yet, though I assumed that it would not be long.

We could not wait for the intermission.

I touched my friend's shoulder and whispered, "Now."

She followed me to the other door with a quiet semblance of footsteps, and, in that precise moment, the man turned his head.

This was unreal. Had he been looking the entire time, somehow seeing without looking as we made our plans and then enacted them? I swiftly pulled Adriana away from the door, causing a slight jolt of surprise, and moved back to our former position.

"I will watch this time," Adriana said firmly. "You

watch me. When I move to take out my cell phone, we go."

I nodded, my heart beating wildly in my chest.

In the ironic duplication of my internship, the cliché of a minute seeming an hour once again resumed.

It was a mad dash that had begun long ago, beginning softly, the narrator cast in unawares.

But now, now it had become the dash.

Adriana moved one hand to her purse, and we slipped to the door.

Once we were out of the auditorium, we ran rapidly outside. Adriana tossed me her phone as we continued to run, nearing the field that we had so leisurely passed through only minutes before.

Her message was clear and had already been implanted in my mind.

I lifted the phone to my ear as we passed over the mound of grass and flower. With a single finger, I dialed the number to the police station.

And, in a single instant, a hand was placed firmly on my mouth, knife at my throat.

The phone crashed to the ground, filtering into nothingness as a large foot stamped it out of existence.

Chapter 43
Of Fallen Angels and Rising Stars

The dark gray form of a Jaguar convertible steered its way across the street until it reached an unkempt, brick-layered building, quiet and small in its surroundings of little else.

The man turned off the ignition and closed the door behind him, reaching for the back, where we lay struggling on the floor. He pulled me from the car, and then Adriana, rough hands with callouses that tinged my own with pain.

He pulled the gag from each of our mouths, a mad smile dashing its way across his face.

"Don't say a word," he intoned under his breath, yet still with the smoothness that I had learned to expect from him. "Or you will die earlier than expected."

I sucked in my breath, and then was thrown into the room in what seemed like a single bound of chaos.

The room appeared to be even smaller from the inside. It was sparse, with a few chairs about and a long, rectangular table at the very back. Dirt and dust were spread liberally throughout the surroundings.

It was clear that no one lived here.

Except for today.

The man roughly pulled our arms behind us, tying them to the back of the chair with the cords of rope in his hand. I managed to move my wrists slightly apart, a memory surfacing. I took a deep breath, expanding my chest, and glanced sidelong at Adriana with my shoulders pulled back. In an instant, more rope extended across the chest.

I struggled uselessly, my knuckles already beginning to throb from the burning sensation of the rope.

"Let us go!" Adriana growled, flailing her arms and feet about desperately.

The man cocked his head thoughtfully, as if considering, and then reached into his pocket, pulling out a roll of duct tape.

A smile curled at his lips as he slowly moved forward, fastening a generous piece of the tape across Adriana's mouth.

"I would be careful with your words, little one," he intoned smoothly before taking a step back.

Adriana glared at him, but made no attempt to continue.

I opened my mouth to speak, but closed it. I did not know whether communication would do either of us any good. But, if it did, if it could, communication would be our downfall or our success.

I intended it to be the latter.

"Don't worry, *Rebecca*," he said, his eyes alit with cool amusement, as he emphasized my name in bitter tones, "we want to hear what you have to say . . . at least, for now."

The man circled around the room, eyeing his two prisoners with satisfaction, the careful watch of a hunter observing his prey. His eyes focused intently, taking in every angle and detail, a sweeping gaze from the minute details of the rope clinging to our hands behind the chair to the way my shoe fell against the floor, to the larger portrait and vision of the entire room as it was.

An icy coldness attacked my chest, realization dawning upon me.

He was not simply observing us to make sure that everything was in order.

He viewed this scene as his masterpiece.

I shuddered involuntarily, a sick feeling creeping its way across my stomach and into my lungs.

"You know, Miss Veritas, I was satisfied with just failing you."

The trickles of cold in my chest intensified, veins of near delirium that filled my entire body, at the new waves of sound that entered the room.

I knew that voice. I had heard that voice many a time, day after day, week after week. It was as familiar a voice as I could ever know. Yet its familiarity offered no comfort or reassurance.

It was a voice that, though calm and collected, offered only panic.

Dr. Yin entered the room, closing an inner door softly behind her, a sardonic smile curling her lips.

"But then you got in my way," she said softly, now looming over me with barely an inch of space.

"Dr. Yin," I began, my voice shaking, "I am just an intern. What harm could I possibly give you?"

A loud outburst of laughter, hollow and empty, filled the room. Dr. Yin raised an ironic eyebrow.

"Do you take me a fool?" she uttered, her eyes

plastered on my face.

Through the shaking of my body, a strength and resolve burst through, warming my heart.

"You are the mentor; I am only the intern," I quoted, my eyes unwavering.

Dr. Yin's eyes flashed briefly, and then they were stilled, an immediate calm after the storm.

"Yes," she said, her voice level, "you will never be more than an intern."

Was that a threat? Or simply her measurement of humanity?

A memory surfaced in my mind, and with it a revision.

Knowledge detached from Truth is irrelevant.

And yet I now lived in a world where that actuality had no place in reality.

I took a deep breath, my heart pounding in my chest. "Then why keep me here if I am so . . . useless?" I cringed at the word but held onto it.

"Because you live."

The words echoed throughout the room, a plunge into depths of the unquelled emptiness of a vacant abyss.

"Because you are innocent."

"Because, where you are present, I cannot step."

"Because," she spat out the words, "I hate you."

How did she become this? I wondered, staring at the cold, assured woman before me. *How?*

"But," she said, her face relaxing and calm resuming in her voice, "you are probably more interested in a precise measurement of your crimes." A cutting smile once again tore across her face, distorting its every feature.

Your crimes.

"Then tell me," I said.

That moment filled the room and, with it,

disappeared all trace of my best friend and the man who did Dr. Yin's bidding. Only two figures remained.

Yin and I.

"Poor, poor Rebecca," Dr. Yin offered me a pitying glance, "you really thought that I would leave a poor, hapless bookstore owner as the sole assurance of my security? Really, now, I thought you were better than that . . ."

My mind returned to a hushed conversation with Adriana in front of a store bookshelf, my breath quickening.

Of course. Dr. Yin was too intelligent, too deliberate, too *scientific* for that.

". . . even whispered conversations." Her voice rose in delight at the climax of her revelation.

She leaned forward. "There were bugs throughout the store that would pick up any hint of sound. I pride myself on using sound-sensitive material." Her smile widened.

"Why didn't you just destroy the book?" I blurted out.

"Destroy *knowledge*?" Her voice cut across mockingly. "My dear Rebecca, you don't know me at all."

No, it was more than that, much more than her proclaimed adherence to the glory of knowledge.

This was her chess game, and she made up the rules.

As I looked at the self-assured smile forming on Dr. Yin's face, I realized with horror that I was correct.

A trophy. That's what it was to her. A trophy of how she had outsmarted everyone.

"Now, I will continue," she said with satisfaction.

"At first, I thought that I could handle your 'curiosity' with a warning. After your initial interest in Tara's book, I followed your car . . . to the house of your little teenage friend."

Amelia. My pulse raced.

"I was delighted, really. Here, I was intending to scare you, and the perfect opportunity to do so arose!" She clapped her hands gleefully. "Based on my knowledge of you, your primary concern was with those who you loved. If I simply threatened your life, it would be satisfactory, but not really enough. So, I played a little game with your friend."

Dr. Yin reached from behind the table before us, deep into the closet beyond. When she turned, a large black jacket, cushioned in the shoulders and middle section to an extreme degree, was in her hand.

If put on, it would give the impression of broad shoulders and a constrained chest.

She held it before me, as if modeling an outfit on the walkway. "Lovely piece, isn't it? I simply couldn't have you recognizing me, and I did not want my associate here," she nodded in the direction of the man, who stood, his eyes in rapture, praising her with every sweep, "to do more than watch you at this point."

"Oh, and yes, dear Rebecca," her face glimmered with a clown's smile, "he was watching you."

"Now, let me get back to my story . . . where was I? Oh, yes, the night I gave your little friend a *big* hug!"

The tremors of fear transformed, pulsing into anger. "You coward, picking on children. The twins, and now Amelia."

No. Not just her clients.

"Christy." My voice was hollow as realization dawned upon me.

Dr. Yin's lips twisted into a smile. "Also knew too much, didn't she?" Her penetrating stare measured upon me. "But, really, she wasn't much of a secretary. I am much more pleased with her replacement."

"You are . . ." my body shook, but I was filled with resolve, "*pathetic.*"

Dr. Yin's eyes flashed, betraying real emotion for the second time before her face once again stilled, leaving only a small smile.

"Say as you wish," she said softly. "After all, they are not the only little girls that I play with." She sent me a shooting glance.

I shook my head, a sad smile wrapping around me. *She was evil.*

And, while I was not a little girl as she would suppose, I was still her victim.

"But let's do get back to the story, shall we?" She turned, her eyes appraising, to her assistant. "If there are any more interruptions, punish the black-haired one."

The man nodded, his mad eyes gleaming with delirious desire.

I gulped and remained silent.

"Is that all? Oh, good." Dr. Yin sat down at a wooden chair by the table, casually crossing her legs. "Now, I already showed you my delightful outfit that would give me the appearance of a man. I also wore these shoes," she kicked an outrageously tall pair from under the table, "to mask my height. Clever, wasn't it? Almost as clever as making it into the American Psychological Association." Yin laughed, her voice joined by the man behind her.

She leaned closer. "Or evidence lying in plain sight."

Hail Mary, full of grace.

"I would be shorter than him," she shot another look at her lackey, "but taller than my natural height. And I have connections in the streets, so it was easy enough to find someone who would take my place at the police station."

The Lord is with thee.

"But," her hawk gaze returned in intensity, scrutinizing my face, "you just wouldn't give up, would you? The first time was just to warn you, a little scare. But the discovery on your next visit to Tara's bookstore warranted more . . . shall we say, *drastic* action?"

Blessed are thou among women.

"Which is why we are all here today." She clapped her hands in derision.

And blessed is the fruit of thy womb Jesus.

She leaned forward again. "You were just getting too close, Rebecca."

Holy Mary, Mother of God.

"Far too close."

Pray for us sinners.

"So, now what shall we do?"

Now and at the hour . . .

Her face was an inch from mine, stale breath touching my face, before moving back. "I think it's time to end our little story, don't you?"

Of our death.

The prayer, lifted to a mother who would send it to the Greatest Eternity, swept through my body with the warmth of its Amen. A reel of images flashed gently through my mind, of embers crackling in a welcoming fireplace, "Away in a Manger" lifting through the choirs of angels to a single, small room, Christmas and Easter present together, holding onto me insistently, as they remained, unwavering by my side.

And with them a thought.

"I know that I have no right to ask for anything." I bent my head, as if in shame.

Dr. Yin's eyes narrowed suspiciously, searching my face—

"But, before I leave this Earth, I would like to write a poem."

—but they found nothing.

The raucous laughter of the huntsman spiraled throughout the room, as Dr. Yin shook her head, her eyes cocked in the pretense of being rolled.

"Oh, I suppose," she said, "after all, it might be *entertaining* to read when this is all done."

I would only have one chance at this. I prayed fervently, my heart racing.

Be with me, Lord, I whispered without a word.

With one quick, measured glance in the direction of the chair beside me, I spoke in clear, but unpaced, tones, "The poem could be the *movement* of a song, but I don't think it will end up on *Youtube* by just breathing into existence."

Adriana's eyes met mine.

She understood.

Dr. Yin's back was turned, retrieving a pad of paper from the cabinet behind.

A month prior, I had posted on Facebook a video that illustrated a technique on how to remove rope.

By just breathing.

"You will receive no success post-mortem, be assured, Rebecca."

And best friends were privy to the briefest reference or movement.

I waited, slowly, slowly . . .

The man turned, the briefest flicker of movement, to his master.

One, two, three . . .

I scratched my foot against the floor.

Go.

I breathed in deeply, wiggling out of the rope fastened for a larger form. Chairs tumbled to the floor as we each slipped our hands from the loosened rope.

Faster, faster. I tried to ignore the pulsing in my head

as the sound alerted our captors.

Adriana grabbed my hand, following me toward the window, as they chased after us.

It was foolish, so foolish, but there was no other way.

I overturned a table, striking Dr. Yin in the face, as shots were fired into the air.

Oh, God, protect us.

The man stumbled to the floor, a chair falling upon his feet, before regaining his footing.

We tumbled through the window at the last moment, dashing across the street and into the night.

Amen.

Chapter 44
Of Finality and Continuance

The quiet echo of an abandoned street had no end.
At least here.

Adriana and I continued to run, run without coherent thought except a single purpose, run without anything at all save that, as far as we could before needing, in no exaggeration or lack of scientific precision, to stop.

I breathed heavily, nearly collapsing onto the pavement below, while my eyes darted back and forth, shifting in the measured pace that my feet would no longer employ. They took in a large building with an extensive covering, and, in only another moment, we were running again, reaching it in a final breath of air.

We stood there for a few moments, collecting our breath.

I wistfully cast a look at my shoulder, where my

purse had hung before entrance into a dark gray vehicle.

No cell phone access.

And we continued to collect our breath, intermittent with dry coughs and shallow wisps of air.

I dropped to the ground, and Adriana followed suit.

The shallow display deepened, filling our lungs with greater depth.

I closed my eyes in relief, before opening them to the winter of night that I could now feel.

"I thought you liked your men mysterious."

We sat, shivering, beneath the overhang of the old and shambled building.

"Not *that* kind of mysterious!" I snapped.

Adriana played with her jacket zipper.

"I'm sorry, Adri. You didn't deserve that."

"It doesn't matter." She waved my words away. "I was just trying to lighten the mood." She laughed without humor. "Dumb idea."

"No, it wasn't."

There was a moment's pause.

"Do you think we got away?" Adriana asked.

"I guess that depends."

"On what?"

"On whether we're in a horror movie, inspirational drama, or family film."

Adriana laughed, a bit of a real laugh trickling in as it came. "Yeah, I guess so."

"It's cold!" I complained, keeping the measured flow of distraction.

"Well, it *is* January."

"I want my parka."

"You're insane to even *own* a parka in CA."

"Freak-dork-nerd-geek, actually," I said.

She tilted her head. "Freak-dork-nerd-geek?"

"I'll explain later. Now . . ." I took a deep breath, "we

have to go. We can't take any chances."

"And," I pointed toward the gutter lying in wait a few inches to the right of the building, "I'd hate to say it, but I think *that* is our best chance."

"Great."

"Just . . . think of it as your latest theatrical assignment."

"Have any hand sanitizer?"

"No."

"Too real for theatrics then."

With a sigh, she opened the creaking metal grate. She descended, inch by inch, until all I could see were two round eyes above the criss-crossed bars. Those eyes widened in concern like those of a small child, and then she was gone.

I had spoken too soon about movies.

As I breathed a sigh of relief and moved toward the grate to follow my friend, I heard the sound of footsteps in the distance.

Big footsteps. Big footsteps of boots. Big, cliché footsteps.

I looked back and forth, my heart racing, between the sewer system and the shrouded expanse ahead.

If I moved quickly, I might make it under the grate in time before the man approached.

But, if I were only a minute—even a moment—off, he would see me as I stepped down to follow Adriana . . . and thereby know her whereabouts.

Leaving now, running as far and as fast as I could, would be giving my best friend her best chance.

And so I ran.

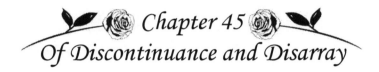

Chapter 45
Of Discontinuance and Disarray

The echo of laughter fell away, revealing nothing but silence, a silence that knew no peace.

It was only a few steps before I made out the form of my predator, jogging behind me in an almost mockery of my frenzied run.

God, please protect me.

He remained behind me for nearly a block before large arms swung around me, nearly knocking me to the ground with their weight.

His eyes shifted to my face, leering maniacally, as his lips twisted in the semblance of what could have been a smile.

"You shouldn't have even tried," he said, his gun lifted as he thrust me forward, his hand sinking into my back with cruel lines a reminder of my captivity.

"Please, no." I backed into the wall. "I know that Dr.

Yin told you to do this, and I know that she probably paid you a lot of money to do it—at least, that's the way it's done in movies—but please don't kill me."

The man laughed. "You really are little." He moved his face closer so that I could smell his foul breath. "Little. Crushable. Just like a paper doll."

I tried to distract him. "Actually, I'm 5'8"."

His eye glinted with something that I could only call evil. "You will always be little. A little girl who will be pushed down by big girls and boys. Until . . . now." He smiled, his lips curving so twisted I could barely see their human form. "Now you will be a fallen paper doll. An unsung paper doll. You will die, and I will throw you in the biggest ditch, far away where no one will find you. You will be forgotten."

"No," my voice cracked, "I will never be forgotten. My name is written in the beyond."

The man tilted his head, seeming to not comprehend my words.

"And, no matter what you do to me, I will be safe. Safe in His arms."

The confusion on his face turned back to ice. "Religious freak. I hate them. This will give me even more pleasure."

He moved closer again, tracing a line across my brow. "So pretty."

I shivered involuntarily.

He laughed. "Scared you."

I recalled when Adi and Abi had said the same thing. And so differently.

He caressed his weapon lightly with one hand.

His hand moved toward the trigger.

God, I love you. And I love my family. My friends. And I love—

I closed my eyes as I heard the gunshot.

Chapter 46

Of . . .

But I felt no pain.

I opened my eyes again to look at the taunting eyes of the man. As I turned around, I noticed a bullet shot in the wall to the left of me.

"Scared ya."

How did someone get that cruel?

He grabbed me roughly, pulling me down the abandoned street, his gun at my throat. "This is not your gravesite." He cocked his head, grinning madly.

I had no choice but to follow. I prayed a silent prayer.

We moved down another dark alley. My stomach heaved. He seemed to be aware of it, too, because he smiled even more widely.

He stopped, my body roughly hitting a wall. I bit my lip, trying not to focus on the pain.

He let go of me, still pointing the gun in my direction.

"Where is your little friend?" he taunted. "The job target was two, but your little friend got away."

"She is somewhere safe," I managed, knowing in my heart that, no matter what the cost, my best friend needed to stay safe.

He focused his weapon on me. "Tell me or you will die now."

"You're going to kill me anyway." My voice was shaking. "Why would I risk my friend's life, too?"

"Because, if you tell me now, I will spare the life of your family."

I gulped, searching for air. *They couldn't possibly kill my family . . .*

"We know where they live. Let's just call it a casualty of war."

"You can't just—" I couldn't talk.

He laughed again. "I will blast to shreds the entire apartment on Ember Street."

He had seen my brother. He thought that was the family's apartment.

I tried to keep myself from smiling in relief. "People will see it. You will be found."

"Unlikely." He laughed bitterly. "I am not so foolish as my own."

An opportunity of delay.

I pressed him to continue, tempering my eagerness in the appearance of the idle prattle of a shaking prey who spoke without premeditated thought.

"What do you mean?" I said slowly, as if lack of comprehension dulled my words.

And to some extent they did, but, for once, I had little concern for curiosity.

Anger flashed through his eyes briefly, but it was

not an anger directed toward me. He looked off into the distance for a nearly unmeasurable moment before turning his eyes back to me.

His fingernails pressed harder into my back, ripping across the skin, as my spine throbbed.

I winced, screaming out involuntarily in pain, and he smiled widely.

"See," he said, as if proving a point in a planned debate, "I am not as foolish as they are."

"Oh, you want storytime, little girl?" he lifted his cool blue eyes to my face as my own addressed him inquisitively. "I really don't have the time."

"You seem really angry," I continued. "Obviously these . . . people of yours were very foolish to make someone like you feel that way."

His chin jutted back and forth, his eyes crazed, nearly involuntary in their aspect.

He had known it too long.

"My brothers," he said, speaking rapidly as what seemed to be a memory tapped against his nerves, "they . . ." and here he glared in a madly frightening way, "let them live. And now they are in jail for their foolishness."

"Not a mistake," the man said, cocking his head wildly, "that I will make."

He lifted a foot and aimed for my leg, when another mad smile broke across his face. "But not here either. There is another friend who must die, isn't there?"

"I do wonder," he said, peering into my face with the feigned curiosity of a friend himself, "if he is your boyfriend?"

He spat in my face before leaning back, laughing, as my chest throbbed.

"Oh, yes, *my* girlfriend Donna was all too willing to tell us of the little incident with your *international* friend. I picked her up at a bar one night a few months ago, and let's just say that she was smitten," he added as an almost casual afterthought.

"Oh, and Rebecca," his smile widened beyond the confines of his face in twisted form, "I'm sure you'll be pleased to hear he is on his way back. He received an *ever* so urgent message from a Rebecca Veritas, begging him to return immediately, and, you see, he's on his way now, to meet the same fate as you." He laughed mockingly.

And then I trembled, tears burning my eyes.

Peter.

"The train conductor was *all* too accommodating when it came to bribes, and he informed me that your friend would arrive, oh, right about," he cast a theatrical glance at his watch, "*now.*" He grinned again, his entire face a serpent's throne as its tentacles lifted across its surface in abandoned disarray.

"So," he roughly grabbed my arm again with searing pain, "it's time that we make a trip to the train station."

On and on, we moved, his foot aimed at one soft body part after another, burning with agonizing pain.

I struggled to stand, held only by the weight of my aggressor, as my body crumpled into itself.

"Faster." He delivered a piercing kick to my back, as I fell to the ground, unable to move farther. "Move it!" he yelled.

I moved from the ground, breath seeping out of my lungs and onto the ground that I left.

I could not survive this.

The train station stood before us, tracks lined in precise mathematical arrangement by its side in orderly submission, the train itself stopped, halted in action on the steel gray surface.

No one left the train.

We stood for a few moments, and still no sound or

movement occurred.

Of course.

A sinking feeling settled at the bottom of my stomach, which was still throbbing in agony.

His agreement with the head of the train staff was far more extensive than a simple request to spy on one of its passengers.

He intended sabotage.

The man grinned wildly at me, a knowing look on his face.

Oh, God, please . . .

"We shall wait for the train station 'master' to arrive. It shouldn't be too much longer now. I worked with him in Canada some years back. Fine fellow," he said conversationally.

The sick feeling wrapped itself farther, lifting itself to the depths of who I was. *Corruption on all corners.*

"Your friend should be escorted by him any minute now. And then, oh my, what *fun* we shall have!"

Please take care of Peter, my Lord. I matter little next to him. I couldn't bear it if . . .

The sound of a siren pulsed through the air, ringing with the ecstasy of a wedding dance.

It was so raw, so piercing.

It was *beautiful.*

But it was only in my mind.

My body tilted between air and dirt, reality and disillusion, uncertain of where it stood. Dizziness overcame me, and through that blur, I saw his maniacal smile, lifting across the haze that I could not penetrate.

"You don't have to . . . do this," I said weakly, my vision blurring further, sending a piercing pain through my head.

"Oh, but I *do*, Rebecca," he said. "This is what I do."

His career. His pastime.

His life.

Away in a manger, no crib for His bed, the little Lord Jesus laid down His sweet head.

"But we'll wait for him, don't worry. You two lovers should die together. How *romantic* that would be, don't you think?"

The stars in the sky looked down where He lay.

Distinct figures blurred out of recognition, a smudging of light and darkness, obscured from form.

Figures.

I love Thee, Lord Jesus. Look down from the sky . . .

They moved, flashing between hues of every color, understated, but real.

And stay by my side 'til morning is nigh.

I looked up and saw him.

"Hey there, old friend," I said softly.

Then I fainted.

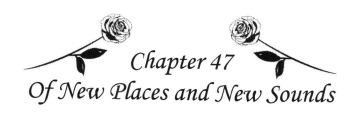

Chapter 47
Of New Places and New Sounds

I blinked, opening my eyes tentatively as a sharp pain in my back accosted me. As my vision cleared, I saw a familiar figure seated in a chair by the hospital bed.

Hospital? What was I . . .

Then I remembered. The fight for my life in true movie drama form . . . the fall . . . blacking out . . . and someone's strong arms lifting me up.

"Hey." Peter looked up from the book he was reading. "How are you feeling?"

"I," I considered his question, "I'm alive."

Peter smiled, the lines in his face pronounced as if they had not held a smile in days. He leaned forward and lightly touched my hand. He opened his mouth as if to speak but closed it. He just kept looking at me.

I broke the silence. "Dr. Yin?"

"In jail." Peter's voice returned to him, filled with a sense of triumph, as he moved back in his seat. "She won't be bothering you or her clients anymore."

I smiled, a wave of relief washing over me, but a stab of pain interrupted it with the movement of my jaw. I winced.

"Rebecca, are you okay?" Peter moved toward me again, his eyebrows furrowing together.

"Yes. It . . . must just be a bruise from the fall or something."

Peter nodded, sitting down. "Yeah, the doctor said that you might have some aches and pains for a bit. But," his eyes met mine reassuringly, "nothing too serious."

"Then . . . why am I here?" I blinked in confusion, trying to sort everything out in my somewhat disoriented state.

"Your asthma . . . kicked in for a bit. We weren't sure if . . . well, the doctor wanted you to stay here for a few days to be monitored. Just in case . . . it became a problem again."

"What do you mean?"

Peter's eyes flashed with pain briefly before clearing and returning to my own. "You had a lot of trouble breathing, Rebecca," he said gently. "But the worst is past."

"Isn't that what . . . asthma is?" I knew that he wasn't saying everything.

"You . . . stopped breathing."

I almost stopped breathing when he said that. "What?!"

Peter sighed. "I knew it would freak you out. That's why I didn't want to say anything."

"Sorry." I finally managed a laugh, a laugh that was worth the pain that ensued. "Guess I'm always too obstinately curious for my own good."

"That you are."

I raised an eyebrow. "But it did make you say 'freak out.' Not a very Peter-esque word, now, is it?"

"Hanging around Californians for too long can do that to you." Peter's signature grin finally broke out. "First it was dude . . . now 'freak out' . . ."

"If you stay a bit longer, you can become a knight of California, too," I whispered.

Why was I whispering?

I looked up, and saw something change in Peter's face. No visible movement had occurred, yet it had changed. The reason that I had whispered was the reason that . . . I shook my head in an attempt to clear the confusion racing through it. I had just been in an accident. No need to think.

But a thought pressed in my mind, refusing to be ignored. "Peter," I said quietly, "when I fainted, how . . . how did I get here? I don't . . . remember it very well . . . and then I blacked out, so . . . I remember nothing except . . ."

Except what seemed like a dream.

"Oh, that. I . . . found you lying on the ground and carried you to the hospital."

So, it was true. Snapshots of scenes ran through my hazy memory. A walk that never seemed to end. But a walk filled with security. A walk where I felt safe. Completely and unreservedly safe.

"You walked," I said slowly, "all the way to the hospital."

"Yes." Peter's eyebrows moved in puzzlement. "Not sure how you remember that, as you were completely out of it, but . . . yes."

"What happened, Peter?" I asked quietly.

"It's a long story," he said.

"And I'd like to hear it."

Peter nodded. "Okay."

I waited in silence, allowing it to flow over me, rather than fighting against it.

He finally spoke. "Something in me made me feel . . . unsettled about the trip that I was making. I instinctively chose an earlier train. You see, I was not quite in Alberta yet, having taken a few days to visit with some cousins in Denver. And, so, I naturally headed first to see you. I don't understand what made me return to the train station." He paused. "I just knew that there was no place that needed my attention more.

When I saw the man holding you, I had the advantage of surprise. I waited, and when you . . . fell to the ground, I moved in. But, after I knocked him from behind, it was only a partial blow; he recovered rather quickly, jumping to his feet. We struggled for a few minutes, and, at a time of momentary advantage, I took the Swiss Army knife from my back pocket. But I knew that it would not be enough; his eyes mocked me with the knowledge of his superior weapon. One brief move, and he might regain it. I injured him, but only superficially, before he bit my other hand, causing me to momentarily jolt back. He reached for his gun—now only an inch away—as I regained my grip, and, in the struggle, it went off . . . his own shot intended for me ultimately firing at himself."

There was a moment's pause as I took in the news.

Yin's henchman, The Man with the Cool Blue Eyes, who had shadowed me with his leering presence for so long . . . was gone.

Gone—indirectly or not—at the hand of Peter.

"Thank God you are okay," I finally broke through the silence. "But your hand . . . "

"I'm fine." Peter waved away my concern.

"But you could get an infection! Did you have the doctor—"

"Yes."

"Okay." I settled back in the bed reluctantly.

"It's strange, though," he paused. "He almost . . . looked familiar."

"You knew him?!" I blurted out.

"No, I don't think so. Not sure . . . what it was. It all happened so quickly."

My eyebrows creased together. "I know."

He waited, but I had nothing further to say. And so he continued.

"When I reached you, you were barely coherent, and soon drifted into unconsciousness. You . . . didn't look too well. There were voices that rose from within the train—likely due to the commotion outside. I didn't know who was in control of the train and recalled my misgivings about taking the later train, so I decided to get you out of there as soon as possible."

"The people," I interrupted, a thump in my heart. "There were innocent people on that train—"

"Adriana," he said gently.

I nodded, understanding. *She had made it to the police.*

"If I had known for sure that there were innocents on the train . . . But I couldn't be certain, and knew that you needed medical attention—"

"Peter, don't."

He would not have this on his conscience.

My eyes met his, bidding him to finish the story.

"You were in the middle of nowhere, my phone had died, it was a worst case scenario . . . I gave up trying to locate a 'quicker' route and just thought that it would be quicker to take matters into my own hands."

I smiled. "Literally."

Peter shook his head with a smile. "At least you still

have your sense of humor."

"But that had to have been at least . . . three miles."

"I didn't mind."

I smiled down at the hospital bed so that he wouldn't see my face growing red for no apparent reason. "Thank you, Peter. Thank you for . . ." I suddenly felt the urge to get up. "For . . ."

Peter's eyes narrowed. "No you don't. You need to rest."

"I'll be fine." I pushed myself up, ignoring the pain that shot through my leg. "I promise to just be up for a minute. Okay, doctor?"

Peter raised an eyebrow, but, before he could speak, I began to fall. He rushed forward, catching me, his arms pulling me into a standing position. Yet, somehow, it still felt like my feet were off the ground. Above the ground.

Our eyes met.

"Thank you for catching me again, Peter," I said softly.

He smiled and reached up to push back a lock of hair that had fallen into one eye. "Wouldn't have it any other way."

I caught my breath. *Must still be having asthma . . .*

"Hey, I should let you get some sleep." Peter moved back slowly, picking up his book. "I'll be back tomorrow."

"Okay," I said, looking at his foot. "Thank you."

"No problem."

As the door closed quietly behind him, my vision lingering at his retreating figure, I caught, out of the corner of my eye, the sign-in sheet for visitors. My hand reached for it.

He had been there all night.

For three days.

Chapter 48
Of Friends and Foes

I looked up to observe Adriana tumbling into the room with as much expedience as a medical facility would allow.

"I'm tired of clichés," I grumbled before setting my head back against the pillow.

"Dude," she blinked, still standing before me, "you almost died."

"Yeah, I know. But he was still *cliché*. His appearance, his demeanor, his actions. He was all wrong for a villain . . ."

Adriana sat at the edge of the hospital bed and stared at me. "You almost died for the *second* time in *two months*."

". . . and," I dismissed her words, "he would never make it into a serious novel. He just isn't believable. I don't care what I've said before . . . clichés *do* exist, and they must die before they fall!"

"So . . . what medications are you on?"

"Lots, why do you . . . Adriana Hanson, I am not under the influence of drugs!" I glared at her fiercely from beneath the stark hospital sheets. "I am simply dissecting the world around me!"

"Though I am a bit groggier than usual," I admitted with a sheepish grin.

"Hence the heightened insanity, evident irritability, and opposite perspective effect."

It was my turn to stare.

"Hey, you're not the only one who can play psychologist!" She grinned. "Anyway . . . where were we in this most-bizarre-of-post-almost-death-reunions-in-the-history-of-the-universe?"

"We were discussing clichés and how," I stated firmly, "Yin's henchman was too much of one."

"So obvious as to escape notice?"

"But not snobbery."

"Yin wasn't cliché," she said quietly, staring at the hospital bed quilt.

"No . . . she wasn't." I paused, following her study of the quilt in measured silence.

If she had been, this would be easier right now.

Adriana looked up, searching my eyes briefly before sighing deeply. "It's all right, Rebecca. It may not be all right now, but that's okay. One day it will be. And somehow, somehow I think that makes it all right now after all. But maybe I'm just insane."

She squeezed my shoulder. "Feel better, dude."

There was a slight squeak as Adriana got up from the hospital bed, and then, in tiptoes of motions dichotomously contrasted to her entrance, she turned to leave.

"By the way, Adri," I called, "what happened after

I left you?"

She cringed briefly. "I followed the sewer system. I'd rather leave it at that."

"Sounds . . . delightful."

"Yep. But . . . I'd take that over what you went through."

She paused, and then turned to leave, closing the door quietly behind her.

And, once again, I was left with my thoughts, until my mother arrived, smiling me into my sleep.

Rock-a-bye, baby, on the tree top.

The baby reached for the top of the tree, and, with it, the stars.

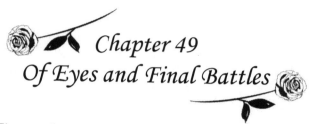

Chapter 49
Of Eyes and Final Battles

"Time to depart," Amelia pronounced triumphantly as she offered me a hand.

I took it, finding that I only barely winced now when reaching a standing position. The nausea of the past week had also dissipated to a low hum of recognition.

Peter remained in the chair near the hospital bed, his head hung downward with the rest of his body tangled in a comical display of slumber.

Peter, always dignified and formal, caught in a less presentable state.

"Should we wake him up?" Amelia indicated his sleeping form with some impatience.

I shook my head and smiled. "No, let him sleep."

Amelia nodded. "Okay, let's be on our way then."

I followed my honorary little sister toward the door, her hand squeezing mine with what I suspected was a fear that she had not been able to express to me verbally. I squeezed it back. I had almost lost her once, too.

And I had lost her in another way long ago.

She turned and, after a brief moment of hesitation, threw herself toward me in a fierce hug.

"I'm so glad," she said simply as she drew back, her eyes moist.

"So am I, little sis. So am I."

When we finally reached the door, I glanced back at Peter's bent form, my mind caught in recollection.

He had remained there every night of the hospital stay, save the one that my mom spent by my side. Every morning — or afternoon — when I woke up, my vision cleared, and he was there.

Strange. There had been a time when I questioned his presence in my life . . . only to find that he was more present in it than ever before.

I turned away from the scene before Amelia could catch something in my eye.

"Shall we?" Amelia pointed toward the door with a dramatic flourish.

I couldn't help but smile and nodded.

The crowd in the hallway reminded me of my surprise eighteenth birthday party.

Except for the absence of Vulcan ears.

"Welcome back, dude!" Adriana rushed forward as if she had not seen me in months. "Time to make a jail break!"

I cleared my throat, casting a seemingly desperate look about the hall. "I hope there is no hospital staff around to hear your thoughts."

"Oh, don't worry about them . . . I took care of the matter." Adriana winked conspiratorially.

I laughed. "You are absolutely insane."

"As are you."

"Thank you."

"Nice to see you again, A2," Amelia patted Adriana's shoulder.

"A2?" I raised an eyebrow.

"Um, yeah." Amelia blinked as if it were the most obvious state of affairs. "I'm A1 . . ."

"And I'm A2," Adriana finished. "We keep you safe."

"I didn't know that . . . I had bodyguards."

"Now you do."

I smiled. *How nice that my dearest old friend and my honorary little sister were hitting it off.*

How nice indeed.

My parents slipped their arms around my back, squeezing me affectionately. Alexander was close behind, tousling my hair before I saw a single strand of his own fiery locks.

"Glad to have you back," he said. "Even if you do cheat at PIT."

PIT was an old, rather rambunctious card game based on the stock market.

I glared at him. "I *never* cheat."

Alexander laughed. "Take it easy, little sis. You can dish it, but you can't take it, huh?"

"Our next match is scheduled for Friday the 23rd," I said firmly. "I would suggest that you bring a significant supply of tissues."

Dad offered me a knowing look. "Yeah, if it's anything like our Crazy 8s games, you'll want to supply enough tissues for your sister."

"Hey!" I protested, a smile weaving its way across my face despite my efforts to the contrary.

"Now, everyone, let's give our patient some rest." Mom touched my shoulder lightly, her face resolute. Teresa, who had been offering a long distance hug for the duration of this exchange, nodded in agreement.

Mom turned to me. "Are you sure you can walk okay?"

I nodded. "I'm a bit wobbly now that I've been standing for a while, but otherwise have been just fine—"

"Which is why I made sure that there would be something for you to sit in." Mom moved aside to reveal a wheelchair, labeled with hospital insignia.

Of course she didn't really mean the question, "Can you walk?"

"Mom, that's really not necessary—"

"Oh, Rebecca, just get in!" Amelia took a position behind the chair. "I'll push you."

I reluctantly obeyed, sitting down. "Just because it's long distance. After all that time in the hospital, I'm itching to walk around . . ."

". . . and run in flip flops, yes, we know," Dad interjected. "But let's hold off on that last part for a bit."

"Or, better yet, an eternity," my brother mumbled.

Mom took her place next to Amelia, who stood resolutely behind me. "Ready?"

As we turned to make our way down the hall, I heard a rustling from the direction we were leaving and craned my neck for a better look.

Peter, his eyes cast madly to and fro, scanned his surroundings in search of something before they rested on us. His countenance was still brushed with remnants of sleep, half a daze holding him in surrender despite the urgency that cast it aside.

His eyes met mine and relaxed. "Oh, hi."

"Hi, Peter," I said.

In a moment, he had reached us, standing before me uncertainly with his head slightly lowered. "I just didn't know where you were when I woke up."

My face flushed. "I understand. And . . . thank you."

We did not have much more time to speak, for

Amelia was taking her position as Bodyguard: Subsection Wheelchair Guardian very seriously.

"We really can't deal with interruptions, Peter," she implored. "Do get in the waiting party and hurry up!"

Peter obeyed, a glimmer of a smile in his eyes.

We set off for the second time down the hall, and, this time, when a new sight stopped us in our tracks, even Amelia remained silent.

A middle-aged woman, donned in flowing blue garments, stood in the middle. Her eyes, once restless and nervous, were still self-conscious, but had in them a certain peace. Her long, dark hair fell in jumbled strands about her, yet were more a part of her than ever before.

To her right stood a more elderly man, slightly bent. His clothes were tattered and worn, but I barely noticed because his eyes too held something different.

Eyes.

Two eager pairs of identical, yet singular, eyes peered at me openly. They collided with shape and form until they formed distinct figures.

Stacie, Albert, Abi, and Adi.

Behind them, Diana, a tall, young woman with wavy blonde hair, and Tybalt, a staunch fellow with broad shoulders and daring green eyes, also stood.

Dr. Yin's patients.

My clients.

Abi and Adi ran to me, hugging my knees. "Oh, Miss Rebecca!"

I affectionately tousled their hair before looking up again at the figures who surrounded them.

Albert stepped forward, holding my eyes. "Thank you, Dancing Girl."

Tears threatened to fill my eyes and cascade across my cheek. "You're welcome, Albert."

Albert nodded, his eyes shifting again.

I knew all too well that healing took its time.

But its beginning also mattered.

"Albert," I said quietly. "What did Dr. Yin do to you in the dark room beyond her office?"

It was a while before his eyes once again met mine. Stacie stroked his shoulder comfortingly, a gesture that could only be imparted by fighters of the same war.

A war that took him beyond the battlefield and yet beyond still its resulting scars.

Some scars were formed in places accustomed.

He looked up, his eyes misty and shaken. Yet he nodded, a firm gesture that I had never learned to associate with Albert.

"War," he said simply.

A petite figure, iron-pressed into perfection, stood before a small tape player. The darkness of the room overshadowed her figure in the illusion of cadence and silhouette.

Her hand reached for the "Start" button.

When she left the room, a delirious smile on her face, there was only sound and space, no light.

And a single figure tied to a chair.

Gunshots filled the room, littered with the screams of those disembodied from anything save pain and anguish. The screams shifted, turning into desperate sobs, as lives faded into the distance.

The man held his head, trying to find coherence out of chaos.

"You did not survive the war," a smooth, confident voice rose about the smoke and tin of the battlefield. "You are home, but that is irrelevant. You will never survive here. You are already dead."

My eyes overflowed with tears. "Oh, Albert."

I reached for his hand.

The smell of freshly baked bread filled my nostrils as soon as I entered my old house.

Home.

I turned toward my mom. "Mom, thank you so much."

She waved my words away. "It was Grandpa, actually. He's at the grocery store with Grandma at the moment but will be back shortly."

I breathed it in with all the contentedness of an Italian heart.

"It's nice to be back." I sat down at the table and let out a sigh.

Mom said nothing, but simply reached around my back and hugged me.

I glanced down at a pile of papers on the table. "What's this?"

Bodyguards A1 and A2 burst on the scene, as if they had been standing there all along.

"Simply unnecessary for a recovering monarch." Adriana grabbed the papers and handed them to her associate, who organized them neatly into a pile.

"Um . . . okay?" I looked up at my friends, my eyebrow cocked. "What's going on?"

"Just business that can be discussed later," Adriana said cheerfully.

"I have plenty of time."

"Have some bread, Rebecca." Amelia put a dish with piping hot bread in front of me.

Muffins were to Alexander what fresh bread was to me.

"Thank you."

The phone rang.

I moved to leave my seat, but my mom shook her head and walked quickly toward it.

I turned to my friends, my tone firm.

"Amelia and Adriana, tell me this instant what is going on. I am a dissector. I note individual characteristics and anomalous reactions. I know something is up."

The two girls exchanged looks.

"Well?"

"Rebecca," my mom stood in the doorway, "they lost your paperwork for the internship. We think that Dr. Yin destroyed it all before they took her away and—"

With voices a buzz in the distance, I looked up at a vase near the kitchen sink. Delicate pink petals circled in wide, elegant strokes.

The rose had reached full bloom.

Chapter 50
Of Scattered Dreams and Distant Memories

Her face, iron smooth with black tendrils struck against her cheeks, surfaced. She looked at me, her eyes cool and surmising, her face the impassive surface of a china doll that I saw on my first day in the building. She reached out her hand, and I fell down, down, screaming blindly until the night became a day that knew only the darkness of night . . .

I jumped up, my head reeling, as the images of the nightmare fluctuated, spinning around me as they dimmed into incoherence.

For the past three nights, I had suffered from the same nightmare that woke me long before it was time to arise for the day. It was always Dr. Yin's face floating before my vision, carrying with it the deepest anxiety I had ever known. I was lucky if I was able to get back to sleep within an hour of that terrifying dream; more often than not, I waited with the moon for the stars to scatter and the sun to arise, bringing with it the comforting light of dawn.

I lay my head back down, wiping the sweaty palms of my hands against my pajama shorts.

She was in jail. This I knew. I knew that she would no longer be able to harm me, to harm her clients, to harm anyone as long as she was there. It was as Peter had said. Momentary shifts of worries passed, unwanted weeds of doubt, as I recalled the fact that Dr. Yin had escaped from jail before, and surely then it was within the realm of possibility that she could do so again. Yet, even if it had not been for the additional security measures that I had been reassured were taken, I somehow, deep within, understood that she was there to stay. This worry was only a fear, a fear that seemed far less real than the nightmare that plagued me every night since my stay in the hospital.

No, she would not escape. I did not know why I knew this, but of it I was certain.

And, when the shadows of my dreams passed by, lost in the later hours of the morning light, I endured the daily toll of the time left. But there was something more, something that traveled through my head when fear did not keep me from thinking, or, perhaps, when it did most of all.

Saint Pope John Paul II had visited the man who had shot him in jail and forgiven him. Dr. Yin had not wedged a bullet inside my body, but she had metaphorically done so time and time again. It wasn't the same, and I had far less to forgive . . . less to forgive than Pope John Paul II and less to forgive than Dr. Yin's clients. And yet the thought of visiting Dr. Yin in jail was so incomprehensible a matter as to be immediately dismissed as it weighed out in my mind.

I pursed my lips, staring up at the ceiling. It was not a matter of forgiving her. No, that was difficult, but not impossible to achieve.

It was that, no matter how much I wished to visit her in jail, I was incapable of completing the task. At least, at least for now.

I had the strength. Time against time had weighed that truth so that I could hear it myself, hear the song that I called my own. But it wasn't enough to have the strength. It wasn't.

Her appearance poisoned my heart in its memory, searing its way to my very bones, penetrating the depths of who I was with a horror and terror that I had never previously known. That Fr. D'Angelo had warned me about, that he himself wished that I would never know.

I could not face my nightmare again. One day, I wished that I could.

But that day was not today.

I closed my eyes, suddenly brought in that motion back to another time.

At age 12, I don't think that I had ever cried myself to sleep.

But, on the night of April 1, 2005, as Pope John Paul II lay on his deathbed, I got about as close as you could get.

And, as the tears streamed down my face, turning into sobs, there were—whether spoken or unspoken— three words resounding in my heart:

I love you.

No, I had never met him . . . in person.

Yet, between Pope John Paul II and me—from my heart to his—was a profound spiritual connection difficult to explain.

I closed my eyes, recalling a baby girl due to be born in the year 1999.

We loved her. We loved her from the start.

"It's more than a feeling," I whispered to the darkness of my room, "and . . . even more than a choice. It is a *conviction*. And a mystery. A beautiful, beautiful mystery."

I propped my head up against the pillow, broken into awakenness by my fervency.

He spoke in a voice that was gentle, yet unwavering—filled with peace—his eyes were overflowing with the deepest love, and his actions showed the depths of his character, his soul, and the person that he was, and remained.

No, it wasn't just that I loved Pope John Paul II. It was that I knew that he loved me, as he did all of God's people. He chose to follow the Mystery of Christ's Love, no matter how difficult that path would prove.

Who would love Yin?

Memories shifted, pausing only briefly before they hurried to a later moment in time that was not my own.

A young child tiptoed around the dinner table . . .

Thousands gathered in Rome, outside the papal apartments, in quiet prayer during the final hours. United, as one people.

"I have looked for you. Now you have come to me, and I thank you," he said.

. . . her ebony black hair standing in stunning contrast to the paleness of her skin.

"Non omnis moriar." Not all of me will die.

A smile danced across her face, innocent and pure.

And six days later saw the funeral of one beloved . . .

It knew no evil and chose none.

At the very moment of his burial, large rain clouds appeared, yet not a single drop of rain fell that day, nor the entire week in which pilgrims and locals stood in wait. So too the last hours of his life, when many kept vigil in the streets.

It was as if the heavens held their breath in tribute to the passing of a great and holy man.

She moved to the melody of a dance that she would later forget.

Almost immediately after the funeral, rain began to fall steadily . . . like heavenly tears.

. . . forget for what reason I did not know . . .

And then . . . the moment, the moment of canonization, as I watched the coverage from Rome from my computer screen late into the night.

. . . but perhaps was not lost forever.

There was a sense of anticipation, a sort of excitement, but beyond it all . . . there was a sense of majestic peace.

It transcended time itself in this sense of . . . greatness.

She was only eight, or ten, or six.

Echoed beyond Time itself.

And one day she could remember.

Beyond "common" history to a history that spanned decades, transcended human understanding, and took us on a journey that once again united us with Christ.

One day she could unite herself with that little girl again.

I closed my eyes, the image of Dr. Yin as a young girl, sweet and pure, floating through my mind.

Saint John Paul II, I whispered, *please pray for me, that I go when it is time.*

When I can.

"I suppose you want to know what happened."

"No, I . . . know some of it. And I . . . I'm tired."

Tara's eyes met mine. "As am I. It's just as well then."

I paused, my keys scattered, as my right hand froze an inch from the door handle.

It had been long since I had lingered in nightfall without reserve.

But tonight beckoned me to stay.

I leaned against the car, collapsing against its surface in relief. A cool night breeze shifted against the friendly shadows of tree and leaf, refreshing and alive. I drank it in hungrily, the marathon runner dehydrated after a long race across the track, gulping for more and more as it lifted softly across the dry parchment that had become my throat. After a few moments of this simple balming flight, I turned my attention upward.

Tiny chandeliers of the night sky quietly scattered, trickling across its expanse.

Doubt thou the stars are fire . . .

They blinked, aware and softly echoing. My mind shifted through lines and thoughts, and I allowed it to simply be, too drained of energy to do anything else.

Doubt that the sun doth move.

Oh, when I had told her I was tired, how true that was now, yesterday, and every moment since . . .

Even now, as I bathed, my body could not move.

Doubt truth to be a liar.

No, it was not over yet.

The starry night sky echoed across my thoughts, the expanse of my own void filtered in its quiet solitude.

If you are what you should be—

Chapter 51
Of Last and First

I splashed water liberally over my face, allowing it to drip down unchecked, spilling onto my neck, before I took a towel from the rack to dry it.

Somehow it made me feel more alive.

I put down the towel with a sigh.

How silly I was to think that the past two years could change everything. No, it was the past year that had changed everything, and I wasn't sure where that left me in the grand scheme of things.

Battle scars were not a commodity that I was accustomed to selling, least of all to myself.

Yet there they remained. I had never been given the choice. No, not to be given the fight. But, as much as I regretted — and would to the end of my days — not having spoken up sooner, I had made the choice to speak.

And, while I did not understand all of the implications yet, I knew that I was irreversibly changed as a result.

And maybe, I thought as I closed the medicine cabinet, *now I simply must learn how to live with the scars.*

I glanced at the clock and ran. Some things never changed, I told myself ironically. I was just as susceptible to being lost in my own thoughts with little notice of anything else as I ever was.

As I dashed across my room, throwing on a pink peasant top that I had not worn in ages, scattering blush across my cheeks, the thoughts followed, bringing me to today.

It had escaped my notice for as long as I could dare, but the fact remained that today was a day that could—forget scars—determine the presence of a fresh wound. And I wasn't sure if I was ready for that, but I would have to be.

I had spent countless hours over the past five days agonizing over how to face the meeting that would ultimately determine whether my entire semester of coursework and internship would be tossed out of existence as if I had never been scarred at all. As if I had never met Albert, or Stacie, Abi, Adi, Diana, or Tybalt. As if it were all a dream of a long night, forgotten in the careless buzz and busy chaos of city life.

I had returned to Yin's office two days prior, despite my inner trepidation, in hopes of finding some evidence of what had occurred there. But it was wiped clean, free from any sign of inhabitance, let alone paperwork from my internship.

They had been thorough.

Should I have expected anything less?

As I walked forward, spinning around the place

in the steps of a dance that could only bring me to the dark terror of the underground, tendrils of my former existence here followed me with every step. I moved, moment after moment, cast in the frigid surrender of swerving icicles whispering remnants of an unearthly melody. When it came time for me to leave, unsuccessful but unable to do more, the desire to take a shower overwhelmed my mind, and, so, upon entering the car, I squirted hand sanitizer into my hands with little restraint.

I did not want to return there as long as I lived.

I shuddered and put the keys into the ignition.

And, now, today, I stood before that same car in momentary pause, struck by how the sun reflected upon its surface. I had never noticed that before, not really, not in its full quality. The mixture of the natural and the man-made instilled in me a new sense of what could be done when humans used their God-given intelligence to mold something new.

To mold something new out of incoherent scrambles.

If today, I lost everything, I would have to be that new reflection. And somehow I would be able to live with that.

I put the keys into the ignition and drove.

When I arrived at my old school campus, the campus that had seen the fulfillment of my undergraduate years, culminating in a joyous moment of victory in my graduation, I turned off the engine, slowly reaching for my purse.

In five minutes, all would be determined.

I felt unease at the pit of my stomach—distinctive from the pains that had followed me in the battles I had faced among those who were untrustworthy—but still unsettling.

How could I face Dr. Everson? He was more mentor than the mentor I had been given, more than anyone I had had the pleasure of knowing during my college experience. *Would he trust that?* Heat rushed through my body, filling me with embarrassment. How could I face him, with these half-truths and inconsistences, with the absence of any verifiable work? Would he know me? Surely he would. Surely he would know that I would have been responsible, that any ill rumors circulating were incorrect, that I would have completed my internship duties to the best of my ability.

I hope.

But I realized, as I locked the car with a quick, precise click of the keys, that that would not matter. In a court of law, the truth was irrelevant in the absence of evidence. Only Christy could have verified the transference of that paperwork, and she was dead, tossed aside so easily as the victim of a calculated scheme that no longer had any room for her in its enactment. Moisture stung my eyes, and I closed them briefly, recalling her kind face and pleasant demeanor.

As I walked to the psychology complex, a distinctive structure with green, translucent windows, visions of three dancing figures followed me, tearing the moisture across my face with insatiable deployment.

Let it be done according to Your will, I whispered at the threshold, opening the door. *I place it all in Your hands. All of it. With nothing held back.*

Dr. Everson's office was at the far end of the hall. *It almost heightens the drama of the situation*, I proposed to myself, nervous energy filling the void of fear temporarily.

Yet, when I stood before his office, the name "Dr. Everson" neatly engraved, any such sense of relief departed from me, leaving only a breathless traveler, her heartbeat quickening in calamity.

I knocked on the door and, upon hearing the familiar voice, stepped in.

Dr. Everson sat at the head of the table, his sharp, blue eyes immediately taking in my presence upon my arrival. His colleagues, Dr. Everett Brighton, a professor emeritus with thinning white hair and wire spectacles, and Professor Magdalene Flueque, a distinguished woman in her early forties with short brown hair, sat at either end, nodding in greeting as I entered the room. I knew little of them, having taken most of my coursework from Dr. Everson and others. But, from the few classes that I had taken from Professor Magdalene, I had come to respect her for her sound reasoning and vast knowledge.

She was also known as a stickler for the rules . . . a stance that I would normally approve.

I sat down, my thoughts weighing upon me as I did.

There was a great silence, as the three psychology professors examined a portfolio each in front of them.

A copy of my records, more than likely.

I waited, each moment stabbing at me with piercing reality.

Dr. Everson cleared his throat, filling the silence, and finally looked up. "Rebecca, we have gathered here to go over your academic status, most specifically in regards to your internship."

The formality of this professor who was more like a friend scared me.

I nodded, unable to speak.

"We have here your records for this university, both in terms of graduate and undergraduate studies. I'd like to go over them today." Dr. Everson looked at me over the portfolio in front of him.

"Sure," I said with more enthusiasm than I felt.

"Miss Veritas," Dr. Everett Brighton was speaking now, eyeing me with an academic stare that reminded me of my college days, "before we continue, is there anything that you would like to say?"

I stared ahead, a lump in my throat.

What would I say?

There was too much to say for there to be room for anything to be said at all.

"No," I said quietly, resuming my attention on the board.

"Very well." Dr. Everson nodded, removing the necessity of attention on me with one quick movement. "We will continue then."

"May I?" Dr. Magdalene interjected, a questioning look in her eyes. Dr. Everson nodded.

"Certainly."

"Rebecca," Dr. Magdalene's eyes transferred to me, "I see that your academic record has been uniformly excellent in your undergraduate studies, consistent with what I witnessed when you were a student in my class."

Was this a good sign?

"Thank you," I replied, the quaking in my chest subdued slightly.

"Unfortunately, reports of your post-graduate work have not been as uniformly excellent."

No, that was too easy.

She turned toward Dr. Everson, who took out a piece of paper from the green folder in front of him.

My chest throbbed, pulsating in anticipation.

"According to the evaluation Dr. Yin sent upon the mid-semester period, you were, and I quote, 'a disruptive presence in the practice, disrespectful of her mentor and unable to manage the day-to-day functions of a clinical psychologist that may occur in a typical client session.' She went on to say," Dr. Everson's eyes rose to study mine, "that you were 'ill-equipped to participate in the psychological field at any determined date in the immediate future, pending official evaluation at the end of the semester.' "

And so it begins.

They waited for me to speak, but I simply sat there, immobile, unable to speak or even think beyond the confines of a single sentence.

"Rebecca," Dr. Magdalene finally said, "we understand that the practices of Dr. Yin have been called into question, leading to drastic action on the part of the authorities. However, we also need to be honest with you now about any details of your record that stand apart from that."

"I understand." I swallowed, tears inching toward my eyes once again.

No, Rebecca, you cannot cry. Not here.

No, it would not be professional.

At this, my thoughts widened, taking shape into a sense of cohesive structure.

I looked up. "I reiterate that my analysis of the situation, as reported at the end of the semester, stands."

Dr. Everson nodded, glancing over at me one last time before casting his eyes downward, a thoughtful expression on his face.

"We have here the final evaluation as conducted by the university," Dr. Brighton spoke for the first time in a while, sliding a thin, stapled packet of two sheets of paper toward my end of the table. "As a reminder, due to the high emphasis placed on field work at this university, your undergraduate internship work counts toward the 3,000 hours of supervised study required by the BBS, with an average of approximately one third of that measured by graduate work."

I caught the packet in one hand, forcing my eyes to

address it.

It was the standard form, the same method of evaluation that I carried in my own internship packet, lying nearly unforgotten on my apartment desk. As I scanned the first page quickly, before the professors would speak again, measure upon measure took in the pen-dripped assignations of empty space, incomplete areas tempered slightly by the weekly internship reflections that I had emailed without fail to the university.

It would not add up. I swallowed, reaching to turn the page, when Dr. Everson continued.

"There are areas in which you could use improvement or further practice," he continued from his study of the page, "as you can see clearly highlighted in this piece."

"Yes."

"In particular, I recommend working on your use of session time. It was another area cited in your mid-term evaluation that seemed rather specific."

That was true enough.

I nodded.

"If you would turn the page . . ."

I hesitated, my hand finally dropping down to the corner, as I held my breath.

I knew what would soon occur, but somehow the idea of seeing it made it even worse.

It would become too real.

The second sheet of the evaluation was only printed about halfway across the page. As Dr. Everson detailed each specific criterion, shifting between advice and recognition of criteria meaning, it slowly faded to the distance, a quiet hum of half-understanding that soundtracked my lost thoughts.

". . . and, so, we come to the final score for this

evaluation period, which stands at 265 points."

My heart thumped, dropping down my stomach and to my toes. *Oh. Oh.*

265 points. I looked down at the page fervently, certain that I had mistaken his words in my distracted presence.

But there the numbers remained, written neatly in clear black flourish.

No, perhaps the passing score was 275 . . . It had been too long, and I had forgotten the correct criteria.

"Which," Dr. Everson looked up, his eyes meeting mine, "is the bare minimum for a passing score."

"You . . ." I fumbled, unable to keep the emotion from my voice, "you found the missing paperwork."

The three professors exchanged looks. "No, we did not."

"But the part here, on the second page! It refers to information that you could only have received had . . . had the information from Dr. Yin . . ." My voice trailed off.

I could not breathe. But, this time, that state of affairs was the most beautiful thing I had ever experienced.

"The information stands in its accuracy."

How could it? How had this . . . An effervescent smile burst across my face, as I shook my head, my eyes filling with astonished wonder.

"I hope you will understand," Dr. Everson continued, "that, due to the circumstances, I will be unable to write a letter of recommendation . . ."

I brushed aside his words, still lost in the reverie of the news. "Yes, I understand! Of course!"

"And pending your scores in the licensing exam, your final status in the field remains inconclusive."

There was a time in my life in which tests actually held a certain level of preoccupation. His words flickered in my mind only briefly before they escaped, giddily spilling outward in speckles of insignificance.

I barely heard him. "Oh, yes, of course!"

"Then, if there is nothing further that you wish to discuss," Dr. Brighton took off his spectacles, placing them into a thick black case, "this meeting is adjourned."

I rushed from my seat, nodding politely at them, my heartbeat quickening as I hurried to the door.

"Oh, and Rebecca," Dr. Everson called, his booming voice once again arising in the comfort of familiarity.

"Yes?" I turned back quickly.

A wide smile surfaced. "Congratulations."

I breathed deeply, hints of a smile tiptoeing across my face, and turned to open the door.

Cools wisps of a breeze greeted me in the soft beacon of their balmy flight. I walked quickly, stopping only briefly every now and then, to brush tears from my eyes. I laughed, spinning around and around, breathless and exuberant, free and flown from time, beneath the encompassing web of a great redwood tree that led to the parking lot.

It was impossible, every bit of it.

And yet the impossible had occurred.

With a single movement, I thrust my phone into my hands.

He answered.

"Peter? Oh, Peter, you have no idea what just happened . . ."

The Silver Rider took me to the familiar white, concrete structure—the name "St. Vitus" neatly imprinted—without incident.

I thanked it, abundantly clear of how utterly insane that was, and lifted myself from the vehicle.

The presence of the Holy Spirit filtered through

the air, weaving its way through bristle and stone in tangible reality, filling me with a deep peace that I had not known in so very long.

I approached the church, taking in its familiarity and distinctive presence of beauty with contentment of heart and mind.

A distinct perfume sifted through the gentle breeze, its enigmatic breath overtaking me. I turned around.

On either side of the church, petals of soft hues swirled before my eyes, circling and circling until reaching the middle with a final stroke.

My hand flew to my mouth, tears involuntarily streaming down my face.

Dozens upon dozens of roses surrounded me on either side, as if lying in wait.

In this place of sweet surrender . . . I—

I fell to my knees, my hand touching a delicate petal brushed in light coral.

And the shower of roses spun around me, inviting me to take part in their ever-present waltz.

The figure, quiet and unseen, stood at the threshold in watch.

A knowing smile crept across the worn lines of age.

Before the kitchen window, spiraling out of a translucent glass vase, stood the rose, its petals turned to dusty pink in the passage of time, yet still brighter than the age that they held. The pink petals shyly peeked up from the portal of nature, timid, yet unafraid to show their humbly regal beauty. They whirled around in the light dance of a duchess entering a ball—majestic yet understated—a spiraling splash of purity of color that took shape under nature's watch. A newly-sculpted garden burst forth, glistening in an afternoon sun. It welcomed the dusty pink rose, who stood beside its fellows, basked themselves in their own serenity of white, triumphant red, or cheery yellow. It swayed in the breath of a wind, caressing each and becoming more. It was a mixture of quiet and thunderous, light and dark, shyness and boldness. It was a mixture of the quiet strength and overwhelming courage that the human soul might wish to one day possess.

And, tiptoeing gently from its mother, a small, thin stem sprouted, young and green, giving way to a tiny, intricately-spun bud.

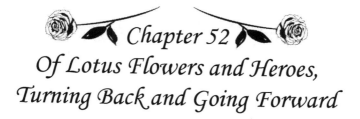

Chapter 52
Of Lotus Flowers and Heroes,
Turning Back and Going Forward

"Bless me, Father, for I have sinned . . ."

After I finished my confession and received my penance, a huge weight, as always, lifted.

I looked up. While there was a sense of peace, newly found, another matter still circled in my mind. A matter that was not mine to confess.

"Father?"

Father D'Angelo looked up. "Yes, Rebecca?"

"I know that people can change. But . . . what about someone who allowed evil to consume her heart? Could such a person . . . ever really change?"

"St. Paul did."

"Yeah," I said slowly. "Yeah, he did."

Father D'Angelo's eyes met mine. "We all were given the gift of free will. Some use it for good. Others abuse it. They make the choices. But," he looked at me intently, "that doesn't mean that we cannot help them. Sometimes by our own direct actions, but . . . there's always something else that we—all of us—can give them."

"Prayer," I said quietly.

He nodded. "Prayer. Prayer has changed the hardest of hearts and allowed the light in."

I nodded. "Thanks, Father." I got up to leave. As I was at the threshold of the door, I turned back.

"I want her to heal." A tear slipped down my cheek. I wasn't even sure why.

He smiled. "I know. You have a heroic heart."

I shook my head. "I . . . I don't feel heroic at all. In fact, I feel so imperfect, like a half-bent flower that doesn't move with the grace of its fellows. I always feel like I'm not enough, like I could be better." I shrugged.

"And that is what makes you a woman of courage."

A woman of courage.

I didn't feel like that either, but, in that moment, every ounce of my being was resolved to become that.

Like a lotus flower.

"It is the littlest of flowers that fly the farthest," Father D'Angelo spoke, as if reading my mind. "That have the *courage* to fly the farthest."

I smiled, blinking back another unexpected tear. "Thank you."

Father D'Angelo nodded.

I moved again to leave. *I'm sure those waiting in line for Confession must love me.*

"Rebecca?"

I turned back. "Yes, Father?"

"What prison is Ms. Yin being held in?"

I told him.

"I'll visit her."

"Thank you," I said sincerely.
A man of courage.

As I left the church, the doors coming firmly to a close like the pages of a book, I looked ahead.

Blue sky. Beautiful, brilliant blue sky.

I breathed it in.

I heard familiar footsteps, and soon a hand was squeezing mine.

"Hey," Peter said.

"Hey." I looked at him.

He hesitated slightly. "You don't mind if I hold your hand?"

"No," I paused, "no, I don't. It makes me feel . . . safe after all that has happened."

Peter nodded. "Me, too. I was scared . . . that I was going to lose you." His eyes reached mine. "You're my best friend."

I felt moisture in my eyes for the third time that afternoon. "You're dear to me, too. Very dear."

He looked ahead with a smile. "I hear that there is a playground over at the St. Vitus School. Think we might find some swings?" His eyes, in all the brightness of Peter, returned to me.

I laughed, and let him lead me.

Misty visions of yesterday
Dance across the orchard floor
Gliding like nymphs and fairy folk
They beckon us to worlds once known.
A dandelion, bright and full,

Blows softly in the gentle breeze
A memory caught in its flight
Of rosy cheeks and chubby hands
Popsicle sticks and water balloon fights
Laughter that echoes throughout time.

I stand at the portal anew
And before my very eyes
Images shift and collide
Not with chaos and calamity
But true story's tapestry.
The years soar by
Each summer day spent
Turning, spinning
With the sun's bright glare
Until its gaze softens
Its mad dash halted
The air, still, hushed
Yet a distant melody.
And you and I, hand in hand,
Walk through the orchard fair
Our eyes lost in the splash of waves and ocean breeze
Like sea creatures forever of the shore.
Our feet firmly planted on the ground
Safe in an embrace
That speaks of golden summer days.

- "The Summer Orchard"
    By Rebecca Veritas

Acknowledgements

First and foremost, I would like to thank God. Without Him, none of this would be possible. He inspires me with the Beauty of His Creation and gives me strength when I am facing seemingly insurmountable difficulties and struggles. I also thank His Mother, Our Lady, for her love and prayers, and all the saints . . . in particular, The Little Flower, St. Thérèse of Lisieux, and Saint Pope John Paul II.

I would like to thank my mom for, once again, reading and critiquing an early draft of my latest novel. Thank you for your support, encouragement, and love. Thank you, most of all, for being the best mother in the world. No matter what, I know that I can count on you. You are one of the most giving people I know. You are a voice of reason, steady and true, never swayed by the times . . . but remaining firm in who you are. You are a kindred spirit with whom I can share my excitement over so much, from fairy tales to foreign languages. You are my role model. I love you, Mama.

To my love, Vinnie, for being another early reader of *The Rose and the Sword*. You kept me laughing with your random sidenotes and kept me thinking with your suggestions. Thank you for your patience in my in-depth questioning sessions, and for believing in me. Most of all, thank you for being you. I think what I love most about you is that you care. You care about the things that matter, and love deeply and truly the people that matter to you. You are the authenticity that society lacks, and that I am so incredibly blessed to call mine. I fall more and more in love with you all the time. Each day is a reflection of the first, and each moment is a new summer day found in winter.

To my honorary little sister, Catherine. My dear sorella, I may not have a sister by blood, but God gave me a true sister in you. You may be very different from Amelia, but the bond is the same. Thank you for your sweetness and love. Thank you for reading *The Rose and the Sword* early on and providing your reflections, as well as entertaining commentary from the perspective of the ringleader of Team Peter/Rebecca (as for the question of that team . . . I guess you will have to wait and see.) May you always be as courageous and steadfast of heart as you are today. I am so proud of you.

To my dad, the final reader who always notices little things that escape everyone's notice. Thanks to you, we added the character diagram to the beginning of *I Thirst*. Once again, your keen eye has been a tremendous help. Thank you also for being a wonderful father. Your sense of humor and fun adds joy to my life, yet the sparkle in your eyes goes beyond that. Ever since I was a little girl, you showed by example and word how I should be treated and respected as a handmaiden of the Lord, as a daughter of not only you, but of a King whose family truly stretches to infinity and beyond. Even now, I continue to see your chivalry in the little random things that you do for my mom on a daily basis. I am, and shall always be, your little girl.

To my big brother for just being himself. You are seriously epic. I am so proud of you for your talent, creativity, and loving heart. Keep reaching for the stars. I think that you can do anything, and will be truly incredible in your chosen field. Through it all, you also continue to amaze us with your other passions, in particular your incredible skill as a musician. And maybe, just maybe, you'll still create that spaceship after all as a side job. ;) Why not?

To Jansina of Rivershore Books for continuing to believe in me and for saying, upon reading the first excerpt that I shared with her from *The Rose and the Sword*, "I love seeing my friends again." You are truly the best. As always, your attention to detail is impeccable. Thank you for your patience and support. I am not only proud of being one of your authors, but so thankful to be able to count you as a friend, too. How many writers are that lucky?!

To my grandparents, for their unconditional love and generosity. Thank you for making Italy come alive for generations to come. Grandpa, thank you for the essence of your poetry—that is, not only the words conveyed in your beautiful verse, but the meaning it takes in your everyday life. Thank you for your words of wisdom from the perspective of a psychologist— for, in that, you take the perspective of a human being. Grandma, you are beautiful and brilliant. Thank you for the love that you pour into your cooking and for your timeless wisdom. You are inspirational in all that you do. How many eighty-eight year olds still participate in a book club and don't bat an eye at the prospect of reading one thousand pages?! Enough said.

In memory of Uncle Eddie and Fr. Joe. Uncle Eddie, you were one of the first people who encouraged me as a writer. Thank you for always believing in me. Fr. Joe, thank you for the palm rose. Thank you for helping me better understand meditational prayer with your peace, and for reminding me one long night that a host of angels surrounded me. I love you both dearly and am afraid that I will never stop missing you here on Earth.

To Christopher and Diana for their insight into the field of psychology. Thank you for your assistance! The data you provided was very helpful. Thank you also for your friendship.

I would like to thank my family—including other honorary siblings—and all whom I name "friend." Thank you for your continual love, support, and encouragement. It means the world to me.

And to the fans—you are incredible. You remind me of why a young, shy girl dared to one day show the world her writing. Thank you for your kindness and enthusiasm. Stay tuned for the next chronicle.

Author Bio

Gina Marinello-Sweeney is the author of *The Veritas Chronicles*. The first book in the series, *I Thirst*, received the 2013 YATR Literary Award for Best Prologue from Young Adult Teen Readers. This is the second volume. Gina has been writing ever since she was a little girl and turned her bedroom into a "library," complete with due date slips and a check-out stamp. As her own stories were "checked out" by family and friends, she dreamed of a day in which her stories would be available in public libraries worldwide. Gina is also an avid poet in both the English and Spanish languages. In 2009, she was asked to present some original Spanish poems at an international literature conference in Costa Rica. Although unable to attend this event, a presentation of the poems was well-received at another scholarly event that same year. Graduating summa cum laude, Gina completed a degree in liberal studies, an elementary school teaching credential, and a minor in Spanish. In her spare time, she enjoys producing videos, going to the beach, reading, and traveling. Gina lives in southern California, where she is at work on the next volume in *The Veritas Chronicles*, as well as a short story collection. Visit www.ginamarinellosweeney.com for more information.